DOUBLE DOWN

A FRIENDS WITH BENEFITS, BASEBALL ROMANCE

ERIE CITY HAWKS
BOOK 2

KC BROOKS

For the ones whose happily ever afters didn't turn out as they planned, this story is for you. May you find someone who fuels your fire, instead of trying to tame it.

PLAYLIST

1. Heartbroken- Jessie Murph & Polo G
2. Honest- Song House & Kyndal
3. What You Do- James Gillespie
4. Wicked Game- Theory of a Deadman
5. Hello My Old Lover- Dove Cameron
6. Is There Somewhere?- Halsey
7. Fear on Fire- Ruelle
8. Lost- Luz/Mahogany
9. Say So- St. Lundi
10. Parachute- Soundhouse & Kyndal

AUTHOR'S NOTE

While this book might be a baseball romance, it is a romance book above all else. While it is the author's intention to honor the sport, some rules, timelines, or guidelines may have been tweaked to allow for the characters' relationship to thrive.

This book also contains on page, sexually explicit situations. It also contains elements of infidelity (not between the main characters), divorce, emotional abuse, manipulation, and violence.

While it is the author's intention to broach these topics with sensitivity, it could still be triggering for some readers. If that is the case, please skip this book.

Protect your peace, lovelies.

ONE

Damien

"Want to tell me again why we're doing this?" I pressed on the brake, sliding my car into the guest parking space. Looking over my shoulder, I stared at the school behind us. The nondescript building had clearly seen better days, with peeling paint and rust gathering in the corners of the front doors. On the higher levels, kids waved from the windows. *Shit, they looked so excited.* And yet, I couldn't hold back my grimace. Not that I had anything against kids—hell, my five nieces were my entire world—but I had something against waking up at the crack of dawn on our one day off this week.

Cam just shook his head, tossing the bag at his feet over to me. "Told you. Means a lot to Hadley. And with everything she has going on right now, it's the least we can do." He pulled open the passenger door and climbed out of my car. "So get your ass out of the car and put a smile on your face, D."

I chuckled as I joined him, popping the trunk to grab the rest of our gear. "You're beyond whipped."

"Don't care, man. She's it for me, and I'm done playing

it safe on the sidelines." He grabbed the bag of signed balls we'd picked up at the stadium. "Anything I can do to make her smile, I'm gonna do it."

I closed the trunk with an audible thud. This kid was a fool. Sure, deep down, I was happy he'd finally admitted his feelings for Hadley. Cam Seda was a lot like me when he first joined the team as an outfielder this season, full of pure love of the game and fierce determination to earn his spot. But over the last few months, he'd also fallen for a new girl, one who just so happened to be his ex's best friend. Their situation wasn't ideal, and for a while, they tried to hold back, but it was useless, and he'd finally let himself fall hard and fast for Hadley.

He dashed over to the school, smiling at someone waiting on the other side of the glass. There was a lightness to his steps that hadn't been there a couple of months ago. It made even my calloused heart root for love, made me believe they'd make it through the trials and tribulations of our seasons.

But there was also a darker beast, one that warned of broken promises and long nights alone, of returned rings and fractured hearts. Our schedule—*our lives*—weren't for the weak, and personal experience taught me most people weren't willing to stick it out.

No one else understood why we'd pick love of the game over everything else.

Except for my sister, her wife, and my nieces, baseball came before *everything* else. I'd missed birthdays, holidays, recitals; you name it, I'd had to skip it because of a game or training, but that was the sacrifice we had to make. Baseball was more than a sport—it was my livelihood. It helped me provide for my family while also letting me live out my wildest dreams. I'd sacrificed too much to get here to let go just yet.

Especially for something as temporary as a relationship.

Heaving the last bag over my shoulder, I joined the rest of the guys. As they talked about our upcoming series in Colorado, I shifted toward our second baseman, Jace Lyons. He stood off to the side, not bothering to make eye contact with any of the other players. As I got closer, my eyes scanned his frame, checking for any signs of distress.

Dark circles lined his eyes, and his normally tanned skin had turned more pallid. He'd even lost weight over the last couple of months.

I frowned, unease and uncertainty creeping into my chest. It'd been almost two weeks since Jace confided in me about how the pressure was getting to him, the unhealthy ways he coped. He'd tried to clean up his act multiple times, but each night on the field stripped away a little piece of his soul.

What first started as small comments had shifted into loud outbursts, and it was beginning to mess with the team's dynamic. Jace didn't have the best reputation when he joined the Hawks, and he wasn't earning any allies with his gruff demeanor. If you'd asked me a couple of months ago, I was ready to write him off too, but we'd spent some time practicing one-on-one, and I'd gotten to know the guy underneath the arrogant smirk. Jace meant well, but he was lost, and as his captain and his friend, it was getting harder to sit by and watch him drain himself to the bone.

Sure, playing professional baseball was the dream. Many people would never get to experience walking out to thousands of fans screaming your name, and I was so fucking grateful I got to live this life. But if I'd learned anything over the past decade, playing at this high level wasn't for the weak. Getting called up to the majors was only the first half of the battle.

No, the other half played out once you got your shot. The desperation to keep it soaked deep into your bones. We saw it way too often—guys who worked their whole lives to get to this level, only to let the pressure destroy them once they had it in their hands.

As Jace nodded his chin up at me, I frowned. "You good?"

"Yeah," Jace said, his voice scratchy. "Late night."

"Seems like that's been a trend lately."

His eyes narrowed at me. "Been keeping track of me, cap?"

"Just checking in as a friend," I said as I clapped my free hand on his shoulder. "If you need to talk to someone, try the team doc. They can recommend a therapist—"

"Don't." Jace's throat bobbed as he looked around, making sure no one else was listening. His eyes darkened as he glared at me, his mouth twisting into a tight line. "Told you. I don't need a fucking shrink."

"Couldn't hurt," I said. "You can't keep going this way, kid. You're going to drown under all that pressure. Talking to someone helps. It sure as fuck helped me."

Jace swallowed heavily as Cam and Parker led the rest of the guys toward the school. "I'll think about it." I frowned at him, and he just smirked. "C'mon, cap. I said I'll think about it, and I mean it."

Knowing when the battle was done, I clapped his shoulder and joined the rest of the guys. They nodded as I walked by, calling out different versions of my title. *Team Captain.* The shit still made me smile. Most league teams didn't bother with captains, but the Hawks were such a green franchise, upper management wanted a strong voice to get everyone on the same page.

As the most senior player, most people assumed I'd be their pick, but I didn't believe it until Benny Weber, our manager, pulled me aside and asked if I'd lead these guys to victory. Fuck yes. I never questioned it, just automatically jumped in.

After that day, I'd made it my mission to make our team as strong as possible—not only on the field, but off it as well. Too many guys burned out, and I didn't want that to be our legacy. We'd already implemented some changes to protect the players, including mandated sessions with the team therapist, but there was a lot more work to do. Pressure mounted on my shoulders, but I pushed it down as we approached the school, buried it under an easy smile, like always.

The front door swung open, and a woman stepped out to meet us. As her hazel eyes lifted, the breath stuttered out of my lungs, too captivated by the life circling inside her expression. My eyes scanned the rest of her, unable to look away. She wore a casual outfit—yoga pants that clung to her tight, athletic frame and a Hawks t-shirt that was a couple sizes too big. My gaze trailed along her body; I wished I could pull it back and discover what curves were buried underneath.

"You must be the Hawks." She beamed at Cam, reaching out her hand. "It's nice to meet you, Cam. I'm Brianna, or Mrs. Collier around here. I'm Hadley's co-teacher. She's told me all about you."

"I don't know if that's a good thing or a warning," he chuckled as he shook her hand. As they spoke more about the day's events, my eyes never strayed from our host. Brianna was on the taller side but still shorter than Cam. She'd pulled her long, dark hair beneath a Hawks baseball hat, her ponytail sticking out the back end. She'd dressed for a day with the kids, and it made me smile. I'd spent my childhood at a strict private school, and the rules never would've allowed for a day like this one. Too often, we got screamed at to keep our clothes clean, needing to present a certain front to the world. But no pretense radiated from this woman—only pride over her school.

She looked over the rest of the group. "I'd say I know each of you, but that would be a lie. My baseball knowledge is almost all borrowed from Hadley. But sincerely, thank you for coming here. We're so excited to have you, and I can't explain what this means to the kids." She swiped her badge and led us into the building. "I don't want to waste any of your precious time on your day off, so if you'll follow me, we'll get the stations set up outside, and then the kids will join us."

Brianna led us through the gym, and all of us took in the school and the kids clambering to get a peek at their guests. I waved back at them, already feeling my smile building to match theirs. Ah, fuck. Cam was right. This was what we'd always talked about doing, about ways to give back to the community we called home.

This neighborhood wasn't the best, and from what Cam said, their budget had gotten drastically cut over the past couple of years. But despite the aging building and less-than-pristine conditions, there was still a fierce protective-ness soaking the walls. You heard it in how Hadley and Brianna talked about this place, how much they cared and loved the students who came through their doors.

"Okay." Brianna clapped her hands as we exited the gym and stepped out onto the field. "We've assigned each of you to a station, and you're paired with a teacher. If you need additional support, we have plenty of others walking around. You can also always flag me down if you need something." She paced across the field to where a giant sign hung, displaying all our names. "Each station will be about fifteen minutes, and then we'll switch. You'll hear a bell signaling when it's time to move on."

She lifted onto her tiptoes, searching the crowd. When Ken, our team photographer, stepped forward, she offered him a bright smile. "Before we get started, can we talk? We need to go over which kids can't be photographed."

As Ken and Brianna stepped off to the side, my eyes followed, unable to look away. A sharp crack hit my arm, and I scowled over at Cam as he stared daggers back at me. "Don't even think about it, Ramos."

"Think about what?"

"You know what," he sighed, nodding in Brianna's direction. "She's married. Off limits."

Disappointment rushed through my chest as I finally glanced down at her ring finger. Fuck, there it was. Twin rings. How the fuck did I miss those? It was always the first thing I checked, no matter what. I might not do relationships, but I had a strict rule about meddling with attached women. If you were looking to piss off your boyfriend or spouse, find someone else to fill your time. I'd watched the other end of that situation too many times to bring that level of pain into someone else's world.

I shook off any thoughts of Brianna, turning back toward Cam. "You know me, man. Not gonna go there."

"Probably a good idea," Cam answered, glancing around the field with a forlorn expression. "I wish Hadley was here. Fuck, I never knew I could miss someone like this."

"She'll be back, Cam. And when she finds out about

what you've done," I smirked as I leaned in, "you're going to reap those benefits for years."

He shook his head, but he couldn't hide his grin. "Not about that, D. She works so hard for everyone else. Teaching, helping out with Emilia, and everything she does for me. It's a lot. If I can take a little bit of the burden away, that's what I'm going to do. Even if she never knows about this, it'll be worth it because it matters to her." He ran his hand over his face as if clearing that thought away. "Gotta get set up before the kids get out here. You good, man?"

"Yeah," I said, scanning the poster for my name. When I saw the name written next to it, I couldn't help my smile. Collier.

Almost on instinct, I found her in the crowd, watching as she spoke with the team photographer and our social media manager. She smiled over her shoulder, pointing at the different areas the teachers and team had set up. Something pulled in my chest, forcing all my attention to Brianna.

Married. She was fucking married. The reminder soured all my thoughts, washing them away just as soon as they'd arrived. But no matter what I told myself, it didn't stop the excitement that raced through me as she came over to join my station.

"So, Damien," she beamed up at me, "ready to do this with me?"

TWO

Brianna

Happy, smiling faces filled the back lot of our school, the kids animatedly talking to their assigned baseball players. We'd set up ten stations, one for each player, with different games that incorporated their team drills. Students raced through bases, tossed passes back and forth, and even struck out balls thrown by the Hawks' pitchers.

Even I had to admit, today turned out better than I ever dreamed. When my co-teacher, Hadley first spoke about her ideas for Field Day, it was just fragments, a plan with no defined lines. She'd done all the leg work behind the scenes, but now that she'd be out for the rest of the year, there was no one left to take over her dream.

Until Cam reached out to me. Over the past two weeks, we'd talked constantly, working through all the details about how to make the day a success for everyone. And now, we were seeing it all come to fruition.

Together, we turned Hadley's dream into a reality.

I stared across the field, watching as Cam caught a fly ball. He raced over and changed places with the girl, showing her how to hold her glove just right. He looked over and tipped his hat in my direction, as happy as I was that we'd made all this work. But every so often, when I looked over at him, his eyes sparkled as he glanced around the field, clearly wishing Hadley was here to experience it too.

It didn't take a genius to see he'd fallen for Hadley. Hard. That kind of deep love was clear when he spoke about her, how his eyes glistened when anyone else said her name. Even from a distance, she had him under her spell, and there was no one who deserved it more.

As I spun my wedding ring around my finger, I couldn't help but remember the days when I was the one with stars in my eyes, looking forward to building a future with my husband.

Now, seven years later, those dreams seemed further away than ever.

"Heads up, Mrs. Collier!" my favorite second grader, Ashton, called out as he lobbed a ball in my direction.

Crap. I was supposed to be paying attention, catching the balls before they flew out into the middle of the field. Most of them hadn't come close, and I'd gotten too complacent. Ashton, however, swung the bat like he'd been born for it, sending a line drive straight toward my face.

My body froze at the sight. *Who thought this was a good idea?* I was a behind-the-scenes person, all too happy to sit at my desk and analyze data, not to stand in the middle of a baseball field, pretending I knew how to handle the glove on my right hand. That's right! The glove. I squeaked as I held it in front of me, hoping the ball would collide with the smooth leather and not the side of my head.

"Gotcha covered, Mrs. Collier."

The deep rumble broke me out of my stunned state. I risked opening one eye, finding Damien Ramos standing in front of me, as if he'd just stepped out of my wildest fantasies. I might know nothing about baseball, but *everyone* was aware of Damien Ramos. The Hawks' star player was just as famous on the field as he was off it, and I'd spent a lot of time staring at his dashing smile over the years.

But the glossy images in gossip magazines had nothing on the man standing in front of me now. You couldn't sense the power that emanated from his frame—couldn't see the way his corded, inked forearms flexed with each toss of the ball.

"You okay?" he chuckled as he stepped closer, lifting his hand to lower the glove from my face. "Not used to being out on the field, are you?"

"Not even a little," I sighed. "Former orchestra girl over here. No sports on my resume."

"Cello?"

The simple question made my brow furrow. "Huh?"

Damien shook his head with a smirk. "Let me guess— you played the cello."

"Ye-yes," I stammered. "How did you get that off one comment?"

He shrugged one of those muscular shoulders, and my breath caught in my throat. God, he was so...broad, a build only achieved by pouring hours in at the gym. I tried to push away those tendrils of attraction as he continued. "Took a shot. Glad to see I was right, though."

He turned around and tossed the ball back to the kids. Ashton and some of the other kids lined up, ready for a chance to throw to one of the best players in the league.

It was so surreal, watching all these athletes with our kids. When Cam first called, I hesitated, unsure how they'd handle being around our students. Would they only talk to them when the cameras rolled? Would they leave our kids heartbroken, with crushed dreams at their feet?

That was the furthest thing from the truth. The guys were incredible. Even though the kids only got a designated amount of time with each of the players, they never rushed our students away, instead asking about their goals, talking about their own academic careers.

Especially Damien. He was a natural with kids, with that sort of effortless charm that allowed them to open up to him. As soon as Damien found out we had an entire family who'd just moved to America from Guyana, he rounded them all up, asking about their new home. He told them about when he moved to the mainland US from Puerto Rico and some challenges he faced. For weeks, all the teachers had tried to make them more comfortable in their new world, to no avail, and in just one conversation, Damien put them at ease. He even gave them his email address in case they wanted to talk more in the future.

As he walked back toward the kids, I couldn't help but watch, transfixed by the man in front of me. Leave it to me to take my celebrity crush and turn it into full-blown infatuation. He needed to go kick a puppy, steal from the homeless—something to make me forget about how my heart beat a little faster when he came around.

With a shake of my head, I focused back on the task at hand. Hadley would've loved to see this, but with her mom still in the hospital after a heart attack, she had enough on her plate right now. Fumbling through my pockets, I pulled out my phone. Maybe it'd be too much right now, but one day, she'd want to see what Cam had pulled off.

As I scanned the field, taking photos of our class smiling and playing with the team, a text scrolled across the top of my screen.

HUSBAND

Dinner tonight with my boss. Need you
ready by 7.

No question. No greeting. Just a demand, like I was his assistant rather than his wife. Irritation nipped at my insides. How much longer could we keep doing this? For the past twelve years, Todd had been my entire world. When we first started dating, it seemed like the stars had aligned. I gave him everything, supported him through job changes, moves, and everything in between. When we said our vows seven years ago, I'd meant every word, convinced we had what it took to make things work.

But time had a funny way of changing things—shifting your world so your once stable foundation crumbled underneath your feet. What had once seemed like minor imperfections had shifted into something worse, something unfixable.

If we even wanted to fix it.

I groaned as I tucked the phone back into my pocket. I couldn't dwell on my failing marriage right now, not when so much joy surrounded me.

Glancing back at my group, Damien lifted his head and met my eyes. His brow furrowed, as if he sensed the dip my mood had taken, but he was a stranger—albeit a very handsome one. I wasn't his to worry about, and there was no way I'd ever spill my secrets to him. He was better left in my imagination, where nothing would dull the sheen covering him.

He shifted over to the line of kids, dropping to a crouch as he stood behind Abigail, the quietest student in our class. She turned the ball over in her hands, nibbling on the edge of her lip.

"You've got this," Damien said behind her. "Just remember what we practiced."

Abigail's brown eyes met mine, and I nodded, trying not to overwhelm her with too much encouragement. She was the sweetest little girl, but her home life wasn't the best. She needed the time to explore things on her own. I almost said something to Damien, but he read her well, backing off once she looked more confident.

Abigail's lips curved in a slight smile as she chucked the ball in my direction. This time, I remembered to extend my glove, and it landed right in the pocket. I reached above my head with a loud whoop. "That was perfect!"

"Really?" Abigail said, a shy grin forming.

Damien stood to his full height, offering her a high-five. "You've got a killer arm, kid. Natural talent right there."

I swear, this man was making it his life's mission to destroy my ovaries. As I scanned the rest of the field, finding most of my colleagues' eyes glued to Damien and Abigail, I knew I wasn't alone in feeling that way.

"Alright, Mrs. Collier. Ready to do this with me?" Damien called out from the other side of the station.

Nope. Not even a little.

AS I PULLED into the driveway, a soft sigh left my lips. After spending the whole day in the sun, heaviness clung to my body, but my soul felt lighter than it had all year. The day wrapped up perfectly, with the team posing for pictures and signing balls for each of the kids. I pulled my phone out of my backpack, swiping through all the images I had taken to show Hadley. I lost myself in my students' smiles, letting them fill the empty place in my chest.

Tucking my phone back into my pocket, I stared at the unopened garage, trying to muster up the same enthusiasm to walk inside. Even after living here for three years, it still didn't feel like home. It was a beautiful build—a traditional raised ranch like so many other properties in our neighborhood. This development was one of Todd's company's projects, taking open pieces of land and carving out hundreds of identical homes.

When we used to talk about buying a place, I wanted to find something with a little more character, a home we'd both change and develop together. But Todd resisted, especially when the company offered him land as a thank you for years of service.

My stomach dropped when Todd came home one day and showed me the plans he'd developed for us. It looked like every other house on the block, but considering that his paycheck paid for the bulk of the build and the construction loan, he convinced me to give it a shot.

As I looked up at the beige siding, I hated the twist in my stomach. *Ungrateful.* That was the latest word Todd liked to throw at me, and maybe he was right. There were so many people who'd love to live in a house like this one, who would have given up their own style and dreams for a sturdy roof over their heads.

But I couldn't ignore that little voice in the back of my mind asking me if I wanted to keep being a passenger in my life, to keep letting Todd make all the decisions while I just sat back and watched the years pass me by.

What was the alternative, though? Starting over? That was almost as terrifying. I'd loved Todd since I was eighteen years old. I didn't even know what it would be like to date someone else. After all, what we had was fine. It wasn't like he was the worst husband. He never put his hands on me. Tense silence filled our evenings instead of the shouting matches we used to have, as if we'd both given up on the other, content to just let our unease eat us alive. It might not be perfect, but it was what I knew. Safe. Reliable.

With a shake of my head, I dug around my center console to find the clicker to open the garage. No luck. Great—just another thing for Todd to scold me about. Forget the fact that it'd broken three months ago and he'd promised he'd 'take care of it'. No, it would all be on me.

Gathering my stuff from the passenger seat, I opened the door and headed toward the back entrance of our house. As I pressed my key into the lock, a noise came from inside. Shit, Todd was already home. Usually, I had an hour or two to clear my mind before he returned from work. He must have finished his project early and came back here.

Opening the door, I listened for his voice, finding it echoing from his office on the far side of the house. With each step, I strained to hear if he was on a work call, but I couldn't quite make it out.

Until a deep moan broke through the silence.

What the hell?

My steps faltered as the sounds became clearer—moans and grunts I hadn't experienced in months. The blood dissipated from my veins, anchoring me to the spot. What was I supposed to do? Walk in on his private moment? Part of me wanted to rage. Anytime I tried to connect with Todd, he said he needed to focus on work. Was this his outlet instead?

"Oh my God, Todd. Just like that."

The feminine voice ripped through me like lightning, destroying everything around me. I knew that voice, heard it dozens of times throughout the years, shook her hand during my husband's business dinners and listened to her drone on about his work ethic.

All rational thought left my mind when I darted across the house, quietly opening the office door. Todd sat perched on his office chair, his shirt unbuttoned and his tie slung over his shoulder. Normally, he gelled his dark blond hair back, making the long lines of his jaw stand out. Today, it was a mess, as if he'd been pulling on the strands for hours. My eyes darted down when I noticed movement in his lap. *Speaking of pulling.* His hand was clamped over his hard dick, frantically gripping and twisting as he stared at an image on his computer screen.

But when I slammed the door behind me, his eyes darted to me, and his mouth dropped open in surprise. Leaping up from the chair, Todd tried to right himself, tucking his cock back into his pants and shoving his shirt back together, as if he might erase what I'd seen with a wardrobe shift.

"Br-Bri...what are you doing here?"

"In my house?" I bit out.

"I didn't hear the garage."

"Good thing," I said, moving to the other side of the desk to see his screen for myself. As soon as I did, I found my husband's assistant dressed in a skimpy teddy, one of her breasts hanging out. "Wow, Emily. That must be a new part of the job description."

"Mrs. Collier, wait—"

Todd clicked out of the call, leaving his background instead—a photo of us from our last trip to the Cape. Hurt lanced through me. God, how had I been so stupid? Sure, we had our issues, but this? In a million years, I never would have thought Todd would ever cheat on me. We'd talked about it for years, how that was my line in the sand. Any other issues, I'd try to work through with him, but this was the one transgression I'd never forgive.

As he stood and buttoned his shirt, he stepped closer to me. I backed up out of his reach, practically standing in the doorway by the time Todd reached for me. At my flinch, his expression shifted. Gone was the busted man from moments earlier. In his place stood the businessman who'd replaced my husband, the one who valued status and money more than our relationship. I searched his dark green eyes, hoping to find the answer to my question. *Why?* However, there was no apology in his expression—no regret.

"Brianna, we should talk."

THREE

Brianna

ONE YEAR LATER

"This has to be a joke, right?"

The tequila burned as it hit the back of my throat, the sensation welcome after a long day. Well, *another* long day. It seemed like my life had devolved into a series of long, infuriating days over the past year. Turned out, deciding to get divorced was the easy part. Untangling your lives after a decade together? That took time and a lot of mediation sessions with lawyers.

Despite Todd being the one who cheated, I'd walked away with almost nothing. I agreed to let him keep the house, not interested in staying in it after I found out about his double life. He'd taken almost everything he'd brought into our marriage, leaving me with mostly just my clothes and a few sentimental items. I could have fought harder, but I had no interest in sitting in that room with Todd any longer than I had to, watching the man I once loved break down our lives into figures and numbers.

Luckily for me, I'd made a few good friends before the divorce. My newest one, Ollie, insisted I crash in her spare guest room. Her high rise apartment was something I never could have afforded on my own, but she offered to give me a break on the rent, considering she owned the property and my measly rent check was helping cover utilities and taxes. As much as my wounded pride bristled, I was left with no other option.

Almost as soon as I moved in, Ollie and I became inseparable. It had been a long time since I had real friends, with the exception of Hadley, my former co-teacher. Then, she fell in love with a baseball player, and now, he took up a lot of her time. But luckily, Ollie was there to fill in the gaps, insisting we become best friends too. She even paid for my plane ticket to Dallas, insisting I needed to be at the game with her.

A loud laugh broke me out of my thoughts, forcing me to focus on the present. I slammed the glass down on the table then shifted back on the leather couch, happy to escape into the back corner of the dive bar with my friends, Hadley, Ollie, and Victoria. Dallas was supposed to be a good time, a trip to celebrate Hadley's boyfriend, Cam, getting picked to play in the pro-baseball All-Star game.

However, it wasn't the only reason we all decided to tag along. While Hadley had no idea, the rest of us knew Cam planned on proposing during the game, even tucking a ring inside an old baseball.

We'd all been riding high after she said yes and the guys crushed the other team. The night was filled with laughter as we sat in the stands with some of the other players' families. When one of the other player's sisters offered to take Victoria's daughter and the other kids for the night so we could celebrate longer, none of us hesitated, ready to make the most of our trip.

But that was before my mother called and my mood tanked.

"Nope. Apparently, my ex wants me to come to his wedding. Even invited my brother and parents too." I snorted, unable to hold back my annoyance. "Makes sense. After all, I was there when their relationship started. Might as well be there when they seal the deal, pour salt into the gaping wound for everyone to see."

Damn you, alcohol. I'd done a good job of keeping my insecurities at bay, too focused on celebrating Hadley to dwell on my former marriage. But the drinks had another plan, bringing all those buried feelings right back to the surface.

"Absolutely not," Ollie snapped. "You've wasted enough time on that asshole. You are not going to his wedding."

"If I don't, Todd will think he's won, prove I'm nothing more than a sad spinster while he's moving on with his life." As Hadley poured another shot of tequila into the glass in front of me, I winced. "Maybe I'm the problem. It's not like I'm anything special in bed, so I shouldn't be surprised Todd cheated."

All three sets of eyes widened at my statement, their shot glasses still full in their hands, as if I'd pressed pause on the world. Ollie was the first to come back to life, slamming her glass back down on the sticky bar table. Her blonde bob swayed, her dark brown eyes lethal. "Please tell me Todd the Toad did not say something like that to you."

My cheeks darkened at her favorite nickname for my ex. Even though he was the furthest thing from a toad in the looks department, now that she pointed it out, I couldn't help but hear the croakiness in his monotone voice.

I shook my head. "He never said that, but he also never seemed overly enthusiastic when we were in the bedroom. It felt more like a chore, like there was a timeline in his mind. Wednesday? Have sex with Bri." I grimaced as the memories came rushing back. "It's been years since it felt like sex was about us, and I can't help but think I've been doing something wrong, especially now that he's marrying the woman he left me for."

Hadley reached over and took my hand. I gave her a grateful smile. She'd been my rock throughout all this mess. Ever since Hadley showed up at my school last year, a kaleidoscope of glitter and rainbows, she'd been by my side, almost forcing me into her orbit. Hadley had a way of bringing people close, a natural charisma that put everyone around her at ease. She was the first person I confided in about my marital woes, needing an outlet outside of my family.

The fourth member of our crew, Victoria, just sat back, watching the entire exchange in quiet support. Compared to Ollie and Hadley, her response might not be as vocal, but I knew she was always there to lend an ear.

"Fuck that," Ollie said as she signaled the bartender for another round of drinks. *God, my flight tomorrow was going to be a nightmare.* But that was a problem for future Bri. As she handed me a glass, she smiled wickedly. "What you need is a no-strings sex situation to move on once and for all. You're way too hot to only have boring, marital sex." She clinked her glass against mine. "You need to find someone who ticks all your boxes—show you what you've been missing all along."

I downed the shot without further thought, noticing that the burn wasn't as horrendous as it had been earlier. Probably because the alcohol had already numbed all my senses, leaving behind only giggles and warm vibes. After I sucked the juice from the lime and dumped it back in the shot glass, I frowned. "What boxes are we talking about here?"

Hadley and Ollie shared a look while Victoria just smirked into her glass. "Depends on what you're into." Ollie paused, her devious eyes trailing up and down my body. "I'm taking you for more of a submissive type? A little BDSM?" Her brown eyes widened. "Please tell me there's a Daddy kink lurking underneath that quiet exterior."

My cheeks flushed, and this time, it wasn't because of the tequila. I shook my head. "Definitely not. Todd once asked who my daddy was in the bedroom." I shuddered at the memory. "It did not go well."

"What did you say?" Hadley asked.

"Well, he asked, so I answered honestly. Apparently, my dad's name wasn't the answer he wanted."

All three burst out laughing, and I couldn't help but join in. This was what I'd been missing—a group of friends to commiserate during my lows and celebrate my highs. When I left college, I had a pretty solid group, but we drifted apart when our lives started to settle. Between marriages, babies, and more responsibilities, our friendships fell by the wayside. While I wished I could blame it on the others, a lot of it was my fault. I'd poured so much into my marriage, pretty close to co-dependent on Todd for the decade we were together.

It wasn't until our relationship began to fray that I realized how much I'd isolated myself, how much I missed having a life of my own. Making new friends and figuring out what my new normal looked like wasn't easy, but I was determined to enjoy myself.

"Okay, so no Daddy kink," Hadley said. "But there must be other things you've always wanted to explore but never could in your marriage. Any super-secret desires you want to share with the rest of the class?"

I shook my head, heat filling my cheeks. Nice girls didn't talk about sex, especially not in public. It was supposed to be something only shared in the bedroom between two loving, consenting adults—not fodder for gossip circles. Bile hit the back of my tongue. Those words sounded more like my mother's than my own. After a lifetime of indoctrination that sex was a sin, meant for procreation, not pleasure, it was hard to erase that mentality. The women surrounding me helped. While they never talked about their boyfriends in that capacity, they were more than happy to share their past exploits, especially Ollie. While I was a serial monogamist, she had a strict two-week rule, and no one had tempted her to break it yet. We were opposites like that. She never let men stick around for too long, and I'd let the wrong one stay around forever.

If Todd hadn't crushed my heart, I'd probably still be there with him, suffering in silence as my world collapsed around me.

Victoria placed her hand over mine. "If you don't want to talk about this, we don't have to. We're just trying to help."

"I know, and I appreciate you guys." I nodded back to her. It was weird, being surrounded by these women in the prime of their lives while a big chunk of mine had already passed me by, too wrapped up in complacency to fight for anything more. "Truthfully," I sighed. "I'm not sure what I like. Todd was my first, and only, experience."

Ollie spluttered in her water. "What do you mean *only?*"

Hadley shot her a glare, and she smiled back at me

sheepishly. "We're not judging you, Bri. I'm just trying to understand. You're a fucking knockout."

I shook my head. "Not really. Especially growing up. No one notices the girl with her head buried in a book, too consumed with numbers and data to worry about making connections." I sighed and looked up at the ceiling. "I met Todd during freshman orientation, and we instantly clicked. After years of being invisible in high school, I liked that someone saw me, the real me, so I didn't have to worry about that anymore."

A deep sense of grief overwhelmed me, pulling me back to the sting of when our relationship began to sour. For years, Todd had been my constant, the one person I thought would always be by my side. But once that illusion shattered, it was almost impossible to pick up all the pieces, leaving lasting damage nothing seemed to fix. It had been three months since we finalized our divorce; the wound was still raw and festering, and no amount of alcohol would be enough to soothe that ache.

Instead, I just chuckled. "Pathetic, right?"

"Not pathetic." All my friends scrambled to reassure me, but shame coated me. Who lets one man change the entire course of their lives? *Me.* Here lies Brianna Sideris— she lived a lonely, safe life. My mind rebelled at that thought. That would not be my legacy. I might be alone, but I refused to spend any more nights lonely, wondering what could have been. No more hiding behind the walls of my marriage as my life passed me by.

I motioned for another round of shots, waiting until the server passed them out before lowering my voice. "You're right. I have the next nine weeks off, and I think it's time to try something new."

Ollie's eyes sparkled with mischief. "Are you saying what I think you are?"

I smirked back at her. "Tell me more about what I've been missing."

FOUR

Damien

"Please tell me you're not going to another club. Aren't you getting too old for that scene?"

I chuckled as my sister's voice rang out through the speakers of my car. Mari's comments were familiar territory by now. Even though I was the older one by three years, my baby sister had always been the worrier of our family, desperate to solve everyone's problems.

Chaos echoed behind her, children's laughter and screams filling the hotel suite we were sharing for the weekend. Not only did she bring her wife and my five nieces to watch me play, but they'd graciously offered to watch some of the other kids tonight so the players and their wives could celebrate a little longer. As much as I loved my extended family, I sent out a silent prayer that they'd all be in bed by the time I came back. Even though we had separate bedrooms, after a full day playing ball, I needed the rest, and the girls always woke up at the crack of dawn.

"No, Mari," I answered as I hit the blinker, turning into the bar's parking lot. "Just grabbing a quick drink with the guys. You don't have to worry about your brother's virtue here."

"Ha!" Mari barked through the phone. "I'm under no illusions about your so-called virtue. That ship sailed a long time ago."

I shook my head as I scanned the lot, trying to find a spot where my rental car wouldn't get dinged. Exhaustion draped over me, my muscles aching after a long day on the field, but a bunch of the other guys had wanted to go out tonight, and I was a team player at my core.

Even though we only had a week break for the all-star game, I missed my teammates. We spent almost all our time together, especially now that I'd been the captain for over a year. The Hawks got together at least once a week for a team meal, and we spent a lot of time hanging out after the games as well. Our families were so intermeshed, they'd all practically merged into one larger one—the Erie City Hawks family.

But here in Dallas, I only had a couple of the other guys from my team with me. The league sent three of us this year, and I was beyond grateful they'd picked our third baseman, Parker Drobrek, and our new short-stop, Cam Seda. Not only were they solid players, but they were also two of my closest friends, making the trip even more exciting.

"When are you going to meet a nice girl?" my sister asked, her voice tinged with disappointment. "Your nieces are dying for some cousins to play with. I met the sweetest woman in the stands today—"

"We've had this conversation a million times, Mari. Not gonna think about that until I retire." I turned off the ignition and pulled the phone to my ear as I walked toward the bar. "Besides, I've already got my hands full with your crew. You guys are all I need."

Mari ticked her tongue in agreement, even though she'd never admit it. When she first married her wife, Angie, she said she wanted a large family. Ten years later, they had five girls, their house a blur of chaos and love. But as much as I loved visiting them, I couldn't handle that right now, not on top of the team, all our away games, and trying to manage my sponsorship deals.

"And we love you too, D, but it's not the same. What happens if you get hurt? I don't want to see you alone just because you're too focused on baseball."

I paused, closing my eyes as I measured my next words. Mari might have been there for the end of my last relationship, but she'd only seen what I wanted to show her. She hadn't experienced the fights, the guilt, all the things that fucked up my game more than I wanted to admit. I'd tried like hell to make things work with Talia, but in the end, she still walked away, leaving my ring on the counter as she started a new life—one without baseball and constant travel and the fear of being moved to a new city at a moment's notice.

A life without me.

After that, I'd sworn off relationships, not needing to go through that ever again.

"Mari, I promise, I'm fine," I said. "Stop worrying about me."

"Never gonna happen, big brother." Something loud crashed in the background, and Mari swore under her breath. "The twins are terrorizing the villagers again. I gotta go. Love you."

I clicked off the call, heading across the gravel parking lot into the bar's front entrance. Mari's words flashed through my mind, but I shrugged them off. Ever since Talia left four years ago, professional baseball had been my entire world, and it would stay that way until they dragged me off the field. Too many people never got this chance, dreaming of playing under the lights until time or their bodies failed them. I wasn't about to squander this gift because my sister was worried about me.

When I pushed open the door to the bar, the air shifted. All the patrons by the door turned, eyes widening as they took me in. I'd been in the league long enough to be recognizable, especially after my years on the New York City Rebels. Even though the Hawks had a smaller following, most major fans recognized me even off the field. Most of the time, it didn't faze me.

But on nights like tonight, after spending a week playing nice with the press and spending time with all the fans, I was done. I just wanted to share a beer with my buddies, and their stares seemed invasive, like people wanted to cut out a piece of me.

A hand jutted out from the crowd, and I smiled, finding my teammates waiting at the bar. It had been a long week, and we were ready to head back home. At least the stress of the trade window was over. Baseball teams constantly fluctuated, so the stress always mounted when it was open. Luckily, while most of the Hawks survived the window, only a few of the guys running out of chances.

Before I left the stadium, I'd called the ones who'd been sent back down to the minors to make sure they were okay. Cam offered to stay behind with me, but I refused. As team captain, this was my burden to bear. Besides—he'd just gotten engaged and deserved to celebrate with his girl.

While I loved being team captain, some days, the weight of that responsibility felt like a thousand pounds on my shoulders. It brought back painful memories, like this time last year, when our second baseman, Jace, got sent back to the minors. After mentoring him for months, it killed me to watch Jace clear out his locker. He'd been trying to outrun his demons since the day he'd walked onto the field, and they'd finally caught up with him.

At least the change seemed to benefit him. He was thriving up in Maine, and there was talks about bringing him back to the pros. But as much as I wanted that for him, the last time we spoke, he still had some issues handling the pressure. I owed him a trip up to Portland, but right now, I had too much to do with the team, especially with playoffs coming up.

Shit, I needed a beer.

As I leaned against the dark wooden bar, Cam clapped my shoulder. "Hey man, how're you feeling?"

"Like shit." I raised my hand to the bartender, asking for the same beer as the rest of the guys. "Feels like I let the guys down."

Cam shook his head. "You did everything you could, cap. They know it, and so do the rest of us. Hopefully, they'll be back next season."

I hoped so too, but I pushed the thought out of my mind, instead focusing on the group surrounding me. The low pulse of a country song wailed through the speakers, and the air smelled of stale beer and popcorn. It was a far cry from my usual haunts, but when the rest of the guys picked the place, I refused to complain. Besides, Mari was right. I needed a break from the club scene. I loved the atmosphere—getting caught up in the rush of dancing and lust in the air—but the last week had been exhausting, and my body needed rest, not another distraction.

My phone chirped in my pocket, and I smiled, seeing

my five nieces' faces smiling back at me. A message sat in the middle of the screen in all capital letters.

MARI

FAMILY DINNER WHEN WE GET BACK.
NO EXCUSES.

I chuckled as I replied with a thumbs-up. My little sister was relentless. Hopefully, she wouldn't bring another surprise guest like she had for the last few dinners, all available women, whom she sat right next to me.

For a moment, the idea of settling down crashed through my mind. What would that even look like? The game would only last so long—I had only a few more seasons left before my body broke down. This season, it was already getting harder to shake off the muscle fatigue and pain. My right knee throbbed after every game, and my joints stiffened when I climbed out of bed each morning. Shit, I was already maxing out on sessions with the team's physical therapist. Maybe Mari was right, and I *should* think about retirement.

Fuck that. No way I'd leave my team anytime soon. We had too many games to play, and I had at least one more championship in me.

"Ah, shit," Cam chuckled, turning around with a wide grin. It didn't take a genius to see where his attention had drifted. His brand new fiancée, Hadley, had made an impromptu dance floor in the middle of the crowded bar, screaming the words of a classic song at the top of her lungs. He turned over his shoulder, glaring at the bartender. "Dude, I thought I warned you about the tequila."

He just shrugged. "She tips better than you."

Cam shook his head but didn't hide his smile. He was so

gone for his girl, it wasn't even funny. "Your funeral. Next, she's going to be up on the bar."

I smirked as I sipped my beer. "You going to stop that?"

"Nope," Cam said. "She's having fun. I'll intervene if any fucker tries to touch her, but Hadley can handle herself."

Heart beams practically shot out of his eyeballs; he couldn't look away as Hadley winked over her shoulder. I might have had my reservations about mixing relationships with baseball, but they were living proof it could work.

"Still can't believe she said yes," he muttered, smirking as he took another pull from his beer.

I clinked the top of my bottle with his. "Not surprised at all, Cam. That girl loves the hell out of you. Good thing she hasn't realized she can do so much better than your cranky ass."

Cam shook his head. "Don't I know it."

I laughed at his words, letting my eyes scan over the rest of the crowd. Okay, a distraction for the night might not be the worst thing. I might be determined to stay single for the foreseeable future, but that didn't mean I had to spend all my time alone. After all, what was the point of keeping my body in peak condition if I couldn't use it occasionally?

Although lately, my one-night conquests had left me wanting. It probably sounded cocky, but I'd never had a problem finding someone for the evening. The issue was finding someone I wanted to stick around when the sun rose.

God, I sounded just as pathetic as Cam. I loved my life, loved all the perks of my career choice. The women, the money, the lifestyle—all of it was a bonus. I already got to spend my days playing the game I loved, which was more than most guys got to say. And now, being at the top of the pack?

It was a damn good feeling.

A couple of women snuck past our group, staring at us like predators assessing their prey. The joke was on them; I played the game as well as the rest, but there was nothing meek about me. After a decade in the league, I could sniff out a jersey chaser from a mile away, the ones who saw the dollars attached to our contracts and got gold bars in their eyes. Another reason to keep that single box checked. If I couldn't tell a person's intentions, I kept them as far away as possible.

But when a long-legged brunette peeked back over her shoulder, nodding toward the bathroom, an easy grin formed on my face. Okay, not a great idea, but I was only a man, and there was nothing like a quickie in a bar bathroom to take the tension out of my bones.

I downed the rest of my beer and followed, but my steps faltered when I took in the new additions to Hadley's dance party. Two of the women, I knew well—frequent guests in the outfield. Ollie was Parker's best friend, and all the guys on the team knew better than to mess with her. As Parker's girl, she was strictly off-limits. Not because the dumbass had said anything about having feelings for her—he was too far in denial for that shit—but Parker was my friend, and Ollie was his everything, even if she couldn't see it. None of us would ever hurt our teammate like that.

The other woman was Cam's ex, recently married to a movie star. *Another in the no column.*

As I moved past them, my mind was singularly focused on the sexy brunette waiting for me by the bathroom—until someone collided with my chest, small, petite hands grasping my shirt like it was a lifeline.

Hazel eyes widened as they looked up to meet mine, surprise coloring her cheeks.

Brianna.

My fists clenched at the sight of her, trying to ignore the pull in my chest. It had been over a year since we'd stood in the same space, yet it was still there, daring me to get closer to her. Since the field day at her school, she'd become a regular member of our outfield gang, but I never let myself get too close, not with that wedding ring sitting on her finger.

I glanced down at her hands, still planted against my shirt. *No ring.* Interesting. Her fingers toyed with the lines of my jacket, as if she needed the support to stay standing, and I took a moment to study her up close. Brianna had cut her hair since the last time I saw her; now, it only dusted the tips of her shoulders. It was sexier, edgier than it'd been before, and seemed to suit her.

When Brianna realized what she was doing, she pushed against me, giving us some much-needed space. My body still thrummed from her touch, and it was way too tempting to reach back out to her.

"God, I am so sorry," she said, covering her face with her fingers. Her *bare* fingers. "I knew shots were a bad idea. Please ignore me while I go crawl in a hole and die."

"Nah, Brianna, nothing to be sorry about."

Her brow furrowed. "How do you know my name?"

I smirked, leaning in closer. "Am I that forgettable, Mrs. Collier?"

FIVE

Brianna

Mrs. Collier

My tequila-fueled brain latched on to the name—the one I'd used for the past decade of my life. As soon as Todd and I separated, I went back to my maiden name. Sideris suited me better than Collier ever did. Step one of reclaiming my future. That, and the drastic haircut I'd instantly regretted. At least it was growing out now, almost touching the tips of my shoulders. Thank God Ollie talked me out of bleaching out the color. Blonde would not have looked right on me.

Damien chuckled, and for a moment, I wondered if I'd said all that out loud. Freaking tequila shots. Even now that the alcohol was wearing off, it still clung in the corners, making everything around me feel fuzzy and warm. Or it might have had more to do with the slow, sly smile radiating from Damien Ramos.

Of all the men I could have run into, why did it have to be Damien? I'd noticed as soon as he entered the bar—he didn't blend in with the rest of the crowd. Not only was he one of the tallest men here, but he had a larger-than-life presence. The man oozed sex appeal, or, as Ollie would say, massive big-dick energy.

His eyes met mine, and my memories latched on to our first meeting—back when Cam convinced a bunch of his teammates to visit our school for Field Day. Even a year later, it was one of the best days of my career. I thanked every one of my lucky stars that Damien and I had been paired up at our station. We spent the entire day laughing, bonding with all the students. They still wrote him letters, and, to my surprise, he always wrote back.

My crush might have started long before that day, but it became all-consuming as I watched him up close. Oh shit. Did that make me sound like a stalker? I'd never done anything about it, but whenever I watched one of his games, my eyes sought him out, entranced by his power and precision. We hadn't spoken since Field Day, and every time we found ourselves in the same room, Damien made a convenient excuse to leave. I'd thought we'd gotten along when he visited the school; however, he seemed to have little interest in getting to know me any better.

It was probably for the best. After the train-wreck of my divorce, I wasn't looking for anyone to date—especially with someone who had the power to crush me like Damien.

He chuckled as he stepped closer. "You alright, Brianna?"

I shuddered as he said my name, loving how easily it rolled off his tongue. There was just a hint of an accent there that made each of his words sound more seductive to my alcohol-addled mind. A whoop from my friends pulled me out of my staring contest, and I took a giant step back.

Which was a mistake.

Just as I sputtered out that I was fine, my heel wobbled, and I almost landed on my ass. But before I could make a fool of myself *again*, Damien reached out and pulled me back to my feet. He smirked as I steadied myself. "Think it's time to call it a night. Do you have a ride back to the hotel?"

I glanced over my shoulder to find my friends still dancing. *God, bed sounded like heaven right now.* I'd never ask them to leave because I was about to fall asleep. Turning back toward Damien, I shrugged my shoulders. "I rode over with the girls. I'll just call a car to get back to the hotel. It's not too far from here."

Damien's jaw tightened, clearly unhappy with my words. An apology sat on the tip of my tongue, a habit from the past few years. But Damien didn't let me, instead reaching down to take my hand in his much larger one.

"Where are we going?" I asked as Damien guided me through the crowd.

"You said you wanted to go back to the hotel," he said, pausing so I could catch up to him. Fuck, he was a giant. My legs were about half his size, and it took everything in me not to topple over. He shook his head. "I don't like the idea of you in a rideshare this late, especially when you've been drinking."

"It's fine." I tried to let go of his hand, but he held tight. "It's only a couple of miles away."

"I know. I'm staying at the same one." He placed his hand on the small of my back. I shivered at the touch, savoring the rough callouses against my skin. Hell, when was the last time someone put their hands on me? *Too freaking long.* As much as I loved the new toys that filled my bedside drawer, the one thing they couldn't do was replace a man's rough touch.

Damien nudged me into the night air, a warm, sticky breeze blowing around us. It had been blaring hot all day, and apparently, it had no plans of breaking anytime soon.

We moved together until we reached a sleek sports car, one that did *not* belong in this dingy bar's parking lot.

My hand flew up to my lips, trying to hold back my giggles at the sight. It was like a diamond in the middle of a pile of dirt, so out of place, it was comical. Damien stopped, turning to stare at me with one of his brows cocked. God, he was so handsome. There were a lot of attractive guys on the Hawks' team, but no one made my stomach somersault like Damien. His dark eyes spoke of delicious, dirty promises, especially with the devastating smirk on his full lips. He was the polar opposite of my ex-husband, with his preppy attire and gelled blond hair. Todd might be attractive, but Damien's smoldering good looks were soul-shattering.

Shaking my head, I forced those thoughts away. This wasn't me. I was the girl who always chose the safe option. Must be leftover lust from my conversation in the bar. Ollie opened my mind to so many new options in the bedroom. Most didn't appeal to me, but I had to admit, a few of them had my thighs clenching together. *Please tell me I packed my favorite toy.* Between our conversation and my closeness to Damien Ramos, I really needed to take the edge off.

"Do you need anything before we head back?"

Damien's rich voice shocked me out of my thoughts. "I, uh—"

Just as I opened my mouth, the world around me shifted, and my knees buckled. My stomach twisted, and I slammed my mouth shut. *No, dear God, please do not let me lose my dinner next to this man. I will do anything.*

Suddenly, Damien shifted us, pressing me against the passenger-side door. My hand reached behind me, slamming against the glossy paint. My chest heaved as I looked up at him, and the unease in my stomach twisted into something else entirely.

I inhaled, soaking up the warm leather scent that wafted off his jacket. Being in this man's presence was more intoxicating than any of the drinks I'd had, making my heart pound and my head spin. Oh, wait, no. That might have been the tequila.

Damien frowned. "How much did you have to drink?"

"Me?" I said. "Too much. I normally stay away from shots, but Ollie convinced me otherwise."

"Celebrating or commiserating?"

The question brought Todd's wedding invite back to the forefront of my mind, and I frowned. Fresh shame rushed through my cheeks. My ex had won. *Again.* While he tasted cake samples and erased our marriage from his mind, I was drinking like I was back in college, perseverating on the end of our relationship.

I shifted away from Damien, not wanting him to witness anymore of my pathetic state. "Have you seen my purse? I should call a rideshare."

"Already told you, Brianna. I'm driving you back."

"But why?" I shook my head. "It's not your responsibility to make sure I get home okay."

"No, but I still want to do it." He shrugged. "You're a good friend of Hadley's, and she's part of the team. No way am I letting you hop into a stranger's car in an unfamiliar city, especially when you've been drinking." He reached behind, and for a moment, I thought he was leaning in to kiss me. I froze, unsure of what to do. Did I lean into his touch, letting him erase the memories plaguing me? Was this the opportunity to have some fun, like Ollie suggested?

Before I could figure out my answer, Damien's hand found the handle, pulling it open for me. *Oh God.* Shame washed over me. At least I didn't lean in to him or make a move to kiss him. That would have been the actual end of me.

"Do me a favor," Damien said as I climbed into the seat. "If you get nauseous, let me know so I can pull over. This car's a rental."

Fresh mortification filled my cheeks as I nodded, unable to meet his eyes. Damien's spine straightened. "Shit. I didn't mean to make you feel bad, Brianna."

"It's fine," I said, brushing off his concern despite the tight knot in my stomach. I was too old for this nonsense. When was the last time I even got drunk? It was so far in the past, I couldn't even remember when I'd had more than one glass of wine at a function. "For what it's worth, I have a pretty iron stomach, so your car is safe."

Damien smiled down at me. "Full of surprises, aren't you?"

No, not even a little. I'd never been the girl with the layers, the one who got more interesting the more you got to know her. Damien must have seen the defeat in my eyes, because he knelt and took my hand. His thumb swiped over my bare ring finger—like he wanted to know what happened. But I couldn't talk about it, especially not with this man. He was used to spending time around the most beautiful women in the world, not pathetic divorcees hiccuping cheap tequila. He didn't need to be exposed to my mess. Besides, when I cried, I turned into a red, splotchy raccoon. That was a sight no man wanted to see, especially not Damien.

"We should get going," I whispered, tugging my hand out of his.

With a frown, Damien shut the door and walked around the front of the car, God, my head throbbed. I should've skipped the last couple of shots. Tomorrow was going to be a nightmare, especially with my mid-afternoon flight. I'd much rather spend the day binging a bunch of the newest crime documentaries.

But all thoughts of tomorrow died as Damien closed the driver's side door, sealing us inside. As he turned the key in the ignition, he leaned over, tugging my seatbelt to check if it was secure.

"You ready?"

No, I was not.

SIX

Damien

What the fuck was wrong with me? My car sped along the empty city streets, passing through the streets of Dallas. The established city made me miss home. Erie City wasn't the biggest city in New York, but it was growing constantly. What had started as a small port city near the border was becoming a modern metropolis, and I loved getting to see it grow. I'd lived there for only three years, and my neighborhood had already shifted before my eyes.

As we turned off the main strip toward the hotel we'd called home for the past week, I snuck a peek at Brianna in the passenger seat. As much as I wanted to ignore her presence at my side, it was impossible, not with the way her subtle floral perfume filled my car. How did this woman pull me in so easily? Was it because she'd been off-limits before we met, or was it something about her?

Brianna stared out the window, almost consciously trying to keep a wall up between us. Even after drinking for most of the night, she sat straight up in the chair, as if someone had placed a taut spring along her spine. She needed to relax, to breathe, but I wasn't close enough to her to say anything.

Hell, this was the first time we'd been alone together, and I practically had to force her into my car. Which was surprising to me. I'd tried not to make assumptions, but experience had taught me that if I offered a woman a ride home, she'd usually make a move on me.

As I hit the turn signal, I turned my head to check for oncoming traffic, but got caught up, staring at Brianna. The streetlights highlighted her sad smile. There was an extra edge to her, one I hadn't noticed when we first met. Jaded—like life had done a number over the past few months.

She sighed and shifted toward me, her short brown hair spreading out over the headrest. "I'm guessing this isn't how you wanted your night to turn out."

No, it was not, but for the first time in a long time, I was okay with leaving the bar early. Celebrating with a new woman in my bed would have been fun, but lately, I'd woken up too many times with an emptiness inside my chest. No matter how many beautiful women traipsed into my life, it never seemed to fill, and each one-night stand only made it burrow deeper.

I cleared my throat, burying those emotions before smirking at Brianna. "Hanging out with a beautiful girl like you? I've had worse endings."

Brianna shook her head, hiding a slight smile under a lock of hair. I'd seen that look before—doubt and a little self-loathing. My jaw tensed, and I hated the darkness that wafted off her. "Once, when I was a rookie, a bunch of the guys pulled a prank on me. Took my clothes when I was in the shower and removed all the towels from the clubhouse. Had to run through the stadium naked, covering my goods with part of the mascot's costume."

"And you drove back to the hotel like that?"

"Yup." I grinned. "Walked right on the team bus and plopped down next to the coach. He almost had a heart attack right then and there."

Brianna let out a soft laugh, covering her mouth as her giggles dissolved in hiccups. I reached behind her and grabbed a spare water bottle from my bag in the backseat, twisting off the cap before handing it over to her. She gave a grateful smile before taking a sip, holding the bottle in her hands afterwards.

"So," I said as I stole a glance over at her. "Gonna tell me what happened to the ring?"

"What ring?"

I smirked. "You know which one, Bri."

Brianna's head snapped toward me. Her pouty lips dropped open as she covered her bare finger. "I'm surprised you noticed."

"I'm getting a little insulted here. We spent a day together, and you think I didn't pay attention to you?"

"Not really." There was no resentment in her voice, just cold fact. "It was just one day, Damien."

"You've also been to some of my games."

"True." She shook her head. "But it's not like we're friends or anything. I didn't think you remembered my name."

"Proved you wrong on that one." I winked at her, relishing the subtle color that filled her cheeks. "But we have a lot of friends in common, so maybe this is a good chance to change that."

Brianna's face furrowed as she glanced over at me, as if trying to read my intentions. When I kept the amiable smile on my face, she sighed. "What do you want to know?"

"When you lost the ring."

She laughed. "You have a one-track mind."

You have no idea.

There was no reason for me to be so curious. Besides my rule about not messing around with married women, there was no reason for me to be so curious about the end of Brianna's marriage. I should have let it go, but curiosity got the best of me, and I needed to know more about what happened.

Brianna sighed and turned toward the window, speaking more to the darkness than to me. "If you must know, I got divorced. We finalized it three months ago. In fact, I changed my name back to Sideris, so Mrs. Collier is no more."

Fuck. That was recent. I tried to read her tone, but she gave nothing away. "How are you holding up?"

"As good as I can, I guess."

"Can I ask what happened?"

"Lots of little things," she answered. "We'd been drifting apart for years, but the nail in the coffin was when I walked in on him jerking off on a video chat with his assistant. I told him I was done, and he just nodded, told me his lawyer would contact mine, and moved in with the same woman. Turns out, they'd been having an affair for almost a year, and now that we're officially divorced, they're getting married." Brianna laughed, but it held no warmth. "Aren't you glad you asked?"

"It's not me I'm worried about," I bit out. Who the hell acted like that? I'd never met her ex, but I already hated him. Cheating was the ultimate betrayal, hurting someone you loved for purely selfish reasons. Even before my ex ran off with someone else, it had been a major trigger for me, watching it too often with my parents growing up. They were both gone now, but the image of my mother weeping over my father's infidelity was permanently marked on my soul. "It's his fucking loss." My words took on a harsh tone, one I rarely used. "You deserve better than a cheating man-child."

Brianna nodded, not bothering to turn in my direction. Her jaw tensed, not trusting my words. It wasn't my problem. *Brianna* wasn't my problem. There was no reason for my pulse to quicken, wanting to find out everything about her ex so I could track him down and make him eat his words.

I pulled out into the hotel parking lot, staring out over the steering wheel. "Do you see any open spots?"

"Nope," Brianna said. "You can drop me off if you want, then head back out to meet the team. I don't want to disrupt your night any more than I have."

Searching the lot, I found no open spots. As much as I hated the idea of parking out on the side streets—I hated the idea of her walking alone more. I pulled my car out of the garage and into one of the empty spots on the side of the street then turned off the engine. When I stepped out and moved to the passenger-side door, Brianna stared up at me. "What are you doing?"

"Walking you inside."

Her eyes flared to life, but it seemed more like fear than fight. "If you think—"

"I'm not presuming anything, Bri. Like I said, I just want to make sure you get inside safely." I reached over and held my hand out to hers. "If you're worried about me trying anything, don't. I'm a little terrified of Ollie and what she would do to me if I'm not on my best behavior."

That made Brianna smile. She took my hand and climbed out of the car. It took everything in me to act like the gentleman I promised, but I couldn't help staring at her long legs as they peeked out from the bottom of her slinky black dress. For a moment, the image of her thighs wrapped around my ears flashed in my mind. Shit, I really needed to get laid.

I expected Brianna to scurry off down the street, considering that, all evening, she had seemed nervous in my presence. I didn't take it personally—between my stature and my reputation, many people had the wrong idea. But the idea of making Brianna nervous didn't sit right, especially with the limited information she shared about her ex-husband.

Instead, she stood in front of me, waffling on her heels like she was holding her words back. I shifted a little closer to her and pushed the door closed. Her hazel eyes tracked my movements, scanning my body when she thought I wasn't paying attention.

When I leaned back, her lips quirked into a slight smile. "And if I didn't want you to behave?"

Fuck. The words shot straight to my dick, unable to stop it from thickening at her tone. Brianna's innocent eyes flared to life, and for a moment, I considered what it would be like to cross that line, what it would be like to worship her. If she were anyone else, I wouldn't have hesitated, but Brianna wasn't a random woman I met at the bar. My team connected us, and our paths would cross, at least for the rest of the season. And I also wasn't joking about being terrified of Ollie. I'd watched her step up to grown men triple her size because they insulted Parker. No way did I want to face her wrath.

"You've been drinking, Brianna," I said, my words tight in my throat.

Her eyes darted down to her toes, and her sudden burst of confidence drained by my rejection. Fuck, now I was the biggest asshole in the world. All common sense fled me as she bit her lower lip, a dejected look crossing her features. My body acted on impulse, and I moved closer to her, reaching down to trace her jaw with the back of my fingers. She sucked in a sharp breath as her eyes darted up to meet mine. "If you were anyone else, I'd already have you upstairs, naked and begging for my cock. But you're Ollie's friend, Cam's friend. I don't do strings, Bri, and you're covered in them."

The corner of Brianna's lip quirked up. "And if I wanted something with none?"

SEVEN

Brianna

As soon as the words left my lips, I wanted to take them back. Damien's eyes flashed with fire when he stared down at me with an unfamiliar expression. I'd love to blame the alcohol, but most of it seemed to flee my system when I climbed into Damien's car. The drive, along with the mounting tension, was enough to sober me up.

No, these words were all mine, emboldened by my early conversation with my friends and the ache between my legs. Damien was powerful—alluring. His mere presence was enough to rock me out of my carefully laid plans, wanting to experience what it would be like to be at his mercy.

Damien sucked in a sharp breath, his hands almost shaking as he skimmed his fingers along my bare skin. God, I wanted him to touch me everywhere, to bring my body back to life after so many years of slumber. "Don't look at me like that, Brianna."

Fuck it. Playing it safe hadn't gotten me anywhere, stuck with an expensive divorce bill and living with a roommate again in my thirties. I placed my hands on his chest, and his pulse thundered underneath my touch. It flooded me, making me feel powerful in a way I hadn't in a long time. As I tilted my head up, my eyes darted to his lips, wishing more than anything that he'd bring his mouth to mine.

"Are you sure you want me to stop?"

Damien groaned, the sound so manly and wanting, it made my knees shake. His thumb brushed along my bottom lip, his calluses gliding along the smooth skin. "Fuck, Brianna. Who knew you were such a temptress?"

Not me, that's for sure. I wasn't this girl, not the woman who propositioned men on the side of the road, panting with the need for their touch. I took a sharp inhale, tightening my fingers so they ran along the smooth cotton of his shirt.

"Apparently not." Damien's brow furrowed as the words left my mouth. "You're resisting me."

Damien took a step forward, pressing my back up against the smooth lines of his car. His hips bucked against me, my core flush with his hardened length. His spare hand brushed through my hair, pushing it back until he could whisper in my ear. "You're playing a dangerous game, Brianna. I'm trying to be the good guy here, trying to hold back from fucking you like I'm dying to. You're not a stranger, not someone I can have one night with and walk away." His fingers tightened in my hair, exposing my neck to him. I gasped as his nose ran along the skin, stopping to nip at the shell of my ear. "But if you keep testing me, I'm going to show you exactly what you do to me."

This was the moment—the one when I should run back to my safe and comfortable life. I was in over my head with Damien. Just one look into his darkening eyes was enough to tell me we played in drastically different leagues, but I refused to back down—refused to give in to the fear that pulsed in my veins. Because for the first time, I was less afraid of the consequences than the regrets. Damien's eyes tracked my movements, analyzing each step for any sign of reluctance. I stared back at him, trying to keep my spine straight as I muttered, "Show me, Damien. Ruin me. I want to know exactly what it's like when you come undone."

His fingers tightened on my skin, as if it hurt him to hold back. It was overwhelming, being the subject of his unwavering attention. If his eyes were a pyre, I wanted to climb inside and let his warmth consume me.

With a sudden tug, we were moving, Damien pulling me toward the entrance of the hotel, leaving behind the humid Dallas heat. We entered the lobby, still hand in hand, not wasting a moment on the other occupants watching as we walked by. With the all-star game in town, seeing baseball players wasn't unusual, but Damien drew people in without effort. He did it to me. The moment we reached the elevator, he pushed me up against the sleek chrome surface, his hips anchoring mine in place.

As his hand pushed my hair over my shoulders, he shifted, leaning closer to speak into my ear. "Are you sure? Or is this just the alcohol talking?"

"No," I groaned, shifting my hips to get some of that delicious friction between us. "I want this—want you. Please, Damien. I need to feel alive again."

He pulled back, a smirk forming on his lips as his thumb brushed against my lower lip. "You're so pretty when you beg for me, Brianna."

My eyes darted up to his, giving in to the wanton woman he inspired. "Are you going to kiss me?"

Damien's eyes darted to my lips, looking at them like they could be his absolution, but he shook his head. "That's not what this is, Brianna. If we do cross the line, you need to know a few things. I'll make you come, make you forget your own name if that's what you want, but that's all I'm offering. All I *can* offer. If that's not what you're looking for, walk away now."

His words should have scared me, confirmed I was so far out of my league, I was one move from drowning. But one night of oblivion was all I wanted as well. My divorce bruised me, fracturing my heart into a shell of its former self. Even if someone offered me their whole one, I wasn't in the place to accept it.

"One night," I mumbled as my fingers found his chest. "That's all. When we get back home, we act like this never happened—and no one ever finds out."

"One night," Damien repeated. His hands dropped to my thighs, lifting me so my ass rested on the edge of the railing. His fingers coasted along my skin, stopping when they reached the hem of my dress. The black silk dress wasn't my normal style, but before we went out, Ollie ransacked her closet to find something for me. At first, I doubted her choice, much more comfortable in my jeans and a sweatshirt. But as Damien's fingers skimmed the space between my thighs, I sent out a silent thank you, because it was the most erotic thing I'd ever experienced.

When he brushed against the fabric of my thong, he smirked down at me. "You're dripping for me, Brianna. Is your pussy aching? Waiting for someone to give it what it deserves?"

"Yes," I moaned, shifting my hips to get him closer to me. But he kept up his gentle ministrations, touching me so lightly, yet I could sense it down to my toes. "Please, Damien."

I gasped as his fingers moved past the lace fabric, touching my bare skin for the very first time. My body called out to him, begging him to take everything and more. He sucked in a sharp breath as his fingers explored me, leaving light kisses on the skin of my neck.

The elevator dinged when we reached my floor, and Damien cursed under his breath, removing his fingers from my soaked panties. But before he got too far, the fabric suddenly snapped at my hips. I looked down, finding the black lace of my thong now clutched in his hand.

"D-did you just rip my panties off?" I squawked in disbelief, unsure if the move turned me on or pissed me off. Those were expensive, one of the few luxuries I allowed myself on my measly teacher income.

He just shrugged as he toyed with the fabric before sticking it into his pocket. "Might be only one night, but I already know I'm going to want to remember this one. Consider these my souvenir."

I wanted to protest, but they all died on my lips. We walked to my hotel room in silence, neither of us wanting to break the tension brewing between us. Once the door opened, the game was on. After I turned the key, Damien reached out, stopping me before I could open it. "Before we go inside, I want you to make sure this is what you want, Brianna. If you've changed your mind, I won't hold it against you. Fuck, if you change your mind at any point, all you have to do is say so."

I shifted, pressing my back against the wood so it opened. Reaching out, I took his hand and pulled him into my room. As the door closed, I stood against it, needing the strength to keep standing. Too much desire filled the air, too much promise of what would come next. There was no backing down, not for me. "I'm not changing my mind. But the same goes for you. It's not only about my comfort here, Damien."

His eyes flashed, as if I'd struck an unintentional nerve. Any hesitancy was gone, replaced by the longing I'd seen earlier. His hands found my hips, shifting us so I was up against the door, his body keeping me tight against him. "I've wanted you since the first time I saw you, Brianna. Something about that innocent smile," he thumbed my lower lip, "made me want to corrupt you. And now that I have you, that's exactly what I'm going to do."

EIGHT

As Brianna's angelic eyes widened at my words, my gut screamed. *This was a mistake.* The smart thing would have been to walk back out that door, to ignore the way Brianna's sweet pussy wept for my touch, to go back out into the world and find someone else to warm my bed for the night, someone I'd leave without guilt or my conscience screaming at me.

However, from the moment I saw her at the bar, the die was cast. I might have a lot of strengths, but walking away from Brianna right now wasn't one of them.

Brianna's hazel eyes watched as I lowered to my knees. The fucking hem of her little black dress had been teasing me the entire car ride, shifting just enough to expose the delicate skin lurking below. Now that I'd touched her—felt her reaction—there was no backing down, no hiding.

My hands bunched up the skirt of her dress until Brianna's bare pussy was in my face. The delicate skin called to me, glistening with her desire. I groaned as I dove in, nothing tentative or tender about my touches. I shifted to hitch one of her legs over my shoulder, giving me more access to what I wanted. When my mouth sealed over her aching cunt, Brianna moaned, the sound electric to my ears. Her dark hair spread out around her face, and she looked like an angel on the verge of damnation. *My* angel.

Her taste consumed my senses: sweet and delicate, just like the woman in front of me. Brianna was a fortress, hiding behind her eyes and placating smile, but I sensed the damage lurking just beneath the surface, the kind no one bothered to look for. It called to my darkness, to the doubts and fears I locked behind in the night. For tonight, I'd hide them away, too consumed with pulling as much pleasure from Brianna as possible.

As my fingers dipped into her core, her hands fell to my hair, tugging me closer. She gasped in realization, pulling away as if I'd shocked her. "I'm so sorry—"

I silenced her with another long lick of my tongue. "Don't you fucking apologize, Brianna. Grab me, hold me, do whatever feels right. Let me know you're enjoying yourself."

"Yes," she said breathlessly. "Fuck, Damien. This—you. It's too good. Don't stop."

I couldn't even if I wanted to. Not with the soft press of her thigh into my shoulder, her succulent warmth squeezing my fingers like she never wanted to let go. Everything about this moment was like poetry—overwhelming, confusing, and yet the most beautiful thing I'd ever witnessed.

With another suck and curl of my fingers, Brianna fell apart in my arms, pleasure overtaking her like I'd never seen before. There was nothing soft about how she came, her screams loud enough to wake the entire hotel. How had anyone ever let her go? She was a fucking goddess when she fell apart, and all I could do was sit back and bask in her heat.

When she stopped trembling, she chewed on her lower lip, her doubts erasing her earlier confidence. Her eyes darted down to my rigid cock, pulsing, hard and heavy through the dark material of my jeans. "I, uh, I could take care of that for you."

I lifted from my knees, shifting to press her back into the panel of the door. "You're going to, angel. I'm going to bury myself so far inside you, you'll feel me for days." Her cheeks flushed, but for the first time, it didn't seem like nerves. It was more like excitement. Her pulse pounded under her slick skin, and I ran my fingers along the column of her throat. I forced myself away from her long enough to look around the hotel room. It was similar to my set-up, with a small living room and two bedrooms off it. "Which room is yours? Unless you'd like me to fuck you right here?"

Brianna's mouth dropped open, and then she was pushing back on my chest, rushing through the room without looking over her shoulder, as if she knew I'd follow, which I did without hesitation. Honestly, nothing could have turned me away at this point. When was the last time a hookup left me this needy?

I enjoyed sex, don't get me wrong, but lately, it turned into an itch to scratch, a way to lose myself for a couple of hours. And while I always left my partners satisfied, it was more about chasing my high than anything else.

But not tonight.

When Brianna placed her hand on the doorknob and led me toward her bedroom, electricity crackled in the space between us. Tonight was different—not about chasing my pleasure or forgetting about my stress for a few hours. It was all about Brianna, about bringing her more pleasure than she could handle. I brought my fingers up to my lips, sucking down the last of her. She tasted like the end of a rainstorm, the moment when the world was washed clean.

I entered the bedroom right after her, not wasting any time to look around the space, as tempting as it might be. This wasn't about getting to know Brianna on anything other than a primal level, and I needed to remember that. One night. That was all I had to offer, especially at this stage of my life. Give her everything this one time, but when I walked back out that door, we were done, nothing more than a passing memory.

And if that was all we had, it would be one she'd never forget.

Brianna stood at the edge of her bed, toying with the edge of her dress, unsure what to do next. That wouldn't do. I moved in front of her, lifting the fabric from her trembling fingers. With a hand on her shoulder, I turned her around, pulling down the zipper until the black fabric lay bunched around her ankles. When Brianna turned back toward me, her arms were wrapped around her stomach. *Protecting herself.*

I arched a brow, running my fingers along her clenched arms. "Why are you hiding from me, Brianna?"

She shook her head. "My body...it's probably not what you're used to. I'm older—"

My hand darted up, forcing her trembling chin up, so she'd meet my eyes. "You're fucking gorgeous. Every single inch." My spare hand took hers and placed it over my weeping cock. "You feel that? That's because of you. Because of your fucking gorgeous body, angel." A smug smirk curled on my lips as her mouth dropped open, unable to pull her gaze away from me. "Now, are you going to let me have you? Because I can't take you in all the ways I want if you're hiding from me."

With a resigned sigh, Brianna brought her arms to her side. Her fingers still twitched with the need to cover herself, but she fought against it. I leaned down, pressing a soft kiss to her breastbone. "Good girl, angel. Now, undress me." Her eyes widened, but she did as I asked, unbuttoning my shirt until it slid off my shoulders. With my chest bare in front of her, she stopped, her eyes jumping up to meet mine. "Now the pants."

Her fingers fumbled with the button of my jeans, twisting until the fabric loosened on my hips. Brianna's eyes traced every inch of my body, studying the ink that started at my wrist and climbed up onto my chest. Five angels—one for each of my nieces—sat on my arm, watching over me, just as I pledged to watch over them. But I didn't give her that story, not when she looked like a vision pulled from my filthiest dreams. I leaned down and lifted her by the knees, depositing her onto her bed with a soft thud. She giggled as she bounced on the mattress, the sound so soft and light, it made me smile.

I tugged down my jeans and boxers as Brianna's eyes tracked every one of my movements. When my cock came into view, she sucked in a sharp breath. "Damien, I—" She tucked her lip between her teeth. "I don't know if I can take you. That's—" She laughed and covered her face.

I climbed over her, brushing her hands away to see her smile. "That's what, angel?"

She rolled her eyes. "Ollie always said you had BDE, but I never got it until this moment. You've *definitely* earned that title."

I shifted onto my haunches, fisting my cock as I looked down at her, sprawled out on the bed like a gift. "You like this dick, angel?" Her eyes flared as she nodded. "Then show me how much you want me to fuck you. Give me your mouth; get it nice and wet before I tear your sweet little pussy apart."

Brianna didn't hesitate as she shifted, scrambling to tilt my cock toward her mouth. The first touch of her hands to my skin was tentative, wrapping around my thick cock like she didn't want to hurt me. "Squeeze me harder, Bri. I can take it."

She smiled half-heartedly as she looked up at me. "I'm not sure what I'm doing, if I'm even doing it right. Todd—"

I reached down and gripped her jaw. "Don't you say another man's name while you've got your hands wrapped around me. This might only be a one-time thing, but while we're in this bed, you're fucking mine, Brianna." My fingers stroked along her cheek. "Do you understand me?"

"Yes," Brianna whispered. "Show me what you like, Damien. I want this to be good for you."

"Oh, angel," I chuckled, brushing a finger along her jaw. "You're going to look so fucking gorgeous with your mouth full of my cock."

She looked up at me, opening her mouth and sticking out her tongue, offering herself to me. The sight was so unexpected, my spine tensed, and I had to rein in the urge to ram myself down her throat. Instead, I coaxed forward slowly, teasing her with only the tip. As I gave shallow thrusts, Brianna's tongue jutted out, circling the head of my cock. Goddamn. Her apprehensive touches felt like heaven, but I wanted so much more. "God, Bri. So fucking good." I ran my hand through her hair, pulling her mouth off. "But I need you to take me deeper, angel. Can you do that for me?"

"Yes," she moaned, her hand twisting around the base of my cock. "Take my mouth, Damien."

Fuck. Four words, and I was coming undone. I fisted

Brianna's hair, holding her tight as I guided her pouty lips over the head of my cock. But this time, I didn't stop, guiding her until she gagged around my length. Pulling back, I searched her expression, but there was only eagerness looking back at me. "If it gets to be too much, smack my thigh." Brianna nodded, and I resumed my movements, pressing in a little further each time. Despite her insistence that she didn't have any experience in this area, Brianna's mouth was a gift I didn't deserve. She moaned as she took more of me, her tongue brushing up along my shaft like it was the sweetest treat. When her cheeks hollowed out around me, my knees buckled, almost coming before we'd even begun.

When I pulled her off me, she looked at me, her hazel eyes rimmed red and brimming with tears. "Wh—why did you stop?"

I leaned down and brushed my thumb along her bottom lip, collecting the saliva that had pooled at the edge of her mouth. "You're too fucking good, angel. I'm not missing the chance to come inside you."

Brianna smiled at me, and something cracked inside my chest. She might have been the one on her knees, but for a moment, I wanted to be the one bowing to her, to worship her. Shaking my head, I pushed that thought from my mind. This was one night, one chance to get her out of my system. "Lay back, Brianna. Let me see all of you."

NINE

Brianna

Staring into Damien's eyes, the world shifted underneath me. I blamed Ollie, blamed tequila, blamed everyone under the sun for my situation, trapped under the heavy stare of Damien Ramos. The man had already destroyed my views on sex, and he hadn't even fucked me yet. He'd ravaged my pussy with his tongue, fucked my mouth until I was on the brink of coming again, yet I still wanted more.

He prowled over to his pants and pulled out a condom. My eyes darted down to the impressive length between his legs. He was built like an Adonis, an impressive form that poets and musicians wrote ballads about. Thick, corded muscles covered his entire body while dark ink covered his arms and the expanse of his left thigh. And for tonight, he was mine, and I wasn't about to waste a single moment.

My eyes tracked him as he came back towards the bed, crawling onto my mattress. He sat up against the head-board, watching me with his dark gaze. If it were anyone else, I would have been terrified, but this man consumed me. It was a powerful, heady expression, and it made my thighs slick with my desire.

"Come here," he growled, placing his large hand on my wrist and tugging me closer. I climbed onto his lap, and his hands settled on my thighs. His rough touch sent another wave of lust through my bloodstream. "Climb up, angel. Ride me until you fall apart."

I didn't wait, only hesitated slightly when I lifted my hips above him. The first press of his length to my entrance stretched me wider than I'd ever been, almost like we'd never fit together. "Damien, I—"

Just as I gave up hope, Damien surged forward, kissing my chest and my breasts. His mouth encircled one of my tender buds, and his teeth skated along its skin. A breath rushed out of my lungs as he paid the same attention to the other, coaxing me into a suspended state of euphoria. Just as my head fell back to allow him more access to my chest, his arm wrapped around my middle, bringing me down further onto his length. My mouth fell open as I worked him, swiveling my hips so I could take more each time I lowered myself. Sweat coated our bodies as Damien's mouth and hands worked my body, helping me take him fully.

"Take me, Brianna." His eyes bore into mine with an intensity I'd never seen before. "Take all of me. Every last fucking inch."

"I..." My words came out breathless. "I don't know if I can."

"Yes, you can. You will." His hand gripped my ass, moving me with a newfound vigor. "You look too good taking my cock to stop now. Now, be a good fucking girl and sink down on top of me. Let me give you everything and more."

That command was enough to loosen the last of my restraints. I leaned forward, my nails digging into the hard planes of his pecs. There'd be scratches there tomorrow, but I couldn't bring myself to care. The idea of Damien wearing marks I'd left on his skin only turned me on more.

"Fuck, Bri," Damien panted as his fingers dug into my hips. "God, who the hell knew you were hiding all this under that shy smile."

I let out a moan, loving how his words emboldened my moves. As much as I tried to push Todd out of my mind right now—I didn't want to sour this experience—I couldn't help but compare the two. Todd was always quiet, and I never knew if he liked what I was doing, much less sang my praises. To hear that Damien loved what my body did to him made pleasure curl through my bones, making me almost weightless. As my pussy gripped him tightly, I let out a spluttered curse. "Damien, I'm going to—"

"I've got you, angel. Give me everything. I want you dripping on my thighs."

With that, I crashed over the edge, nothing graceful or subtle about the way I came for this man. For a moment, white spots blurred my vision, and I surrendered to the pleasure cascading through my limbs. It was everything—the piece I'd been missing for so long. It was like it broke the last tether of my old life, and I knew I'd never settle for anything less again.

As soon as my mind climbed out of the clouds, Damien roared out his own release, screaming my name into the night sky. He'd come unleashed, and his groans of pleasure echoed through my chest like a medal of honor. I'd made this man—the one who made legends cower when he walked onto the baseball field—lose all control. His fingers dug into my skin, his touch almost painful, but I loved every second.

When he came down from his high, Damien's eyes met mine, and something like adoration flashed back at me. His eyes flickered down to my lips, and for a moment, I wondered what it would be like to have his mouth on mine. But we couldn't—he wouldn't. That was the one line Damien had drawn, and I had to respect it. Besides, it wasn't like this was relationship, or the start of anything meaningful between us. Damien might have shattered all my past sexual experiences, but he was only mine for the night.

I'd just broken free of the chains of one man; no way I'd willingly surrender control to another, no matter how amazing the sex had been.

Slowly, I climbed off his lap, collapsing onto the pillows by his side. Damien just watched me, his eyes tracking every inch of my still-bare skin. As the sex haze wore off, self-consciousness wrapped over me. This man might have seen every inch of my body before, but that was when we were hooking up. Now, it made me feel vulnerable, like he'd switch his words since he'd gotten what he'd wanted.

I chewed my lower lip. "If you want to grab a shower before you go, you can use mine."

Damien chuckled as he rolled over, kissing my bare shoulder. "No need, angel. I'll wait until the morning."

"Are you sure? That was—" I cut off, unsure how to finish the sentence.

"I'm positive," Damien said as he shifted to the side of the bed. He grabbed my ankle, dragging me closer as he lowered onto his knees.

"Wh-what are you doing?" I asked.

He arched his brow. "You agreed on one night, remember?" I nodded. He looked over my shoulder at the sheer curtains covering my window. "Don't see any daylight yet, angel. We still have a few more hours together, and I have every intention of going until you can't take anymore."

I GROANED when I woke the next morning, my head still fuzzy. Damien kept me up most of the night, making me come more times than I ever had in my life. After the fifth mind-bending orgasm, I crashed—hard. If it weren't for the lingering ache, I would have chalked it up to a drunken sex dream. But even hours after Damien headed to his room, the space between my legs felt used and worshipped. God, what I wouldn't give for a bath right now.

When Todd and I bought our house, I'd always dreamed of an antique clawfoot tub. It was the one thing on my wishlist, but it never came to be, pushed aside for more practical things—like Todd's gym. Annoyance prickled through my skin, hating that my thoughts turned to him at every chance. Maybe this was the penance for walking away from your decade-long relationship—it tainted every new thought, every piece of your new life.

I turned over onto the spare pillow. Even though I had an entire bed to myself now, I still slept in a ball, uncomfortable if not tucked into the corner. When I'd last closed my eyes, Damien had been there, watching me as I drifted off to sleep. All I'd felt was a light kiss on my shoulder when he left, but I had no idea what time he'd left. He'd made good on his promise—the sun was rising when I tapped out. He'd wrung every ounce of pleasure from my body, and its effects would haunt me for days.

Reluctantly, I climbed out of my bed, stretching my arms over my head. I walked into the ensuite bathroom, checking myself out in the mirror. I ran my fingers over the marks on my hips and thighs. It was a reminder of last night; I hadn't imagined Damien. They'd already begun to fade, and I hated it, wanting to hold on a little longer.

After grabbing a quick shower, scrubbing the remnants of last night from my skin, I headed into the sitting area, in desperate need of caffeine. I had a few hours before I needed to head over to the airport, and I was planning on using every moment to relax until it was time.

Thank goodness it was the summer, and even when we got back, I had weeks before I had to think about returning to work. On school days, I was up before the sun, needing to get everything settled before the kids arrived.

As a special education teacher, my job was almost always in flux, especially now that Hadley had left to pursue her dream of opening an early childhood center.

Every year, I'd change grade levels, fitting in wherever they needed a co-teacher. I was at the mercy of the general education teachers, with them deciding who wanted to take on the added responsibility in their classroom. Most years, it worked out well. I'd worked at the school for eight years and had good relationships with most of my colleagues. My work ethic spoke for itself, and I'd dedicated myself to my students. However, I had a couple of colleagues I'd never gotten along with, our personalities and disciplines too different.

The worst one? Brad Fitzman. He was the type of teacher who made a mockery of our profession. After almost a decade of working together, I couldn't find a redeeming quality in him.

Guess I'd have to try harder when we shared a classroom next year. I didn't even know why he agreed to the assignment—probably thinking of me more like an additional set of hands than a co-teacher. At least it was only for one year; then, I'd move on to someone who actually cared if their students' succeeded.

The sudden rush of anxiety made my fingers itch, and I glanced around the hotel room. Even though we'd only been here for a week, clutter covered every inch, thanks to Ollie. While I'd never be able to thank her enough for opening her home to me when I needed one, the girl was a slob. It was like the chaos in her mind spilled out around her, and she left a trail wherever she went. You could see the piles of things she started to sort before she lost focus, moving on to another task she'd never finish.

I tried to relax as my coffee brewed, reminding myself it was summer vacation and I'd earned some time to rest. But my body refused to settle, knowing there were things to be done—clothes to pack, reservations to double check, and snacks to buy, all the small things that used to trigger my ex-husband if I left them to the last minute. My jaw tensed, sucked into flashbacks of the many times Todd had walked through the door, barely taking his shoes off before berating me. It didn't matter that my career was just as demanding as his—Todd thought our house was my responsibility. Even though my day started at five in the morning and didn't stop until long after I got home, none of that mattered to him, and he made sure I knew it. It became so frequent, I couldn't relax with chores hanging over my head.

Just as I started to pick up Ollie's stuff, the door to the hotel room burst open, Ollie juggling her bag and two giant coffees in her hands. She squeezed her phone between her neck and her shoulder, talking to someone about an account that needed to be revitalized. I just shook my head, always impressed by Ollie's ability to multi-task. In the past couple of months, Ollie had started an online marketing firm, focusing on local athletes. She'd planned on keeping it small, but Parker had recruited most of the guys in Erie City to check out her services, so her roster was already becoming too much for her to manage alone. The work never stopped, but Ollie loved it, enjoyed swooping in to make sure her clients' reputations were pristine.

As she walked into the kitchen, she dropped her bags on the counter, shot me a glare before looking down at her shirt in my hands. *"Don't you dare,"* she mouthed as she nodded into the phone. "Yup, that campaign sounds good. Send me the details, and I'll get everything set up. *Yup.*" She rolled her eyes at me. "Listen, Theo. You either learn to trust me or find someone else to work with, someone your clients will pay double the price for half-ass work. Now, leave me alone so I can enjoy the rest of my morning."

With that, she hung up her phone, tossing it back in her purse. Her knowing smirk filled the lower half of her face. "It smells like sex in here."

My mouth spluttered open. "Wh-what are you talking about?"

Ollie rolled her eyes. "Dammit, I was hoping that would trip you up. Way to squash my dreams that you'd gotten down and dirty last night."

I shook my head, hoping to hide the blush that colored my cheeks. While I wanted nothing more than to tell Ollie everything about Damien, we'd promised not to say anything, and I was determined to keep my word. "What about you?" I asked, changing the subject. "Why didn't you make it back last night?"

"Nothing scandalous," Ollie groaned as she dropped onto the couch. "After we got everyone back to their rooms, Parker and I stayed up talking. You know Park—can't leave the game on the field."

I nodded, trying to keep my mouth shut. Ollie was

always an open book—except when it came to her relationship with Parker. If anyone asked if they were more than friends, she'd instantly shut them down.

There were moments I tried to broach the subject, but right now, when I had a secret of my own, I kept my mouth shut.

Damien

Most days, I lived to be on the field. I loved the sounds, the smells, the turf underneath my cleats. I even loved how the sun beat down on my head, reminding me to keep my mind focused. Days spent like this one—on the field with my team—were what kept me going.

Today, however, an ice pick had lodged itself into my brain.

As I headed over to the baseline, I groaned and ran my hand over my face. God, I was getting too old for this shit. After the all-star game, we'd headed back to Erie City, only to jump back on a plane the next day to play a series out in Phoenix. We'd won it in a clean sweep, and we'd spent the last night celebrating our victory. Now, it felt like lead filled my bones.

There used to be a time when I stayed up all night and still walked onto the field with a smile on my face the next morning. Not anymore. Once I hit thirty, if I didn't get a solid night's sleep, my body ached all damn day. My eyes stung under the lights, desperate to close for a few hours.

Glancing down at my watch, I cursed under my breath. No way that would happen soon.

As I closed my eyes and let my head fall back, my mind instantly drifted to last week, when I'd spent the entire night exploring every inch of Brianna's body. It had been the beginning of this long stretch, and it definitely started me off on the wrong foot, but I wouldn't trade it for anything.

Being wrapped up in Brianna felt right—more so than anything else had in a long time. Pretty sure that woman drained me dry, keeping up with me long into the early hours. Right before dawn, when her gorgeous eyes finally fluttered closed, I lay in her bed, staring as her chest rose and fell. I waited for the usual itch—the one that told me to leave before she woke up. Instead, I had to fight the urge to snuggle up to her, to wrap my arms around her and pull her close. That threw me off enough to get me to move, to head home. I'd only gotten three hours of sleep before it was time to meet the guys at the airport.

"Ramos, get your head out of your ass and start running. No fucking around before this weekend."

I groaned and forced my legs to move. Baseball didn't give a shit about my exhaustion, and our manager, Benny Weber, cared even less. The man was a hard ass, already coming to our team last year with a decade of experience and a legendary temper. It was getting easier to battle his moods, but he had no tolerance for excuses. Plus, I couldn't tell my team I was distracted because I'd been dreaming about fucking their friend to oblivion.

"Shit," Parker groaned as he approached my side. His pale skin was even more pallid than usual. "Remind me again why we went out last night?"

"The rookies made us," Cam said as he tagged second

base. "Thought it would be a good time for some team bonding because they had a week off before the series."

"Oh yeah," Parker answered. "Remind me never to listen to them again. I feel like shit on burnt toast."

I shook my head, glad all of us were in pain today. Being the old man on the team came with enough shit; I didn't need to bring any more attention to it by limping around the field after a night out. They'd all been ready to celebrate, but I was ready to go home after my first drink. While most of the younger guys were looking to find someone for the night, no one interested me. No, Brianna was all I could think about.

When I closed my eyes, I could still feel her pulsing around me. *Shit*. Not good. Just the fucking memory of Brianna had my dick hardening in my pants. No way the guys would ever let me live it down if they caught on.

And no matter how much I craved Brianna, we were done. One night—it had to be only one night. After only a few hours together, the wounds from her divorce seemed to heal a little. There would always be scars, but eventually, she'd be able to move past them. She deserved it all—the marriage, the white picket fence, the man who would be home every night when the clock struck five. But a beautiful woman like that deserved to be worshipped, and I was a selfish enough bastard to be the one who wanted to bring her pleasure. My job was done.

So why the hell did I suddenly want more?

"D?" Parker asked, pulling me back into the conversation.

"What?" I said, running my hand over my head. "Sorry, zoned out for a minute."

Parker and Cam shared a look. Nope, didn't like that

one fucking bit. Parker dared to ask first. "Does this zone out have to do with Bri? Everyone saw you two leaving together in Dallas."

"Just gave her a ride back to the hotel," I said with a shrug, trying to keep an easy smile on my face. "The girl couldn't handle her alcohol. Not about to let her take a cab in that state."

The lie soured on my tongue. Lying to my teammates was the worst, but sharing personal details wasn't my style. I'd had enough partners in the past share our bedroom stories for a quick payday, so I learned to keep a lot to myself. But even more—I didn't want to share what had happened between Brianna and me. Just the idea of talking about it sullied the memories of watching her chest flush with pleasure as I pulsed inside her.

Cam studied my expression almost as if he sensed the lie. But before the guys said anything else, Melanie, our social media manager, burst onto the field. Benny dropped his head, muttering a string of curses under his breath. While the team might piss him off daily, no one got under Benny's skin like Melanie. He hated all the publicity, a lingering effect of his past on the New York Rebels, and with Melanie as the face of our Public Relations department, the two were always at odds. Despite Weber's surly streak, Melanie was relentless, bullying him into interviews, even though he refused to read the notes and cue cards she spent hours assembling. Still, beneath the animosity between them, there was also a begrudging respect, and Benny didn't tolerate anyone else questioning Melanie's directives.

We all paused, waiting to see who landed in the hot seat. Last year, she spent almost all her time fixing Jace's messes, but now that he'd been demoted to the minors, Melanie had less to do. Still, a major part of her job was keeping our names clean, and that required a lot of hours. Only one reason would bring her down here during practice. Someone had fucked up, and she was going to give them hell for it. We all looked around, trying to figure out who it might be. No one wanted to be the guy she plucked off the field.

"Ramos," she bellowed as she crossed her arms, her dark red nails clicking on her black, tailored jacket. "Come with me."

Unease crept up my spine as she stared at me. Memories of the last few weeks raced through my mind, trying to figure out what had caught her eye.

"You better hurry the fuck up," Parker said, his face a little greener than a couple minutes ago. "She looks pissed."

"How can you tell?" I muttered as I stared at her.

Melanie had a thick skin and was notoriously hard to rattle, but she also radiated *a don't-fuck-with-me* attitude. While she treated the players well, I'd never make the mistake of calling her friendly. She rarely smiled, only plastering on a fake one when the cameras came around. She was all business, and none of us made it very easy for her to do her job. I couldn't imagine how much stress she was under, trying to control the narrative of an entire baseball team.

Each step weighed me down as I followed her into her office in the corporate suite upstairs. It was never good getting called up here. The halls were too sterile, too clean. Upstairs was the opposite of the clubhouse, where it was always loud and just a little chaotic. I followed Melanie into her office, waiting until she stepped around her desk to take a seat. Glancing around the space, unease crept up my spine, reminding me I was an invader. Photographs lined the walls, publicity stills taken over the past season. A large calendar took up an entire side of the office, dates marked for photoshoots and interviews Melanie had to coordinate with players.

As she stared back at me over her desk, my pulse ratcheted up in my chest. I tapped my fingers on my thighs, trying to displace some of my anxiety energy. "Okay, Mel. You gonna tell me why you pulled me off the field?"

She arched a brow at the nickname but said nothing, instead turning back toward her computer. "Do you have any idea how hard it is to manage people's images in the time of social media and smart phones?" I opened my mouth to respond, but she continued. "Pretty fucking hard, especially with the younger guys, the ones who haven't learned people are always watching. *Always*. And I thought you were smart enough to realize that too, Damien."

My jaw clenched. "I am."

"Hmm," she sighed as she kept typing. She turned her computer screen toward me. "Then you want to tell me why someone sent me this video?"

My blood chilled as I recognized the familiar elevator, the one I'd taken almost every day when I stayed in Dallas. But unlike most of the time, I wasn't alone. Instead, my hands were all over Brianna, toying with the hem of her dress. When my fingers slipped under her dress, I reached forward, slamming the mouse down to pause the frame.

"Shit," I hissed as I dragged my hand over my face. "We didn't know there were cameras."

"No kidding," Melanie muttered. "Oh, and it only gets better. There are photos of you with the same girl on the street, getting cozy against your car." She ripped her computer monitor back toward her. "What were you thinking, Damien?"

"I wasn't," I bit out. The images played back in my mind, and a sour taste sat on my tongue. It wasn't the first time my personal life had been leaked to the media, but at least those partners were used to the attention. Brianna wasn't. She was a normal person—a teacher, for fuck's sake. "Please tell me you killed this before it got out."

"Of course I did." Melanie crossed her arms and leaned back. "At least, I killed the elevator video. The social media posts are out there, but there's not too much traction. Lucky for you, some football player cheated on his model girlfriend, so you seem to be in the clear. Keep your head down for a day or two, and I'm sure it'll go away with little attention."

"Thank fuck." My head dropped between my shoulders, relief sweeping over me. Another reason I stayed away from relationships. Most people couldn't handle being in the public eye, especially when they weren't used to it. Just the idea of Brianna being subjected to the court of public opinion made my fists tighten. "Thanks, Mel."

"Do you need me to talk to the girl? Explain how to handle the attention?"

"No need," I said. "She's in the clear. You know my rule —one night only."

Melanie rolled her eyes. "Of course you have a one night only rule. Aren't you a little old to be using the fuck boy handbook?"

"Oh, come on, Mel. It's not like that."

Melanie crossed her arms, staring at me with an exasperated expression, the one that spoke of my potential and how she thought I was wasting it. It was a familiar sight—it was also Marianna's favorite expression. She shook her head, returning her attention to the computer. "I shouldn't say anything, but upper management has been talking about your reputation."

"My reputation?"

She rolled her eyes. "Don't play dumb, Damien. It's beneath you. You're a legend on the field, but your off-field behavior has been attracting the wrong attention. And it's getting noticed by decision makers." Melanie leaned forward. "What do you want the rest of your career to look like, Damien?"

The question took me back. Retirement was a four-letter word in my mind. Although my body might want to slow down, I had no plans of hanging up my bat just yet. I shook my head. "I want to retire here—want to keep playing as a Hawk." My throat tightened. "Are they talking about trading me?"

"No," Melanie insisted. "At least, not yet. Right now, your stats and the fans' support outweighs your reputation." She sighed. "That being said, you are getting older. As you slow down, they might not be able to justify keeping you, especially with your high salary." She leaned in closer, her gaze softening. "If that's not enough of a reason to get your shit together, you should look at this as the team captain, a role model for the younger players. If they get caught in a scandal, they might not bounce back as easily as you."

Her green eyes met mine, and I could read what she refused to say. *Like Jace.* As much as I tried to bury the guilt about my former teammate's fate, it still came to the surface every time his name came up. There was so much more I could have done for him, if only I'd noticed the signs of his downfall sooner.

I cleared my throat. "Okay, Mel, I hear you. No more parading my one-night stands on social media."

She nodded. "That's a start. But I think we need to work on toning down your image in more ways than just that."

"I'm going to hate this, aren't I?"

ELEVEN

Brianna

Summer always brought with it a little guilt. My career was one of very few that provided ten weeks off during the warmer months, but it didn't stop my overactive brain from latching on to a project. In the past, I threw myself into schoolwork, trying to come up with new ways to differentiate the curriculum and familiarize myself with my new students' plans and data.

But for the first time since I started, I forced myself to take a break—to give myself the first half of July before jumping back into planning mode. Since returning from Dallas last week, the days blurred together, a wash of walks through the city, trips to the farmer's market, and spending the nights curled up around my Kindle.

Not to mention—avoid Damien Ramos.

Normally, that would be an easy feat. It wasn't like my world intersected with professional baseball players regularly. At least, it didn't before I moved in with Ollie. But with her business and friendship with Parker Drobrek, the third baseman on the Hawks, the guys came over all the time. Either that, or she spent her nights cheering them on in the outfield with the rest of our friends.

Every time she left the house, she begged me to join them, but I couldn't bring myself to do it. As much as I wanted to forget about my night with Damien, it was impossible, especially when his memory crept into my dreams every night. No, there was no telling what I would do if I spent more time around Damien. It was a toss-up between embarrassing myself like a nerdy schoolgirl with an overwhelming crush or begging him to fuck me again.

Nope. Not going to happen. My life was safe—*albeit a little boring*—but at least there was no room for further heartbreak. Spending time with Damien proved I didn't have the disposition for one-night stands; my tender little heart latched on to that comfort and clung to it with all its might. It was safer to keep myself guarded, to go back to my insular world and enjoy the relaxation.

But by the next weekend, Ollie had had enough.

As I laid in bed, my hair in a bun and my favorite cactus pajamas on, she burst through my door, chucking a dress on my bed. "Put this on."

I looked up at her and shook my head. "Are you insane? It's after ten."

"Please, grandma." She scoffed, plopping into bed next to me. "Most of the bars downtown are just filling up. No one gets there until at least eleven."

"In your twenties," I laughed, tugging my comforter back over my shoulder. "Leave me be. I'm like that aging gazelle at the back of the pack. Let the lions eat me and run free."

"Nope." Ollie ripped the blanket back from me. "The only thing eating you tonight is a hot-blooded man if you play your cards right. Like that guy you did not hook up with in Dallas."

My cheeks heated at her words, trying to keep the guilt off my face. Despite my insistence nothing happened in Dallas, Ollie refused to let it go until I reluctantly admitted I went home with someone. The only saving grace was that she didn't know it was Damien. She might have suspected we hooked up, but she never said the words aloud. Thank goodness, because lying to her about a nameless man was one thing, but denying Damien all together was more than my moral compass could take. As she stared at me, I shook my head. "I told you—that was a one-night thing. My first, and only, one-night stand."

"Ugh," Ollie sighed as she stood. "That's such a waste. You're too hot to waste all your nights tucked into bed alone. You need to find a man who fucks like a God and then milk him for every orgasm he's worth."

I chuckled, diving back into the book on my e-reader. I tried that plan, and it failed spectacularly. From now on, the only men I wanted to obsess over were fictional. They turned you on, said all the right things, and you never had to worry about miscommunication or insecurities. Ollie ripped it out of my hand, reading over the section I had just breezed through. "Brianna Sideris! Are you reading porn?"

"No!" I shrieked as I pulled it back. "Don't defile romance books with the word *porn*. It's smut, if you must know."

"Smut where three baseball players are sharing one girl?" She smirked. "And here I was, thinking we were opening your eyes to all these new experiences. Who knew a little skank was hiding underneath those cardigans?"

"What's wrong with my cardigans?"

"Nothing," Ollie said a little too quickly. She stole my e-reader once again and climbed out of my bed, holding it behind her back. "Okay, tough love. You've been hiding out for almost a week, and it's getting a little too Gray Gardens for my taste. The whole hook-up thing threw you for a loop, but you can't let that scare you away from any new experiences." She tossed the e-reader back to me. "Also, I'm a needy bitch and want you to hang out with me. So if you don't want to go out, fine, but you are leaving this room and spending some time with your roommate."

My cheeks burned as my eyes darted down. Was that what I'd been doing? Being alone was normal for me, especially the last few years. Even when Todd was home, it wasn't like he spent a lot of time with me. My friends were great, but a small part of me always wondered if it was more because of pity than genuine friendship. At least, until Ollie stormed in here.

Climbing out of bed, I walked over to Ollie and pulled her into a hug. Her short blonde bob knocked into my nose, but I held tight. "I'm sorry," I mumbled. "It wasn't personal. I've been alone for a long time, so sometimes, I become a bit of a hermit."

"I get it," Ollie said as she pulled back. "But you're not alone, Bri. Not anymore. You don't have to explain if you want some space, but I'm always going to come check up on you, pull you out of your comfort zone if you've been burrowing a little too long."

The earnest look in her eyes made my heart swell. It might have taken my entire life imploding, but at least I'd walked away with better friends, people who were in my corner, even when I didn't realize it. "Thanks, Ollie."

"Always, Bri. But..." She smirked, leaning down to pick

up the dress from my bed. "If you want to make it up to me —be my wing woman tonight. See if we can make some new friends?"

"No promises," I chuckled as I took the dress from her. "But I'll at least keep you company."

She beamed back at me. "Challenge accepted."

***

"OKAY, CHALLENGE FAILED," Ollie groaned as she slid into the bar's booth, rubbing her ankle. "How was everyone at that club the biggest douche on the planet?"

As the bartender dropped our drinks on the table, I grabbed mine, needing something cool after battling the masses earlier. When Ollie dragged me out to the club earlier, she failed to mention it was the grand opening. Everyone in Erie City under the age of twenty-five had gathered inside its doors, making it almost impossible to find the bar, much less order a drink. After over an hour of trying to flag down a server, we called it quits, heading toward our favorite dive bar.

From the outside, the Rusty Anchor looked like you'd get tetanus from sitting on a barstool. However, that was intentional, keeping away any wandering tourists or the college crowd. But once you walked inside, the place was comfortable and clean, with a vintage vibe that always made me smile. A large mural of a pinup girl filled the wall behind the tables, black iron lights casting the space in a golden glow. Aged wood covered the bottom half of the walls while a dark green patterned wallpaper stretched up to the tin ceiling.

"And the worst part?" Ollie said as she tipped back her

drink. "The bouncer called me *ma'am*. Do I look like a ma'am? Have I crossed an imaginary line into adulthood and didn't realize it?"

"Ollie, you own a condo and have a burgeoning business," I answered. "Why *didn't* you think you were an adult?"

"Okay, when you put it in those terms, sure, I'm an adult. But I'm not responsible enough to call myself one. If an emergency happens, there's no way I should be the one in charge. Way too much responsibility for me to handle."

I chuckled as I grabbed my drink. "Coming from the woman who handles crises daily. Hate to break it to you, babe, but you're an adult. And if you think you're old, imagine how I feel." I winced as the vodka hit the back of my tongue. "Next time, we skip that scene and head straight over here."

"I'm not arguing with you about that." Ollie sighed as she relaxed into the booth. As I took another sip of my drink, she leaned forward. "Have you thought anymore about your list?"

I choked on my drink, pulling over a napkin to wipe the traces from my lips. "What list?"

Her eyes narrowed back at me. "Your spice list. C'mon, Bri. Now that I know what books you read, we can add so many more options."

"They're romance!" I protested.

She held up her hands. "There's no judgment here. In fact, I need you to give me some recs. Real life has been letting me down, and I could use some fictional action to keep my mind busy—the filthier, the better."

"Oh." My anger deflated at her words, too used to getting comments about my reading choices. As I weighed her words, Ollie dug through her purse, pulling out a pen with a triumphant smile. She grabbed one of the paper placemats and flipped it over, writing in bold letters across the top *Brianna's Ho Phase.*

I reached out and snatched it away from her. "Okay, you cannot phrase it like that."

"Why?" Ollie said, taking it back out of my hands. "Everyone has one, and no offense, Bri, but you desperately need a ho phase. Teach yourself what you want when you're ready to settle down again."

"Can't we call it something like *Bri's Summer of Love?*"

"That sounds more like you're going on a cruise for divorced parents." As I continued to stare her down, she relented. "Fine, but I want my formal protest noted."

"Noted."

Ollie nodded then started numbering the side of the paper. When she reached ten, I took the pen away. "I only have eight weeks left of the summer, Ol. I'd like to walk when I have to set up for school."

"Walking is overrated," Ollie mused as she took back her pen. "Now—what is the first thing on your fantasy list?"

I paused, scrunching my face in thought. Was this a normal thing people did? Just list their sexual fantasies out loud for their friends to hear? I wasn't opposed to telling Ollie what I wanted, but after years of my mother making sex sound like the ultimate shame, I struggled to find the words.

Ollie frowned and reached out to take my hand. "If this is too much, we can skip it. It's up to you, Bri."

"I want to do it." Lifting my empty glass in my hand, I called over our server. "Two shots of tequila, please, extra limes."

"Two for me, too," Ollie beamed up at her.

Once the drinks came, I downed both, needing more

liquid courage in my veins. After I sucked down the limes, still feeling the wince of the tequila as it settled in my stomach, I looked over at the list. "Does it make me pathetic if I say I don't know where to start?"

"Nope." Ollie smiled at me, and my stomach somersaulted. "That's what you have best friends for."

TWELVE

Damien

I needed a drink. Scratch that—after tonight, I needed fifteen drinks. Mari was lucky I loved her, because after the stunt she pulled, all future family dinners were in jeopardy.

I should've known something was up when my sister called before I left the house, asking me to wear one of my nicer outfits, and then again after I pulled into the driveway and saw an unfamiliar car parked in my usual spot. After years of Mari's meddling, you'd think I'd recognize the signs of a set-up. But no, not me. I walked in blind, and now, I was eyeing the exit like a dying man.

"Did you enjoy dinner?" my sister asked as she grabbed the plate from her guest.

"Oh yes, everything was delicious," she said. "I haven't had a home cooked meal since I moved."

Glancing across the table, my date's eyes met mine, and she blushed, staring back down at her food. Shit; what the hell was her name? Fuck, Mel was right—I'd crossed into asshole territory. *Gemma.* Nice girl, the kind of woman I wouldn't mind spending more time with normally. She worked with Mari at the veterinary clinic as an assistant and had just moved into town. She was smart, witty, and my nieces all seemed to love her. But as we spoke, there wasn't a connection, no spark between us.

Unlike Brianna.

Fuck. I ran my hand over my face, trying to push the picture of her from my mind. It should have been easy; I'd done it plenty of times before. Maybe it was shitty of me, but there was a long list of women I'd left alone in their beds, barely thinking about them after I left. It was different with Brianna. I couldn't forget the sight of her pleasure; it was etched in my memory from the night we spent together. Every time I tried to block it, she popped up again, stronger than before. Maybe it was a good thing Melanie banned me from all women and clubs after the all-star game. I needed to get my head together.

"Damien?" Mari called from the head of the table. "Can you help me with dessert please?"

All my nieces cheered as we stood, unaware of the glares Mari and I shot at each other. At least the promise of sugar would help the awkwardness of the night. Knowing my sister, she'd made her signature flancocho cake. It was an update of our grandmother's classic flan recipe, but my sister had put her own twist on it, interweaving the classic dish with moist layers of vanilla cake. We all loved it, especially the girls. It was one of the few indulgences I allowed myself during the season.

As Mari pulled me into the kitchen, she kept up her usual jovial smile, but as soon as we were out of everyone's eye-line, she gave me a hard pinch on the underside of my arm.

"Shit, Mari," I snapped. "What's wrong with you?"

"What's wrong with me? What's wrong with *you*?" My little sister glared at me as she walked further into the kitchen. She mumbled something under her breath as she walked over to the fridge and pulled out the cake. "I set you up with a nice girl—tell her all about my charming, *very single*, big brother, and you show up like that? Like a robot has drained all your personality?"

"If you'd told me about this blind date—"

"Don't feed me lies," my sister bit out. "If I told you about Gemma, you would have found a way out of it. Claimed some practice ran over or another excuse."

Okay, she had me there.

"I've told you, Mari. It's not her. I'm not interested in dating anyone." As she pulled the knife out of the drawer and placed it on the tray next to the cake, I hugged her. "Why is this so important to you?"

She sighed and dropped her head onto my shoulder. "You've given up so much already, brother. First for base-ball, then for me. I want you to be happy too." She turned in my arms, looking up at me. "Tell me the truth. Don't you feel it? That missing piece inside your heart?"

I studied her eyes, the ones that almost completely matched mine. If people didn't already know we were siblings, it wasn't hard to figure out. We had the same tanned skin tone, the same tilt to our smiles, but the eyes gave it away the most.

And right now, the concern reflected in them almost made my knees buckle.

Exhaling sharply, I weighed her words. If she'd asked me months ago, my answer would have been a flat no. Though my engagement fell apart, my life never seemed lacking, even if there were a lot of lonely moments.

But lately, the voice in the back of my mind had me questioning my own rules. Maybe it was Brianna, maybe it was Mel calling me out on my shit. Either way, I'd stopped going out and looking for something temporary over the last couple weeks. Did that mean I wanted more? Wanted to be in a relationship?

Did I even know how?

Even if I wanted to be with someone, my schedule would always be an issue. Baseball came first. There wasn't any other option. I refused to let my focus flounder, refused to coast into retirement and obscurity. I'd worked too damn hard to settle for that life.

Instead of giving Mari empty promises, I held her a little tighter. "You know I'm your big brother, right? I'm supposed to be the one worrying about you."

"Please," Mari snorted. "The only thing you have to worry about are the girls destroying every inch of this house. Carmen figured out how to undo all the child locks and decided to paint a masterpiece for the twins on their bedroom wall."

I shook my head. "And that's what you want for me? The chaos you have to experience every day?"

"If you want that, D, then yes. I'm not saying have kids, because we both know it's not the right path for everyone, but I want you to have a family, someone you can confide in when life gets too heavy."

"I have you, Mari."

She shook her head. "And you always will. But it's not the same as what I have with Angie. She's my person—the one I can lean on when life gets heavy, but who also shares in all our joy. It's not just having someone, it's finding that other half of you, the person who makes your life better, even when it's falling apart." She pulled back and searched my gaze. "You give everything your all, Damien. Me, the kids, especially baseball. Don't you think you deserve someone who will do the same thing for you?"

My throat tightened at her words, unable to respond. For so long, the idea of opening myself up terrified me, sure it would be another failure. But maybe Mari was right. Maybe after years of hiding myself in one-night stands and baseball commitments, it was time to step out of my comfort zone and try for something more.

"Mi vida?" Angie called out, breaking the moment between my sister and me. When she rounded the corner and spotted us hugging, she smiled. "Oh good. You had us worried there for a minute. I thought I was going to find you two fighting."

"No fighting." I sighed, pressing a kiss to the top of my little sister's head. "But no more set-ups either. I promise, Mari, when I'm ready to settle down, you'll be the first one I call."

She rolled her eyes, knowing the words were a lie as much as I did, but at least it was enough to get her off my back—for now.

After we settled back at the table, the rest of the night went smoothly. Gemma and I exchanged an awkward goodbye in the driveway, polite but firm enough that she didn't expect a phone call. As I drove back into the city, anxious energy radiated through me, and I wasn't ready to call it a night just yet.

My usual clubs and bars were a no-go, marked off-limits by Melanie. Phase one of getting my shit together, I supposed. Without any of my vices, there was no way I'd be able to sleep, at least not yet. *One drink couldn't hurt, right?*

Driving by a couple of sports bars, I kept going. My face was too recognizable in those circles. But when I found a small dive bar on the edge of the city, I slowed down and pulled into its empty parking lot. Grabbing my hat from the backseat, I ambled inside, not bothering to look around before taking a seat at the counter.

As I signaled to the bartender for a drink, a loud laugh came from the back corner. I turned over my shoulder, catching the eyes of the last person I expected to see here. *Brianna.* She had to be a hallucination. Lord knew I'd conjured her image plenty of times over the past few weeks, but I saved my memories for when I fisted myself in the shower, remembering the sight of her at my mercy, begging for more of my cock.

I wiped my hand over my face, trying to fix my vision. However, when it dropped away, Brianna remained, her hazel eyes wide in shock. My face twisted in a surprised smirk, taking in her features. A knot tugged in my chest, desperate to move closer to her. It had only been two weeks since I'd been in her bed, but it seemed like longer. It'd been too long since her fingernails traced my thighs as her mouth swallowed my length, since I sank deep inside her and finally understood nirvana.

All I could do was stare, taking in Brianna's subtle features. The way the light toyed with her hazel eyes, the soft cupid's bow in her upper lip. I wanted to trace the freckles that lined her nose and cheek, to memorize every hidden detail about this woman.

Fuck, this was too much. I turned away from Brianna as the bartender dropped off my beer. Distance. I needed distance from her. After all, I was no stranger to one-night stands. Even though Brianna clung on a little longer than most women I met, her memory had to fade eventually. There'd be a day when I'd see her across the room and my dick wouldn't instantly get hard—at least I fucking hoped so.

Just as I gathered all my resolve to finish my beer and

walk away, a group of guys crashed into my side, ordering another round of shots. They must have slipped in while Brianna held my attention. There were only three of them, but they were louder than when the entire team filled the locker room. They glanced around the bar, stopping when they spotted Brianna in the corner. One made a comment I couldn't pick up, but the slimy look on his face made my blood pressure rise.

When they started walking toward Brianna and her friend, I couldn't help myself, standing and blocking their paths. As they muttered curses at my back, I kept moving toward the table. Brianna's eyes jumped to meet mine, and she shook her head before ducking down in the seat. Her voice squeaked out from under the table, "Do you think he saw me?"

"Yup," I answered for her friend as I slid into the booth next to Brianna. "Although, that was pretty smooth. No one's ducked me like that in a long time."

She lifted her head and gaped at me. "Damien? Wh-what are you doing here?"

"Getting a drink," I mused, holding up my beer. I glanced at the empty glasses on the table in front of her. "Same as you."

A snort echoed from the other side of the table, and I turned, finding Ollie smirking at me. She beamed hello, her eyes darting between me and Brianna. "How did you even know about this place?"

"Parker mentioned it last week, said it was a good place to go if you wanted to keep your head down. I'm trying to keep a low profile." I motioned for Brianna to move over and slid into the spot next to her. All night, I'd waited for sparks, to see if my sister's set-up was more than met the eye, but there'd been nothing, not even little interest on my end. She was smart, kind, and beautiful, all the things I should want. However, as I slid in next to Brianna, every inch of my skin prickled with awareness.

Ollie's smile turned downright devilish as she looked between the two of us, me with my easy smile and Brianna with the most adorable blush filling her features. "I knew it! You two totally hooked-up in Dallas. No way you found some random guy when Damien was around."

I arched my brow as I turned to Brianna. "Random guy?"

She groaned then turned back to Ollie. "Fine. I might have made that part up. We, uh..." Brianna looked over at me, silently pleading for permission. I nodded, suddenly not caring who found out.

But she didn't get a word out before Ollie held up her hand. "Actually, no. Don't tell me anything. I need plausible deniability if Park asks." She winked at Brianna. "Buuut... this does give me some new ideas."

Brianna shook her head, her cheeks now that delicious red hue I liked so much. As she stayed silent, I looked in Ollie's direction, seeing her scribble on a piece of paper in front of her. When I tried to get a closer look, Brianna grabbed it, moving it far from me.

"What are you hiding from me, angel?" I asked, lowering my mouth to her ear. God, as much as I wanted to stay away, being close to Brianna felt better, like when two magnets finally collided. Her floral shampoo filled my senses, and I stared at the column of her throat, disappointed that the marks from our night together had faded from her skin. It made me want to mark her up again.

"Nothing," she blurted out. "At least nothing you should concern yourself with."

"Aww, I think you should tell him," Ollie said. "He might help you out."

"I don't need his help."

The bite in her tone made my hackles rise. I turned to face her, taking in her sour expression. "Are you okay, Bri? What's wrong?"

If possible, she blushed even harder. "It's not like that... I'm fine. It's just a project Ollie is helping me with."

Now that I knew nothing was wrong, I leaned back in the booth and un-bunched my shoulders. "Sure you don't want to tell me about it? I can be very helpful, after all."

"See, Bri," Ollie said, smirking wildly. "He is *very* helpful. You never know what he might think."

THIRTEEN

Brianna

Torture. Slow, painful torture. Mental images of tossing Ollie into the lake danced through my mind as I glared at my roommate. I might love her, but she deserved it, especially as she sat on the other side of the booth, smirking like she'd just won the lottery. It was bad enough that she'd gotten me to confess some of my deepest, darkest desires, but now, she was baiting me in front of Damien Ramos.

At the thought of his name, I snuck a peek at him. He looked good—too good. He'd gelled back the longer strands of his hair, making the powerful lines of his chin even more pronounced. His short-sleeved linen shirt showed off the tattoos lining his arms, and my eyes traced every patch of exposed skin. The angels called to me, reminding me of the nickname he'd gifted me in the early hours of that morning —the one he'd whispered in my ear along with filthy promises of ruining me for anyone else.

He had no idea how right he'd been.

As his dark eyes turned to meet mine, mischief fluttered in his expression, the kind that spoke of dirty dreams and compromising positions. My inner self told me to back down from his stare. Instead, I steeled my nerve and met it head on, wanting to see if I held as much power over him as he still seemed to have over me.

"It's a sex bucket list," I admitted with a shrug. Ollie's eyes widened with delighted surprise, and Damien's eyes flared with lust. "Figured now that I'm divorced, I should see what else is out there."

Damien's gaze darted to my lips, and I tried not to pull the words back and cower into my safe space. But I'd been that girl for so long, the one who always looked danger in the eye and ran in the opposite direction. While I trusted Damien to keep my body safe and pleasured, my feelings were an entirely different story.

That was the problem. I was still letting my heart lead me through this new phase of my life when for once, I should be listening to my head—or my libido, if the ache between my thighs was to be trusted. If I kept feelings out of this, Damien could solve my problem. He was masterful in the bedroom, and he might be more averse to emotions than me. We had different reasons for avoiding relationships— him because of his career, and me because I was still healing from my divorce—but the results were the same. Just because we weren't looking for happily ever after didn't mean we couldn't enjoy each other's company for now, did it?

"Okay..." Ollie said as Damien and I continued our stare down. "Clearly, my part here is done. I'm going to talk to...someone else. *Anyone* else." She paused as she slid out of the booth. "You two have fun."

As she faded into the background of the bar, Damien shifted closer to me, his breath coasting over my parted lips. "What's on this list, Bri?"

I shook my head. "You don't get to read it. Not yet."

"Yet?"

I chewed on my lower lip, losing a little of my nerve now that he was so close, the hints of his cologne making my head lighter. The smell was perfect on his skin—luxurious, manly, yet comforting. He reached up, untucking my lip with his thumb. "If you're afraid I'm going to judge you, don't. There's nothing sexier than a woman voicing what she wants in the bedroom."

"I want you." The words tumbled out, springing free before I even thought them through. My gaze dropped to my hands, and I felt the blush filling my cheeks. "I shouldn't have said that. We both agreed—"

I was silenced when Damien cupped my cheek, bringing my face toward him. His thumb dusted over my lower lip, tracing the marks my teeth had left behind. "Are you asking me to fuck you again, angel?" When I nodded, he muttered a curse under his breath. "I shouldn't. One taste of you, and you've possessed me. I need you, crave you. Think about you every time I fuck my fist." He inhaled, but his gaze never left mine. "Tell me you've thought about me too."

"I-I have."

Damien's lips curved into a devilish smirk. "Have you touched yourself to the memories of me? Pretended it was me when you stroked your clit?"

"No." His expression fell as soon as I answered, but I scooted closer, practically climbing into his lap. "Not because I didn't think about you. I'm just..." My voice trailed off, embarrassed about what I was about to admit.

Damien's nose brushed the shell of my ear. "Tell me."

"I've never done that." Passing over the list, I pointed to the first item. *Make myself come.* Damien read the list, and then his head popped back up to look at me. I searched his expression, waiting for some sort of shock to fill his features. Instead, his hand reached around my hip, digging into the fabric of my skirt. "You've never given yourself an orgasm, angel?"

"I tried, but it's never quite right. Can't get out of my head long enough to...you know."

Damien's nostrils flared once he understood my words. For a moment, I feared I'd gone too far, shown too many of the cards I normally held close to my chest. But the nerves shifted to excitement as Damien moved out of the booth and pulled me to my feet. He dug through his pocket and dropped some bills on the table before taking my hand again. Searching through the crowd, I found Ollie in the middle of a group of people, animatedly telling them about Parker's last game. When she caught my eye, she grinned back at me and gave us a parting wave. We crashed through the door, back into the sticky summer humidity, and I dug my heels in. "Damien, where are you taking me?"

"To my place," Damien answered as he turned toward me, his eyes a blaring hue of amber and mahogany. "You want to come from your own fingers, angel? Because it would be my greatest pleasure to help you get there."

I HAD no idea what Damien's apartment would be like, but his home was better than anything I envisioned. It was one thing to know someone had money. The Hawks paid him a good salary, but our income discrepancy never quite struck me until he opened the door and I took in the view from the high-rise apartment building. It was a familiar sight on the Erie City skyline. While the rest of the city clung to the turn of the century architecture, this new neighborhood was all steel and sheen. Of all the recent additions, this building stood the tallest, almost like a guardian keeping watch.

But inside was not cold steel. Instead, there were markings of the city's history etched on the walls. Crown molding flowed into an intricately carved fireplace, alongside worn-exposed brick with hints of aged wood. Everything seemed warm—a perfect blend of luxury and rustic comfort.

Without thinking, I stepped toward the floor to ceiling windows, taking in the view from up here. You could see almost the entire city. The streets shone with the dew from the late evening air, and the dark forests lined the outskirts.

Damien stepped up behind me, using his fingers to shift my hair over my shoulder. It barely stayed, too short to obey his commands, but it was long enough for him to place a soft kiss on the side of my neck. "Do you like it?"

"Like it?' I said with an amused chuckle. "This is the apartment of my dreams. I didn't even know places like this existed here."

"Building's only a couple of years old. I got my hands on the first apartment available." He placed his hands on my hips, shifting me to look at an enormous construction site. "In the next five years, the plan is to build three more towers."

"Wow." The awe in my voice was clear, even to my ears. This was a far cry from the home I used to share with Todd, with its cookie-cutter design and pre-fab cabinets. I chuckled as I turned in his arms. "The price tag is a little more than I can afford on my teacher's salary."

Damien's eyes twinkled as he looked down at me and ran his fingers through my hair. "You love it, though. Teaching suits you."

"How can you tell?"

"That day we visited." He shifted closer to me, finding little places to touch me as he spoke. "You looked at those kids like they were your entire world. Others spent more time talking to the other adults or trying to hit on the baseball players. Not you. The only thing that mattered to you was that the kids had fun."

"They deserved it." My eyes whipped up to meet his. "Which teachers hit on you?"

"Damn," Damien laughed, pushing me against the glass. "Didn't realize you had a jealous side, angel."

"I-I don't," I stammered. Was that what I felt? The idea of my co-workers hitting on Damien made my blood boil, but that wasn't fair. He wasn't mine. No matter what happened tonight, or any other night, we needed to know that. I'd spent enough of my life being one man's possession. I wasn't about to walk into another cage any time soon.

"This can't happen again," I said, burning up as Damien's hands coasted along my bare thighs. "This has to be the last time."

"It does?" he asked, his lips finding my collarbone.

"Yes," I said as I pushed his chest away from me. He went willingly, and I could breathe a little easier without his skin on mine. "Dallas was one thing, but here—we can't make this a thing between us. One last time to get it out of our systems, and then we act like it never happened."

Damien chuckled, running his hand over his face. "And if I want more than that?"

"I can't," I answered. "I'm not ready. So if you want something more, I should leave right now."

Damien pushed his chest against my hand, crashing into my personal space like he owned it. His fingers swept across my cheeks. "Not letting you go that easily, angel. If you only want one more night, then that's what we'll do." He chuckled as he leaned in closer. "But I'm pretty sure that's what you said last time."

I shook my head. "I mean it—"

"You say that now," Damien ground out, his voice taking on a much more commanding tone. "But I haven't gotten you naked yet, Bri. Give me a few hours, and then we'll see if you're ready to let this go."

FOURTEEN

Brianna

As soon as the words left his lips, Damien pressed my body up against the cool glass wall. My dress, which was already too short to begin with, rose, exposing the tops of my thighs to his greedy hands. Damien gripped my skin like he needed to hold on, to make sure this was happening.

Or maybe that was me.

Tonight had been pulled from my dreams, the ones featuring the handsome baseball player who took me into his home and claimed me as his own. We might only have each other for tonight, but the power I had over him made my head swim. It was intoxicating, like the first dive into a cold lake. The air was sucked out of my lungs as his hands gripped my skin, needing us so much closer together.

But just as the heat pooled in my core, he pulled back, shifting to take a seat on his couch. Damien spread his arms over the back of it, but his eyes never left me. "As much as I want to sink inside you, Bri, I made you a promise. You're going to touch yourself until you come on your pretty fingers."

My cheeks blushed, the darkening color on display under the bright lights of the apartment. Damien must have read the hesitancy on my face, because he dug into his pocket and pulled out his phone. With a few taps on the screen, the lights lowered.

He nodded to the armchair across from him, but before I sat down, he stopped me. "Give me your panties."

"Wh-what?"

He sat up, his arms resting on his thighs. "You heard me, Bri. Lose the panties and hand them to me. I want to test a theory."

Okay. You can do this, Bri. The man has already seen you naked and appreciated the view. What's the harm in handing him your ruined thong?

Refusing to dwell too much on what was going to happen next, I pulled the lace down my legs and lifted my heels. I placed it in Damien's waiting hand, and he toyed with the triangle of fabric at the center, smirking. "God, angel. These are soaked. You must really want my cock."

"Yes," I said as I hovered over the chair.

Damien arched his brow. "Why aren't you sitting?"

"I—you know..."

"Are you worried your pussy is going to drip on my furniture?" I nodded. "Don't care about that, Bri. Mark that chair. Mark whatever you want in here, just as long as you chase your pleasure. Now, sit your ass down and spread your legs. I need to see every inch of you. It's been haunting my dreams for too long."

Doing as he said, I sank back into the chair, lifting the hem of my dress to spread my legs. As my heels dug into the rug, Damien's jaw tensed, and his eyes blazed in that delicious manner again. He continued to palm the fabric of my panties, but his gaze never left my center. It should have felt dirty, too exposed, but all I noticed was the hum of pleasure skirting under my skin, especially when Damien's eyes met mine. *Obsidian.* That was the best description of the color. Deep, sharp, and all too consuming.

My hands moved of their own volition, stroking the soft skin of my thighs. Damien growled as I brushed my core, the light touch of my fingertips not enough to get my pulse up. "Are you teasing me, angel?"

God, that voice made my spine tingle. So deep, so demanding. I shrugged one shoulder as I parted myself. "Might need some of your guidance, Damien."

"Fuck," he groaned as he shifted even closer. "You're gonna ruin me, Bri."

Without another word, he stood, shifting over to the coffee table. He pulled it right in front of me then sat down, appraising my pussy like it was a priceless work of art. "Spread yourself more," he said, his voice deeper than I'd ever heard it. "Want to see every inch of you."

I did as he commanded, propping my feet up on each side of him to open myself up more. My fingers danced along my clit in concentric circles, applying a little more pressure with each rotation. My breath caught in my throat, soaking up every filthy image as it passed through my mind. With Damien's eyes glued to my hands, a newfound confidence etched itself inside my skin, letting his desire fuel my own.

When my lips parted and a moan slipped out, he clenched his hands and almost reached out for me. Instead, he palmed his impressive cock. God, I wanted it. Wanted it in my mouth. Wanted him inside me. The last time we'd found ourselves in this position, he promised me I'd feel him for days. And he was right. With every step, in the back of my throat—every move I made reminded me how this man had destroyed all my notions about sex in one night.

"Fuck your fingers, Bri," Damien muttered, still watching each of my movements. As I slid my middle and index fingers inside myself, he growled. "Yes, just like that. Feel that fucking perfect pussy? I can still remember it wrapped around me, making me lose my mind. Use your thumb too; play with that clit while you keeping fucking yourself." I didn't even hesitate, following his lead no matter where it might take me. Now, all I could think about was the pleasure igniting my veins, the kind I was giving myself with Damien's guidance.

"Add another finger, Bri." I shook my head, and Damien just chuckled. "Don't think you can? Come on, angel. You took this cock like it was made for you. You can take one more."

I did as he asked, thrusting my fingers inside me. Normally, when I tried this, it was too hard to get out of my head, but with Damien's words and the gruff timbre of his voice, I was already starting to tumble over the edge.

"Fuck, Bri. You're too fucking gorgeous like that. You're doing so good, angel. Such a good fucking girl, fucking your fingers like I asked."

At his words, my walls crushed against my fingers, and my orgasm ripped through me, more intense than anything I'd ever experienced from my own hands. But even as my mind faded into the hums of pleasure, there was no mistaking the real cause—Damien.

As my throbbing core stilled, I pulled my fingers away, grimacing as I tried to stand to go to the kitchen. But before my shame took over, Damien grabbed my wrist, bringing my damp fingers to his lips. He hummed as he sucked them into his mouth like it was his favorite flavor. Blush colored my cheeks as I stared at him, no longer as confident as I'd been only moments earlier.

Shame rushed through me, reminding me of sermons and lectures about the dangers of giving in to temptation. Sin. As much as I wanted to push those thoughts out of my mind, they were embedded deep in my subconscious.

When he released my hand, Damien intertwined our fingers, staring up at me as if he could read my insecurities. "Don't run from this, Bri."

"What we just did—"

"Was fucking perfect," he answered for me. "Don't let anyone shame you for owning your pleasure. Not with me. You're too fucking beautiful when you come to ever believe there's anything wrong with it."

My eyes lifted and met his, searching for any hint of a lie. I knew better than to trust pretty promises whispered after dark, but it was different with Damien—an unbridled truth, begging me to let him in.

"You think I'm beautiful?"

Damien crushed his lips to my forehead. For a moment, I dared to imagine his lips on my mouth, to taste my flavor on his tongue. He held me against his chest, his body chasing away any doubts about his words. His racing pulse, his cock, thick and strained between us—everything screamed how much he wanted me. "You're the most beautiful thing I've ever had in my arms," he answered as he pulled back. "I want to take a picture of you when you come and hang it over my bed."

I chuckled, trying to hide the prickle of unease washing over me. "Might be a little awkward for anyone else climbing into it."

Damien's jaw tensed, the usual humor missing from his

expression. "I don't want to think about that, not tonight." His hands reached down, cupping my thighs to lift me up. My legs tightened around him, brushing his cock against my core. As my mouth opened on a moan, Damien groaned with desperation. "Need you, Bri. Let me have you?"

I smirked up at him. "I thought you'd never ask."

FIFTEEN

Brianna

Early the next morning, my eyes reluctantly opened, taking in the unfamiliar view. Shit. I fell asleep at Damien's. That didn't exactly fall within the scope of our agreement, but in this moment, I couldn't bring myself to care. Forcing my limbs to move, I stretched out on Damien's king-sized bed, letting the sun warm my face. The city skyline was a world away from the brick wall my room faced.

A girl could get used to this view.

Speaking of views, when I twisted back around, Damien's sleeping face greeted me. His expression was so relaxed, so much different from the subtle signs of stress he usually carried with him. To the rest of the world, he might look like the confident leader of the Hawks, but in these quiet moments, it became easy to see how much the pressure weighed on him.

Glancing down, I took in his bare chest, unabashedly ogling the man. His body was a work of art, made up of tight, powerful muscles. His arm jutted out and dragged me back against him. With my head nestled in the crook of his neck, I sighed, relishing how right it felt being nestled in his arms.

Where the hell had that come from?

My stomach rioted at the traitorous thought. Less than ten hours ago, we'd agreed on only one more night. Damien might have teased me about wanting more, but there was no way he actually meant it. Distance. I needed some distance. No thinking about waking up next to Damien, no wondering what it would be like to spend more nights cuddled in his embrace.

That was the old me talking, the one who fool-heartedly believed in fairy tales.

As if a cold shock filled my veins, I twisted away from him. But just as I pushed the sheet off my body, Damien's grip around my middle tightened. My back collided with his firm chest, and as much as I told myself not to, I relaxed into his grip.

"Are you sneaking out on me?" Damien grumbled, his voice still hoarse from sleep.

"We never talked about sleeping over. I really should have left last night."

Damien groaned, running his lips over my shoulder. "Maybe. But you're here now, so why not make the most of it?"

I chuckled as he lifted the sheet, twisting my body so it fit perfectly under his. His gaze turned from tired to turned on in a matter of seconds as he took in my naked body. He smirked as he trailed the back of his fingers along the center of my chest. "Desperate for me, angel? Thought you'd be sore from last night."

"A little," I said, squirming for his hand to continue its path. But he kept up the light strokes, enough to set my blood on fire but not nearly close enough to do anything about it. "Damien, please, touch me."

"Not yet," he said, his eyes lifting to meet mine. "First, I want to hear something else from that list of yours."

My cheeks darkened. I was going to murder Ollie. Slowly. Painfully. But as Damien's thumb traced the outline of my nipple, all violent thoughts flew out the door. He leaned down and sucked the bud into his mouth, teasing me with his tongue and light scrapes of his teeth. "There's nothing to be embarrassed about, Bri." He moved to the other side. "I want this to be fun for you, and I'm enough of a bastard to admit I want to show you new things, want to watch as you learn what turns you on."

"Why?"

He chuckled as his lips skimmed my stomach. "It fucking turns me on, angel. Corrupting you. Watching you find your pleasure. I already told you, there's nothing sexier in the world than when you demand what you want." He leaned back on his haunches, staring at my aching core. Even though he'd barely touched me, slickness drenched my thighs, desperate for him to show me everything. "If you want me to touch you, Bri. You're going to tell me exactly what you want me to do."

Swallowing the last hint of my pride, I sat up and faced him. Damien just smiled, which made me instantly relax. Even in our short time together, he'd never judged me, never made it seem wrong to want more from sex. To crave his touch everywhere, not because it was expected, but because I desired it.

"I want your mouth," I said, refusing to back down from his stare. The sides of his mouth ticked up, and my heart swelled, knowing it pleased him when I used my voice.

"More than that—I want to sit on your face. It's number three on my list."

Fresh shame washed over me, shocked that those words had willingly come out of my mouth. For a moment, Damien's face twisted, and I thought I'd gone too far. At least, until he smiled back at me like I'd just made his day.

"Fuck yes, Brianna." He shifted me to the side of the bed then pushed the pillows away so he could lie flat on his back. Grabbing my hip with one hand, he guided me to straddle his chest. I paused, searching his eyes for any doubt. "Brianna, climb on. I'm fucking starving for you."

"Are you sure I won't hurt you?"

"Trying not to be insulted here, angel." Damien chuckled as his fingers teased me. "But no, you won't hurt me. Ride my face, Bri. Use my tongue to get yourself off."

"And you'll like that?"

Damien's hand shot out and grabbed my wrist, directing me toward his full and heavy cock. "More than you even know. I'm about to come just from the mental picture. Now, climb on, angel. Make my whole fucking day."

Ignoring my inner voice, I shifted to hover above Damien. The last thing I saw before he slammed my core onto his mouth was his wicked grin, one that promised untold pleasure. I reached out, gripping the headboard as he explored me. There was no apprehension or unease with each swipe of his tongue, only the sounds of his enjoyment. It was enough to push me out of my head, instead focusing on the pleasure his tongue brought. When he thrust his fingers inside me, my back arched, and my eyes slammed shut.

Pleasure climbed inside me, coiling until it became too tight to even breathe. But Damien's touch never faltered, and when his tongue traced my clit, stars swarmed my vision. Nothing else existed—not the city, not our friends. The entire world could have melted away outside Damien's apartment, and I would've been blissfully unaware, too busy riding the high he'd gifted me.

His tongue never stopped as I pulsed around him. When my body collapsed onto the bed next to him, Damien turned and nuzzled my neck, his lips leaving a trail along my flushed skin. For a moment, I almost turned my head—almost captured his lips to taste my pleasure on his tongue.

But that was a line we'd established early on, one I refused to break. After all, Damien was helping me, showing me all the different methods of pleasure I'd never experienced. Breaking his one boundary seemed like a pretty shitty way to thank him.

Glancing down at his lap, I shifted to face him, my hand on his aching cock. I don't think I'd ever get used to his size, the way my fingers stretched and still didn't fit around his girth. Just as I shifted lower, Damien placed his hand on top of mine.

"You don't have to do that, Brianna."

I arched a brow back at him. "Who said anything about having to do it? Maybe I want you in my mouth, especially after that epic orgasm."

Damien leaned down and traced my lower lip with his thumb. "You sure? This isn't that kind of situation, angel. I didn't eat your pussy because I expected anything in return. I wanted to do it, wanted you to soak my face. Not because of anything else."

His words made me pause, searching my mind for my motivation. Sure, there was a part of me that wanted to even the score, but it wasn't the reason I was dying to sink to my knees. No, that was all Damien. There was something so empowering about bringing this man to the brink, knowing I was the one making him come undone.

I pressed my hand against his chest, forcing him flat back against the mattress again. "You aren't the only one who gets off on making someone come." My hand wrapped around his cock as I shifted to kneel. "You make me feel so good, Damien. I want to do that for you, need to make you fall apart." I pressed a light kiss to the head of his cock. "Can I?"

Damien growled as his hand jutted out, grabbing a section of my hair in his fist. It stung in the best way, making me come a little more alive. "You never have to beg for my dick, Bri. You can do whatever you want to me. Trust me, I want it all."

My hand reached out, tracing the thick vein that lined his underside. Damien shuddered, and I smirked, loving his visceral reactions to my touch. Leaning down, I traced the tip with my tongue, the salty taste of his pre-cum coating my mouth. "Stop teasing me," Damien said, his voice strained. "Need to see those lips wrapped around my cock, angel."

I did as he commanded, taking as much as I could as I worked the rest with my hand. Damien tried to hold back, but when I dug my nails into his thigh, his thrusts deepened, knocking into the back of my throat. I swallowed him down, resisting the urge to gag on his length. I risked looking up at him, finding his dark eyes staring at me in wonder. "Where the fuck did you come from, Bri? And why the hell are you so perfect?"

I hummed my approval at his words, continuing to work him even as my jaw ached. With a few more rough thrusts, Damien spilled inside me, not taking his eyes off me as I swallowed down his release. When I pulled back, a little trickled from the edge of my mouth. He reached down, collecting it with his thumb before pressing it back onto my tongue. "Perfection," he muttered. "Absolute fucking perfection. You've ruined me, Brianna."

SIXTEEN

Damien

For an hour after Brianna left my apartment, I lay in bed, replaying our morning together. The pillow on the opposite side of the bed still smelled like her—a subtle floral hint that followed her path. Like a chump, I pulled it closer, holding on as if it were Brianna's curves instead.

The woman was going to be the death of me, that was for sure. She might have only wanted me for one night, but after everything we'd shared, there was no way I'd let her go that easily. Maybe I shouldn't be having those types of thoughts, especially when Brianna made it clear she wasn't looking for anything more than a hook-up, but the idea of never seeing her eyes light up in pleasure again made my stomach sour, and I desperately wanted to call her back into my bed.

Looking over at the other side of my bed, I smiled to myself. I'd never be able to walk through my apartment without getting a semi again. She'd infiltrated my space, and for the first time, I didn't mind.

When it came to women, I had a lot of rules to protect myself.

Number one—no one came to my apartment.

This place was my solace, the one place in the world where I didn't have to perform. Being a professional baseball player was the goal, but the cameras and attention drained me. When I was in the public eye, every move was orchestrated, every smile practiced, especially with Melanie's warning about my reputation. I needed a place that was just mine, and this was it. Nestled in the city's heart, it reminded me of what I worked hard to achieve but also allowed me to drop the mask inside its walls.

But last night, I didn't hesitate to bring Brianna here, to let her into my inner sanctum. I didn't want to think too deeply about why that was.

And then, there was her spending the night, a first in a long time for me. Part of always going to the woman's place meant leaving as soon as we were done, no awkward cuddling with a ticking clock above my head. However, when Brianna tried to leave, I pulled her back, unwilling to let her walk out just yet.

What the fuck was that?

An alarm blared out from my phone, alerting me it was time to get ready for the game tonight. As I shifted to turn it off, there were already dozens of texts in our team group chat, trying to confirm our usual pre-game rituals.

> **CAM**
>
> You alive, cap?
>
> **PARKER**
>
> Holy shit. D's not the first one texting?
> Send an SOS
>
> **BENNY**
>
> How do I keep getting added to this
> bullshit?

Benny Weber left the chat
Parker Drobrek added Benny Weber to the chat

PARKER

Our fearless leader needs to be a part of this.

BENNY

Fucking children, I swear.

CAM

Seriously—D, are you okay?

ME

Yeah, slept in a little. Heading to the stadium in ten.

PARKER

Sign of life!

I groaned as I placed my phone back on the nightstand and ambled into the bathroom. Bypassing the mirror, I headed straight toward the shower, letting the water warm before climbing into the glass enclosure. The water rained down from above me, washing away all traces of Brianna from my skin. As much as it needed to happen, I almost wished I could hold on a little longer, unable to get her out of my mind.

I shook my head as I washed my hair. We had a game today, and I needed to get focused. Granted, Houston's team wasn't having a great season, but you couldn't walk into a series thinking like that. Every team had off days, and anyone might get shoved down the rankings if they let down their guard. As the first baseman, it was my job to end runs, especially early in the game. The pressure fueled me, reminding why I'd fought so hard for my spot on the field.

Most days before a game, I spent time alone, maybe in

the gym to warm up my muscles. I never hooked up with anyone the night before a game. I'd done it once in college and played the worst game of my life, and I swore I wouldn't make that mistake again.

But once again, when Brianna's hazel eyes met mine, all common sense escaped me. I lost myself in her, trading my focus to see the smile light up her face.

The smart move would've been to forget about Brianna, pretend I'd never noticed her list. *Focus on baseball, move on to more faceless one-night stands. Less messy.* I stepped out of the shower, and the evidence of our night together met my gaze—nail marks down my chest, fingertip bruises from where Brianna clung to me as she came undone. My hands traced over each one, and I knew there was no going back, at least not yet. I'd been in the game for too long to let a woman distract me, and yet, the idea of walking away from my arrangement with Brianna made me pause. She'd already clawed her way under my skin, and I'd be damned if I was the one who blinked first.

Now was the time I'd normally try to redraw the lines between us, to take us back into that safe and comfortable no-strings attached zone. But my instincts screamed at me to do the opposite, to pull Brianna in close instead of pushing her away.

After getting dressed, I grabbed my phone, seeing a message waiting for me from Parker.

Parker: Ollie's bringing Bri to the game today. Told me to give you a heads up, even though she wouldn't tell me why.

A wide smile filled my face, grateful for the devious little matchmaker. The rules might have said Brianna and I could only be together in secret, but I couldn't deny the spark that burrowed in my chest, knowing she'd be out in the stands, cheering me on.

Damien: Ok.

Parker: Ok? That's all you're going to give me?

With a smirk on my face, I dropped my phone into the bag, feeling a lot more confident about the game this afternoon.

———

GLARING UP AT THE SCOREBOARD, I stretched my arms out, trying to focus as the batter stepped up to the plate. Tied. Fucking tied. Not the way any of us wanted to start off the series. Playing at home was a different beast, and tonight was no exception. When the Hawks first joined the league three years ago, no one knew if the fans would show up for us. There were already several legacy teams in the Northeast, teams that frequently ended up making it to the championship rounds. They had a wicked fanbase— fierce and loyal, no matter how their teams performed.

But Erie City shocked everyone by showing up for our team almost from the start. After last year, when we made it to the final rounds, the stands were filled to the max, and more fans seemed to root for our team every night.

However, with the stadium packed tonight, even more pressure weighed on our shoulders, especially mine. As one of the most veteran players, the media loved to focus on my game and use it as a barometer of our team's performance. If this were ten years ago, it'd fuck with my head. My rookie season was with the New York Rebels, one of the oldest teams in the country. Their legacy was fierce, but their fans were even fiercer. Over the eight years I spent with them, I learned to tune out the outside noise, only listening to my teammates and coaches. You'd never make everyone happy; someone was always on the sidelines, waiting for you to fail.

The only thing you could count on was yourself, and I made it my mission to leave everything on the field each game.

Houston's batter approached the plate and looked right at me with a sly smirk. I'd already stopped two of the players this inning, and I was determined to end it before they got any more runs. Blocking out all the surrounding noise, I focused on the ball, watching as the pitcher wound up and threw it with all his might. The batter swung, but the ball soared past him into the catcher's glove. He cursed as the board lit up with the strike animation, but I blocked it out, focusing on the man's mannerisms.

After so many years on the field, a lot of the newer players bled together, but they all had one thing in common: the drive to prove themselves. So many times, it painted a target on my back, especially when I was up at bat. They wanted to be the ones to strike out a seasoned player, and I couldn't fault them for it.

But I also wouldn't make it easy for them.

My eyes never strayed from the ball as it hurled through the air yet again, but this time, it collided with the batter's swing. The ball glided through the air, over our second baseman's head and into the outfield. As the batter took off running in my direction, Cam did the same, his gloved hand outstretched to catch the fly ball. He did so with ease, twisting before the ball careened in my direction.

Fuck. It was too high. My arm stretched, screaming in resistance as I forced my frame to make up the difference. Muscles twinged and twisted, but I refused to back down, not when the ball was just out of reach. It tried to fly past me, but it hit the edge of my glove, dropping into the pocket.

As if someone suddenly hit the play button, my body dropped ungraciously next to the base, only milliseconds before the runner slid into the bag.

"Out!" the base umpire called.

A smile ticked up the corners of my mouth as the inning ended, in desperate need of a drink and a couple of minutes out of the blaring heat. As I stretched out my glove, my arm still ached, muscles sore and spent after pushing past their limits. I shook it off, hoping it wasn't anything serious. In the past, these aches would be gone by the time I reached the dugout, but now, it was getting harder to shake off. There'd been plenty of horror stories over the years. One wrong move, and guys' long careers were over, trading in their uniforms for surgical gowns and practice for physical therapy.

"Fuck," Cam breathed heavily as he came up to my side. "That guy was too goddamn fast. Didn't think we'd pull that one off."

"Have some faith, kid," I chuckled, trying to stretch out my shoulder. "He was too hungry for the run. Should have waited a little longer for a better pitch."

Cam frowned as he watched my movements. "You good, D?"

"Yeah, just a twinge in my shoulder."

"Shit," he said, stepping closer. "You want me to call someone over?"

"Don't even fucking think about it," I snapped before shaking my head. "Sorry, Seda. It's nothing to worry about. Just focus on getting a good hit."

His eyes darted up to the outfield, smirking when he spotted someone waiting for him. "Gotta. Promised my girls I'd get a run in for them. If I don't, they're never gonna let me live it down."

I followed his eye-line, finding Hadley, wrapped around his seven-year-old daughter, Emilia. The little girl was a spitfire, much like Cam's better half, and she had no problem calling him out if he made a bad play. After growing up on the baseball field, Emilia knew more about the game than most of the rookie players. I'd tried to get some of that love of the game to rub off on my nieces during playdates and family day, but none of them had any sort of interest.

Just as I went to ask Cam about Emilia, someone sat down next to Hadley, holding one of the large popcorn buckets from the concession stand. *Brianna.* Even though I knew she'd be here, I tried to avoid looking in her section, because from the moment I spotted her, I didn't want to look anywhere else. Fuck, it had only been a few hours since she left my bed, and already, I craved her, wanted to feel that plush body underneath mine, to hear her moaning my name.

She was too far away to make out anything more than her smile, but a possessive part of me hoped she'd cheer me on. I desperately wanted her in my jersey, to see my name across her back.

But that couldn't happen right now, not while Brianna swore me to secrecy. So instead, I turned back to the game, doing everything possible to ignore the brunette sitting in the outfield.

SEVENTEEN

Brianna

Watching Damien was like a masterclass in athleticism. The man moved like no other, surpassing even the younger guys on the field. Yet, when he made that last play, he got up slower than before, walking like he'd hurt himself when he knocked out the runner.

Panic swelled in my chest, wishing there was some way to check in on him from up in our seats. But he wouldn't have his phone until the game ended, and there wasn't anyone to ask without setting off my friends' alarm bells. Even though Ollie knew something happened with Damien last night, I refused to tell her anything. The moment I opened my mouth to ask about him, she'd see right through me.

From the second I left his bed this morning, I'd wanted to crawl back into it, getting more of that delicious pleasure only Damien had ever provided. Being with him was easy—almost too easy. He made me laugh, made me more confident, made me want to discover new sides of myself I'd been too shy ever to discuss in the past.

Which was a big problem.

My time with Damien was supposed to be only a night or two, but his touch turned into an obsession—a decade-long itch I'd been dying to scratch. We might have only spent a couple of nights together, but I was already getting attached. Crap. I should've known my soft heart would be too weak to handle him. Even though I tried to keep feelings out of it, they'd started creeping in, making me read too much into our nights together.

This was sex. Nothing more.

As Emilia cheered on the Hawks' batter, Hadley turned toward me. "You okay, Bri? You're looking a little green."

Ollie arched her eyebrow from Emilia's other side. As she took in my expression, she smirked then turned back to watch the game. I glanced over at Hadley. "Yeah, all good. We went out and had a couple of drinks last night, and it's taking its toll today."

Unease settled in my stomach. I hated lying to Hadley, especially when she'd confided in me when things started heating up with Cam. Even though their relationship was a little unconventional, those two were meant to be. When they tried to deny it, they fell for each other fast and hard. It was only a matter of time until Cam asked her to be his wife.

That would never be the path for Damien and me. We were ships in the night, spending a few brief moments together before we returned to our true destinations. Give it a week or two, and Damien would be back scouring the clubs for his next supermodel while I'd return to my world of romance novels and quiet nights alone. And that was what I wanted. At least, what I should've wanted.

So why did the idea of Damien with anyone else make my heart race?

The sound of the roaring crowd ripped me from my

thoughts. I glanced up at the screen and saw Damien heading out to the base, a cocky grin written on his face. The man oozed swagger, like the legends of old Hollywood, but with his gruff facial hair and arms covered with tattoos, he looked more like the stereotypical bad boy.

The pitcher sized him up and tried to look menacing as Damien settled at the plate. God, the intensity made me squirm in my seat, and I had nothing riding on the game. I could only imagine how he felt down on the field, knowing thousands of fans held their breath, waiting to see what their favorite player would do.

I sucked in a sharp breath at the first pitch, watching as the blur of the ball approached Damien. The umpire's 'strike' reached all the way up to the stands, and I winced. Hadley grabbed my hand. "Getting into the game, huh?"

"Yeah," I chuckled. "It's much more intense when you know the guys on the field."

Hadley's head snapped in my direction. "Have you been talking to Damien?"

"What?" I shook my head. "No, of course not. I haven't seen him since he drove me back to the hotel in Dallas."

Great. Now I'd gone from evading the truth to downright lying to my friend. Luckily, Hadley didn't seem to pick up on my deception; she just turned back to watch the next pitch. "Damien's smart. He won't risk swinging at a sloppy pitch."

We all stopped talking as the pitcher released the ball, silent as Damien swung the bat. Another strike. One more to go. His smirk fell from his face, replaced by fierce determination. Now, my thighs clenched for an entirely different reason. Cocky, funny Damien was one thing, but this intense, smoldering version? I wanted to climb down from the stands and mount him right then and there, hoping he'd be just as intense as he claimed me.

Images of climbing on top of Damien filled my mind as the third pitch rang out, followed by the audible crack of the bat making contact. Most of the crowd kept their eyes on it, watching with bated breath to see where it would inevitably land. But my gaze never left Damien as he ran through the bases, too distracted by him to even cheer. When the ball landed in the outfield, it was too late—Damien was already rounding into second base, the previous players scurrying across home. The shortstop tossed the ball back to the pitcher, who scowled at the scoreboard before pounding the ball into his glove.

Damien started to slink off the base, but the pitcher turned over his shoulder, glaring at him. It was enough to stay Damien but not enough to wipe the smirk from his lips. When the pitcher turned back to the next batter, Damien turned, as if he sensed my eyes digging into the back of his skull. His face shifted when he spotted me in the stands, and my heart leaped into my chest at the adoration reflected at me.

Over. This is over.

Except Damien's expression told me he wasn't letting it go that easily.

"ARE you sure I should be back here?"

I paced the small hall, trying not to overthink my decision to follow Ollie to the family and friends area. While everyone else had someone waiting on the other side of the locker room, I had no reason to be down here.

Even though I'd slept in Damien's bed last night, we

didn't have a relationship. We weren't together—hell, we'd barely become friends.

And I needed to remember that.

No matter what happened last night or how I felt during the game, it didn't change our situation. We'd used each other a couple of times; that was it. No emotions, no feelings. Just sex with no strings.

Too bad standing down here, I felt like a puppet, attached to Damien with so many strings, I couldn't even control my own movements.

Hadley chuckled at my side. "Of course you should be here. You're part of our crew. Cam made sure to get you on the list so you could hang with Ollie and me." She paused, turning to look down the hall where Emilia was chatting with some of the other kids. "I swear, that girl's going to turn out just like Cam. She's already begging to join one of the softball leagues with the middle schoolers."

Before I could answer, the door to the locker room swung open, and I jumped, terrified Damien had come out. God, I needed to get it together, needed to find the best way to put distance back between us. No matter what my heart wanted, I wasn't ready for anything more. Honestly, the world's most perfect man could walk in front of me right now, and it would be useless. My heart wasn't ready to get back out there, not when I was still recovering from my divorce. The last time I'd let my heart call the shots, I'd ended up alone, with nothing to show for the past ten years of my life.

That thought sobered me, and I tucked those pesky little feelings into a tightly locked box. By the time Damien came out of the locker room, my mask was back in place, hiding all the thoughts that had raided my mind over the past few hours.

He ignored everyone else in the room, instead heading straight toward me. Instinct told me to run into his arms, to wrap myself around him and tell him how proud I was of him. But fear rooted me to the spot; I only offered a slight smile. Hadley stepped in between us, wrapping her arms around his waist. "Awesome game, Ramos."

"Thanks, Hads." He smiled at her words, but his eyes remained on me. Despite the inches separating us, his gaze was like a caress, cascading down my body until I sensed it in my toes. "Good to see you at a game, Brianna. What did you think?"

Every instinct screamed out for me to praise him, to tell him how mesmerizing he was out on the field. Even after a decade of playing, his joy was evident, even way out in the stands.

Instead, I said, "It was fine. You played well."

The corner of his lip quirked up, finding my dismissal amusing for some reason. "Guess we have to step our game up. Can't have our fans saying we're just playing fine."

Hadley's eyes bounced back and forth between us, as if trying to figure out what was going on. *Join the club, Hadley.* Even though this man had seen me at my most vulnerable, right now, my walls were made of reinforced titanium. I shook my head, turning toward her and edging Damien out of the conversation. Reaching out to hug her, I said, "I'm going to catch up with Ollie. Are you good?"

"Yeah," Hadley drawled, looking over her shoulder at Damien. His presence still burned at my back, but I couldn't turn around. I couldn't keep up this act any longer. My mind might be made up about Damien, but the rest of my body had a vastly different reaction. The scent of his masculine body wash filled my nose, the heat of his imposing frame pressed against my skin.

I glanced over my shoulder, giving Damien a nod without meeting his gaze. "Good to see you again, Damien."

"You too, Ms. Sideris," he responded, his voice taking on that deep tone I loved so much. Shivers scattered along my skin, and from the laugh on his lips, Damien knew exactly how I'd reacted to his words.

By the time I exited the hall, my heartbeat had returned to normal, finally able to take a deep breath now that I was out of Damien's presence. Our lines were there for a reason—one I needed to remember.

EIGHTEEN

Brianna

My heels clacked on the marble path as I darted toward Holy Trinity Church. I didn't even bother looking down at my phone. The lack of people congregating in the gardens already proved I was far later than I'd intended. Freaking alarm.

For thirty-two years of my life, Sundays had always started at church. No matter the illness, the holiday, or other important life event, my mother had one rule: when Sunday morning worship started, your butt better be in that pew.

I sent a silent prayer to all the saints as I snuck in the side entrance, barely bothering to look around before finding my family waiting on the opposite end of the church. After a lifetime of worship at Holy Trinity, the building was an old friend, as familiar as the back of my hand. After all, I'd sat through hundreds of sermons, bored as the priest droned on about sin and redemption. So instead, I memorized the stained glass windows, pretended I was the one decorating the idols and the saints who watched over us. And because church was never a simple affair, I'd hide out in the rafters as my mother socialized, gossiping about the other members of the community with her friends.

But no matter how many times I tried to hide from my mother, she always found me and dragged me back into her world.

As I crossed through the back of the pews, my mother snapped her head around, glaring at me as I tried to make my way through the crowd. Her disapproving frown followed me as I sank into my place next to my older brother, who stared at me with a knowing smirk.

"You better have a good excuse, Bebe. She's on the warpath already."

I knocked my elbow into Jason's side. "You were supposed to cover for me."

"I tried, but I'm already on her list because her grandchildren have the flu. Apparently, that's not enough of a reason to keep them home." He shook his head, probably remembering the time we both had the stomach bug and had to suffer through the hour-long service. He lowered his voice, mimicking my mother's faded Greek accent. "Worship doesn't stop because of a little sickness."

I rolled my eyes but snapped my spine straight when my mother turned to shake her head at me. Nudging Jason, I pulled out my phone, typing in a message without hitting send.

ME: The kids okay?

He nodded. "They're champs. A couple of days relaxing with fluids, and they should be fine. Ella stayed home with them, so I have to leave right after to help her out."

Traitor.

Okay, that might have been unfair. It wasn't like my brother was abandoning me to the wolves because he felt like it. His kids, Abby and Andrew, were only three and eighteen months, a handful on the best of days. While I loved them dearly, they were exhausting. Whenever I babysat, I spent the next few days trying to rebuild my energy, grateful I worked in upper elementary and not early childhood.

Jason opened his mouth to say something else, but the woman in the row ahead of us turned and glared. We both nodded in apology, turning to focus as the prayers began.

Each moment of worship seemed longer than the last, and my mind couldn't help but wander.

And its favorite location lately?

Damien Ramos.

Heat soured my cheeks as last weekend came to mind, when he spent hours worshipping me in his bed, only for us to have to pretend to be strangers at the game. He texted a few times in the days since, but I hadn't responded, unsure how to explain my thoughts even to myself. After all, what kind of person seduced someone and convinced him to keep it a secret, only to get upset when it stayed that way?

Oh, right. Me. That was who.

Honestly, I was more upset with myself than Damien. He'd done exactly what we'd agreed. He'd been friendly when our paths crossed, and I was the one who couldn't manage to string together any coherent sentences. But every time he texted, that tendril of guilt and confusion grew teeth, and I wasn't ready to face them quite yet.

A buzzing formed at the base of my skull, the sign a headache was beginning to brew. I needed to get out of here. After only a few minutes in the church, exhaustion already plagued me from the pitying glances and empty prayers. Maybe I should end this thing with Damien for good. God knows my mother was already praying three times a day for Todd and me to reconcile. If she found out I had multiple no-strings attached sex sessions with someone, much less a man who wasn't Orthodox? There'd be no coming back.

Jason nudged me with his elbow, furrowing his brow in silent question. I smiled back at him, hoping it'd come off more reassuring than it felt. He furrowed his brow but turned back toward my mom, taking her hand. She beamed back at him before looking at me and mouthing for me to sit up. Shaking my head, I focused back on the services. Jason had an easier relationship with both my parents. He'd been the golden child growing up—star of the high school football team, valedictorian, and accepted into an Ivy league university. He even married his high school sweetheart, whose parents were a staple at Holy Trinity. For a long time, I'd tried to keep up, tried to be the girl my parents envisioned.

But even after following all the right steps, my life still fell apart, leaving me alone in the rubble. When my family should have rallied around me, they instead looked at me like I had a scarlet letter pressed into my chest—the pathetic woman whose husband left her for someone else.

Slamming my eyes closed, I forced the tears away, pretending the droning sermon moved me. I'd mourned the end of my past life a while ago, but forgiving my family for letting me flounder? Those wounds would take a lot longer to heal.

DESPITE THE CONCLUSION OF WORSHIP, church didn't end when the priest dismissed us. No, instead, there was always the after—hours of socializing with my mother as she paraded around the community room like the queen of the congregation.

I sat at the edge of the room, poking my room-temperature moussaka with the edge of my fork. Jason disappeared shortly after the priest wished us well, returning to his sick children. Honestly, I'd rather deal with the germs than the empty platitudes I'd received for the last hour.

You should leave.

The voice in the back of my mind called out, sounding suspiciously like Ollie. But despite my annoyance, I stayed seated, unable to leave until my mother dismissed me. Our relationship might be strained at the moment, but I still hated disappointing her, choosing my discomfort over her disappointment.

"Hey, Bri."

My spine straightened as the familiar voice washed over me. *Todd.* As I looked up to meet his eyes, nausea curled into my stomach. It was a good thing I hadn't eaten. Throwing up on his fancy loafers would be church fodder for months. My eyes darted to my mother, who didn't look surprised to see him.

What the hell was she doing?

Todd motioned to the chair across from me. "Can I sit?"

"What are you doing here?"

"I needed to talk to you, and you haven't been returning any of my calls and texts."

"Yes, because we're *divorced*, and you're getting remarried, Todd. There is nothing for us to talk about."

"Come on, Bri," Todd said as he scooted into the seat next to me. My whole body went rigid. "We were such a good team for so long. Our marriage didn't work out, but I'd like it if we could be friends." He sighed, running his hand through his blond hair. "I miss you, miss talking to you. I didn't realize—"

"No." His green eyes darted up to meet mine. For a moment, I almost wavered, hating the anguish in his expression. That primal part of me wanted to soothe it away, to make promises that would ease some of his pain. But I couldn't, not after everything we'd been through. "Our friendship—all of it—died when you chose to cheat, Todd. It's not the end of the marriage that ruined us. No, it was the lying, the deception. If you told me—"

"I tried!"

"Not hard enough," I answered. "The moment you crossed that line, there was no going back, for either of us."

I stood to leave despite my mother's frown, but Todd's voice broke through the din of the room. "I made a mistake." My knees shook as he stared up at me, genuine contrition reflecting at me for the very first time. "Bri, you were the best thing in my life, and for years, I took you for granted. Never realized—"

"Todd, please, don't do this." My voice cracked, emotion clawing its way up through my chest. "It's too late."

Defeat slumped his shoulders, and he nodded. Before he could say anything else, my mother walked over and put her hand on his shoulder. All hope of her standing up for me died when she leaned down and kissed his cheek. "Good to see you, Todd."

"You too, Mrs. Sideris," he said as he cleared his throat and stood. "Thank you for letting me come to service."

"Please, darling, you know it's Olivia. No matter the... *ugliness* that happened, you'll always be family to us. You're welcome anytime."

"Mom!" I hissed.

She narrowed her eyes at me. "Brianna, don't be selfish.

Todd was my son for a long time. I'm not turning my back on him now."

"Thank you, Olivia."

I almost bit through my tongue. Shaking my head, I leaned in to kiss my mother's cheek, unable to stand this exchange for another moment. After a lifetime of playing second fiddle to my brother's accomplishments, you'd think I'd be used to my mother's disappointment, but seeing her kindness toward my ex-husband made my patience snap. "I'm going to go."

My mother's jaw dropped. "But it's so early! They haven't even served dessert yet."

My glare darted between her and Todd. "Lost my appetite."

NINETEEN

Brianna

"Can you believe her?"

I growled as I dug through the fridge, trying to find something to ease the ache in my chest. After coming back from church, I'd tried everything to ease my blood pressure: running, reading, even reality television. Nothing had made a dent, so now, it was time for some caloric therapy.

"Your mother's been advocating for Todd's redemption since the moment you left," Ollie said from the couch. "So while I would love to say no, this seems pretty on-brand for her."

Finding nothing worth eating, I slammed the fridge closed and slumped on the couch next to Ollie. "Maybe, but it's a slap in the face. He cheated on me. I shouldn't have to beg my parents to move on." I leaned over to the side table and pulled an envelope out of the drawer. "Not that I'd ever want him back, but he's getting remarried in less than three months. The ship has sailed. Let it go."

Ollie eyed the invitation I'd tossed between us. "Why do you still have that?"

"What do you mean?"

She picked it up, reading over the pristine gold lettering. "I mean—why are you holding on to Todd's wedding invitation?" Her eyes widened. "Please tell me you weren't serious about going."

"Of course not." I scoffed, tugging it back from her hands. "What am I supposed to do with it?"

"Throw it away! Light it on fire!" Ollie answered. "Hell, rip it into a million shreds and fuck your mystery man on top of it. Do something other than hang on to it like a sad reminder of your past life."

I toyed with the edges, unable to look Ollie in the eye. She was right—I should have tossed it the moment it arrived. But despite the sting, every time I tried, a pang of sadness hit me. Instead, I tucked it into the drawer, leaving it to deal with another day.

Ollie inched closer to me, taking it from my hands. "Okay, let me ask you this—when you saw Todd today, did you want him back?"

"No," I answered. "Even if Todd hadn't cheated, our marriage wasn't working. And while a small part of me will always wonder what if, it's not about Todd. It's more about the life I left behind." Running my hands over my face, I sighed. "Ol, I'm in my thirties, starting over. While everyone else is rushing to the finish line, I'm stuck back at start. It's hard not to feel like a failure."

Ollie reached out her arms and tugged my head against her shoulder. "First—you're not at start. Sure, you might have had to backtrack, but like you said, your marriage wasn't working. I know you, Bri. You weren't happy. As much as you tried to hide it, everyone knew being with Todd drained you." She shifted to face me. "There's no race, Bri. No timeline. Just let yourself be happy and fuck the rest."

"You make it sound so easy."

"Oh, it's not," Ollie answered, her face darkening. "Choosing yourself is never easy, but it'll be worth it."

LATER THAT NIGHT, I'd planned on curling up in my bed, content to hide from the rest of the world after my run-in with Todd. However, Ollie played her best friend card—again—forcing me out of my self-imposed hibernation to socialize with her.

As we sat in the car on our way to Parker's house on the outskirts of town, I stared down at the crockpot in my arms, a frown forming on my lips. "Can't believe you've been holding out on me, Oleander."

My roommate glanced over from the driver's seat, confusion etched on her features. "What do you mean?"

I shook the pot nestled in my lap. "You can cook like a freaking Michelin star chef, yet the only things I've ever seen you make are frozen pizzas and grilled cheese."

"I do make a bomb grilled cheese," Ollie said with a smirk.

"Don't play cute, Ol. You have some serious talent in the kitchen, but you never use it. Why?"

She sighed as she stared ahead, refusing to meet my eyes. "Parker's grandmother taught me when I was younger. She could tell my parents weren't around much and wanted to make sure I could fend for myself." Ollie shrugged. "But I don't love it like she did. Now, I only cook if Parker requests something. No one else has her recipes, and he misses her cooking, so I try to help where I can."

So many more questions danced on my tongue, but I swallowed them down. Ollie and Parker's friendship seemed like more to me, but who was I to question it? Besides, whenever someone tried to talk to Ollie about it, she shut them down. One day, she might see what was right in front of her, but until she was ready, there was nothing any of us could do to help move them along.

Ollie hit the blinker, pulling onto Parker's street. God, I loved this neighborhood. Compared to the rest of the guys' high-rise apartments, Parker's home seemed much more normal. The smaller craftsman's style home matched the other houses in the quiet neighborhood, but his took up the end of the dead-end street. It seemed like a place meant for a family—a home someone could grow into. Parker loved it, and that was what mattered most.

I smiled at the thought—at least, I did, until I noticed all the cars lining the street in front of Parker's home. "Umm, Ollie? I thought you said this was a small dinner party."

"Did I?" She gave me a knowing smirk. "Nope. Should've mentioned tonight's team dinner. Parker asked for us to join the guys and begged me to make something to eat."

My throat dried as I watched members of the Hawks leave their cars, heading up the front porch, holding gigantic bowls and serving trays. After Ollie finished parallel parking, I shot her a lethal glare. "You did not tell me this was a team dinner. We shouldn't even be here, Ol, especially me. I have nothing to do with the guys."

"Relax," Ollie sighed. "It's always a huge affair. And it's never just the players—management and friends come too. I already told you, you're a part of our crew, which means you're required to attend *all* the team functions."

"I don't remember any of this in our friendship handbook."

"Sorry, babe. Snuck in an additional clause during negotiations. Besides..." Ollie nodded behind me. "Pretty sure I'm not the only one who wants you here."

I followed her line of sight and saw Damien climbing out of his car. My eyes roamed over his dark-wash jeans and tight, black, button-down shirt. With his tattoos and dark hair swaying in the wind, he was temptation personified, and my legs instantly clamped together.

As if he sensed my presence, his footsteps slowed, and he looked over his shoulder, meeting my eyes through the car's windshield. I gave him a little wave, unsure what else to do. Damien just shook his head, a smirk at the corner of his lips. I turned, narrowing my eyes at Ollie. "You knew he was going to be here."

"Maybe."

"You are the worst meddler. Remind me again why I love you?"

"Because I'm the best, and you need someone who's going to push you out of your comfort zone. Besides, even though you refuse to admit anything, it's obvious to everyone with eyes that you like him. So, go. Have fun and try to enjoy tonight. Don't worry about what you're supposed to be doing and just let loose for once."

"You're the worst influence."

Ollie chuckled as she reached behind me and grabbed a couple of bottles of tequila. "Oh, I am well aware. Now, let's get inside before the guys start without us."

It was going to be a *very* long night.

TWENTY

Damien

Most team dinners played out the same: shit-talking, drinks, and more food than we'd ever need. We'd spend hours around the table, some of us standing and others seated around the room. Either way, we were all together, sharing tales of our start in baseball, the universal link that tied us together.

When we first started, only four or five guys showed up, mostly out-of-towners who had nowhere else to be that night. But over time, it expanded, and now, we were running out of room in all our homes. Drobrek's was the largest, with an open concept that allowed for pockets of people to gather in different areas yet stay together. It made it the simple choice when we had to decide where to go. Plus, he loved having everyone over. The man lived to host parties, especially when it was our entire team taking up his space.

Tonight, there were more people than we'd ever had before. Almost every member of the team showed up, as well as many of the members of the front office. Russ, the team's manager, sat in one corner, talking quietly with

Melanie. Even Weber came, although he left as soon as they cleared the plates.

And most surprisingly?

Brianna stood only five feet from me, looking all too beautiful with her casual outfit, her hair slung back in a braid. Pieces of it stuck out, the shorter strands not contained by the band. For a moment, her hazel eyes met mine, but she shot them back down, returning her attention to one of the rookies, our new second baseman, Banfield. My jaw tensed. It wasn't like I had anything against the guy, but right now, I could have smashed my fist through his face and felt zero regrets.

Shit. What the fuck was happening to me? I wasn't a jealous guy. I never cared enough to be jealous. But for some reason, Brianna had crawled under my skin, and I hated the idea of her giving her attention to anyone else. I wanted to earn her soft smile, wanted to cause the sweet blush that filled her cheeks, wanted to be the man she sought when she walked into a crowd, knowing my eyes were always going to be searching for her.

As I downed the rest of my drink, someone nudged their elbow into my side. I glanced down to find Ollie smirking at me, a large margarita in a sippy cup clutched in her hands. "You've got a crush..." she sing-songed.

I rolled my eyes. "Ol, I'm almost forty. I'm way too fucking old for a crush."

"Call it what you want," she mused, "but you've hardly taken your eyes off Bri all night. Why don't you go talk to her?"

I shook my head. "She's not interested. Bri hasn't said two words to me since she got here. Not gonna mess up her night any more than I already have."

"Brianna doesn't know what she wants." Ollie shook her

head and lowered her voice so only I could hear it. "She's spent too long on the sidelines, letting people forget her worth. If you want anything more to happen between you two, you're going to have to make the next move. Show up for her. Show her she means something to you."

I lifted my gaze, finding Brianna's eyes fixed on me now. She ducked away again as soon as we connected, but I could see something reflecting at me: the same need, the same longing I was sure was etched into my features like a brand. My feet longed to take a step, to close the distance between us, but something unfamiliar stopped me.

Changing the subject, I tapped the bottom of her cup. "I see Parker hasn't forgiven you for ruining his new rug."

Ollie rolled her eyes. "You spill one glass of wine, and suddenly, you're barred from any open containers." She took a long pull from the squiggly straw. "It's fine. Drobrek might think he's won, but I'm always going to get him back."

"Where is your guy anyway? He's been running around all night, and I want to thank him for hosting again."

"Oh, he's already getting all the thanks he needs." She nodded to where Parker was chatting up one of the front office assistants. I wracked my brain for her name but came up short, only recognizing her because she'd set her sights on our third baseman early in the season. Parker said something, and she swung her head back, laughing a little too loudly to be genuine. Ollie scoffed, just as loudly. "He seems like he's doing just fine over there without me."

"Maybe because the person he really wants doesn't seem to have any interest."

Ollie shot a glare in my direction. "Don't start with me, D. We're just friends and everyone knows it."

Not even close. In fact, Ollie and Parker were the only ones who believed that lie. But even after questions from almost everyone on our team, they both failed to see the spark—the lingering search for *more*.

She whacked her hand against my chest. "Besides, this isn't about me. You're the one walking around like a kicked puppy. Seriously, go talk to Brianna."

My jaw ticked, annoyed at her pushiness. "Why do you care so much, Ol? If Brianna doesn't want to talk to me, I'm not going to force my way in."

Ollie's face softened, looking more vulnerable than I'd ever seen her before. "Brianna is the best person I know. She's been through a lot, and I hate that she let it cloud her perspective. She deserves someone who is going to see her, *the real her*, and not be afraid to put in the work." Ollie nudged my side again. "And you might be that guy. Plus, I really hate her ex-husband, and I get immense joy imagining his face when he finds out you two are an item." She took another sip of her drink. "Think about it, D. If you two are good with leaving well enough alone, then ignore me, but I'd never be able to live with myself if I didn't try."

I chuckled. "For someone who hates unsolicited advice, you sure love to dish it out."

"All part of my charm."

Ollie winked, and then someone else called her. She walked away after squeezing my arm, leaving the unspoken implications in her wake. But before I could think too deeply about it, I was on the move, ready to find the person who'd occupied my thoughts all night.

When I found Brianna, she was standing on Parker's back deck, staring off into the night. With summer in full swing, humidity still clung to the air, making it thick and sluggish. Or it might have been the tension ricocheting through my bones. I almost turned back around when Brianna peeked over her shoulder, shaking her head. "Should've known you'd find me."

"Hiding from me, Bri?" I asked, taking the spot next to her.

"Not exactly," she breathed. "Just trying to navigate how to be around you after everything."

"I know the feeling," I answered. A quip sat on the tip of my tongue, but I bit it back, enjoying the silence between us. There was nothing awkward about it, even with the strange situation we'd found ourselves in. In the past, there was always a line between the women I slept with and the rest of my world, but with Brianna, all of them had blurred, making her a consistent presence. In the past, it would have bothered me. Instead, tonight, I soaked up her companionship, letting the subtle floral scent of her perfume override my other senses.

"I always thought I'd want to live out here," Brianna said. Her voice was quiet, more to herself than to me. "But now that I've been in the city for a little while, I miss the noise—the constant hum of people."

I nodded as I shifted my gaze, watching her bright eyes as she stared up at the sky. While she stayed fascinated by all the stars circling us, she transfixed me, consumed by the peace written on her face. She sighed, closing her eyes tightly. "Do you ever wonder if there is some pre-determined plan? Or if we're all just winging it?"

"Not sure," I said gruffly, forcing my eyes away from her. "I like to think there's some higher purpose, that we're all working toward our end goal, but I've always believed our choices define us—that how we decide to live our lives matters more than any higher calling."

"I like that," Brianna smiled. As she opened her eyes, she turned back toward me. "You were watching me in the kitchen, while I was talking to August."

"Yeah," I admitted, not bothering to hide it with a convenient lie.

"Why?"

I ran my hand over my face. "Because you were smiling at him, not the wide smile you do when you're uncomfortable but the slight one when you find someone funny."

Brianna furrowed her brow. "You didn't like me smiling at someone else?"

I reached out, tucking a strand of her hair behind her ear. "Not for the reason you're worried about, angel. I don't care if you want to talk to anyone else. We both know you're too strong to be kept down. But I didn't like that I couldn't talk to you, couldn't show all the guys how much you mean to me." I grinned at her. "And yeah, I didn't like Banfield shooting his shot with you."

Brianna shook her head. "He tried flirting with me, but I shut it down."

"Why, Bri?"

"Besides the fact that he's almost a decade younger than me?" She leaned forward, pressing her hands to my chest. "There's this other Hawks player I can't get out of my head." Brianna sucked in a slow breath as her hazel eyes shone with vulnerability. "And I might not want to."

I reached down, pulling her closer, eliminating the space that had been there all night. Once Brianna stood cradled against my chest, that unease slid out of me, and I took the first full breath of the evening. "I don't want you to either, and if you can't tell, I've been thinking about you nonstop, Bri. I want more than a couple of stolen nights with you."

"So where does that leave us?" Brianna asked.

"We should explore this," I answered. "Stop putting a timeline on our time together and just enjoy ourselves." Brianna chewed on the corner of her lip, and I reached up, tugging it free. "Tell me what's on your mind."

"I meant what I said—I'm not ready for a relationship. But something casual, I might...I might want to try that."

The word casual sliced a wound through my pride, but I swallowed it down. content for the piece of Brianna I had right now. Ollie's earlier words came back to haunt me, reminding me Brianna needed time and space to feel safe. And right now, this was all she could handle. If I wanted more with her, I had to let her set the pace.

"I'm good with that, Bri, but I have a couple stipulations."

"Like what?"

"No one else." Brianna tensed in my arms, but I continued. "I'll agree to anything else, but if we're going to do this, I want your word it's only us."

"But what if you—"

I reached up, pressing my thumb to her lower lip. "Don't even finish that sentence, angel. There has been no one else since that night in Dallas, and even more—I don't want there to be. If you haven't noticed yet, you're more than enough for me. I'm not looking for anyone else."

Brianna's eyes searched mine before slowly nodding. "Okay. But you have to promise me if you find someone else, you'll tell me." I started to respond, but she silenced me with a shake of her head. "I mean it, Damien. The minute you want this to end, you tell me. No secrets, no lies."

"Deal." I leaned forward, running my fingers along her cheek. "Any other rules?"

"Just sex," Brianna blurted. "We can use each other for

pleasure until we decide to call it quits. No feelings. No jealousy. No one can know but us."

I chuckled and nodded toward the house. "Ollie already knows."

"She might, but I'm not about to give her any details."

"Fine by me," I said. "So are we really doing this?"

Brianna nodded, a wide smile forming on her lips. "Yeah, pretty sure we are."

As soon as the words left her lips, I took her hand, tugging her back into the house and into one of the guest bathrooms. When the door locked behind us, Brianna paused, a question written in her eyes. I stepped closer, dragging the tips of my fingers along the curve of her neck. "Angel, you forgot you showed me part of your list. Don't think I didn't notice public sex on it. We're crossing that one off right now."

"We are?" she squeaked.

"Oh fuck yes," I groaned. "You've been teasing me with that delicious body all night. I'm not waiting another minute until I get to claim you again."

Brianna

No sooner had the words left Damien's mouth, we collided. Our hands, lips, tongues—every part of us was desperate for the other. Every inch of skin was fair game. All except for our mouths, of course. As much as I was dying to claim his kiss, I held back, knowing that was a firm line between us. Despite everything we'd shared, kissing now felt too personal, too intimate. Almost as if the moment our mouths touched, emotions would get in the way, and we'd crash toward our inevitable end.

I pushed that thought out of my mind as Damien hands found the hem of my shirt, tossing it over my head into the corner of the bathroom. He groaned as he took in my black lace bra. "Fuck, Brianna."

I tucked my lip between my teeth. "Like what you see?"

"More than you know," Damien growled, his eyes turning darker with his desire. But his touch was the opposite, slow and tantalizing. By the time he trailed his thumb across my peaked bud, I was ready to beg for a rough touch. "This is going to be fast and hard, Bri. Can't risk any of the other guys hearing the sounds you make, and I'm definitely not going to risk any of them coming in here."

My eyes widened with lust, and dampness coated the apex of my thighs. Damien cursed, reaching forward to untuck my lip from my teeth. "Or is that what you want, angel? You want someone to find you in here, getting fucked rough, just like you want it?"

I wanted to scream out no, wanted to insist what happened in here was for our eyes only, but the idea of someone walking in on me at Damien's mercy made my whole body tense with need. Forcing my eyes up to meet his gaze, I smirked. "I might like that."

"Might?" Damien chuckled, reaching to unbutton my jeans. He swore when he found my dampened panties. "This is more than might. What is it that turns you on, Bri? The idea of someone watching me fuck you? Or that we might get caught fooling around in Parker's bathroom?"

"That one," I whispered as his thumbs ran over my breasts. "That someone might walk in and find us together. Ruin our secret."

Damien chuckled before closing his mouth around my nipple, flicking the peak with the tip of his tongue. I clenched my lips together, desperately trying to hold back the moan building in the back of my throat. He leaned back, running his hand over my thighs, reaching up to cup my core. "That's it. Gotta be a good girl and stay quiet for me. Unless you're ready to show everyone how well you take every single inch I give you?"

"No," I moaned right as his thumb pressed down on my swollen clit. "I'll be quiet, I promise."

"Good," Damien said, continuing his ministrations. "Because if anyone hears us, we're going to have to stop, even if you beg me. Can't risk someone else walking in. I might take out one of my teammates if they see you naked and writhing for me, and I need them to win another championship."

My mouth opened to argue, but Damien shifted, tugging off my underwear and jeans in one swoop. His hands ran along my thighs, getting closer and closer to where I wanted him. There was something so forbidden about this arrangement—me, naked in someone else's bathroom while Damien remained fully dressed. But before I could reach out, he spun me around and pressed my chest against the vanity. I looked up, and all I could see was myself in the mirror, barely recognizing the wanton woman in the reflection. As I tucked my gaze back down to the counter, Damien reached out and tugged on my hair.

"Don't even think about it, Brianna. You're not going to take your eyes off that mirror while I'm fucking you. You need to see this, how fucking right we look together. See why any man in the other room would die for a taste of you." His fingers swept through my core, and I groaned, arching my back to seek more of his touch. Damien's lips skirted along the curve of my neck. "But you're not going to let them have one, are you?"

I shook my head no, still trying to shift my hips to get him inside me. But Damien just pulled back, nestling his chest against my exposed back. "That's right. They don't get to look, and they sure as fuck don't get to touch you. That's my job. Only me."

With that, he tugged down his zipper, and I heard the telltale sound of foil ripping before he shoved inside me. My head fell back at the sudden intrusion, loving the burn that accompanied Damien's size. When he was inside me, everything felt right—and along the way, I'd begun to crave the fullness he provided. My eyes closed on instinct as he settled against my hips, waiting for the pace to increase—but Damien didn't move, just resting his cock inside me.

My eyes snapped open, and I met his gaze in the mirror. He smirked back at me. "Told you, angel. You close your eyes, and I stop. Need those hazels on me as I fuck you." His hand collided with my bare ass, the sudden burn against my skin making my insides tighten. "Do you understand, Bri?"

"Yes, Damien. Please. I'll be good. I'll be so good for you."

"You always are."

With that, Damien resumed his movements, keeping a brutal, frantic pace. It was more hurried than we'd ever been before, and I had to grip the marble countertop to keep up with him, but every slide of his cock inside my core only pushed me closer to the edge until I could barely hang on. Once his thumb darted down to my clit, I crashed over the edge, biting my lip to keep from screaming out his name.

"I got you," Damien whispered as he covered my mouth with his large palm. Then, a primal scream unleashed from my soul, the sound muffled under his skin. It didn't take long for Damien to crash with me, his cock slamming inside me in erratic thrusts.

By the time we both caught our breaths, our eyes met in the mirror, and I couldn't hold back my laughter. With pink painting our cheeks and my hair disheveled from Damien's grip, anyone with eyes could tell what we'd gotten up to in this bathroom. As he pulled away, I hissed, missing him already. Damien cleaned himself up then ran a washcloth under the warm water. He stepped back and ran it over my sensitive core. I shifted, and he cursed under his breath. "Did I hurt you?"

The vulnerability in his words made me turn around to

face him. "Not at all. I loved every second of it. Feel free to be that rough with me anytime."

He studied my expression for any hint of a lie then shook his head. A smile played at the corner of his lips. "Gotta say, Bri, you shock me at every turn. Who knew the good girl liked to be fucked so dirty?"

"I didn't," I laughed. "But I'm really glad you showed me."

Damien's gaze softened as he looked at me then reached up to tuck a lock of my hair behind my ear. Even after everything we just shared, the subtle move made my pulse race, suddenly all too aware of the intimacy of his touch. "Damien, I—"

"Yo! Open up. I gotta take a piss."

August's voice broke through the tension, and I sobered, realizing I stood there naked, the rookie I'd spent most of the night with waiting on the other side of the door. We'd spent almost an hour talking about our shared love of romance novels, and I'd been in the middle of my list of recommendations when I caught Damien's annoyed glare across the room. Maybe his jealousy should have turned me off, but truth be told, I relished in it. For so long, I'd been ignored—taken for granted. Knowing how much Damien wanted me was a powerful aphrodisiac.

Damien helped me scoop up my clothes, and I hurried to get dressed. As August pounded on the door, I frowned at Damien. "How are we going to play this?"

He ran his hand over his face. "You owe me for this." Before I could ask what he meant, he yelled out over August's bangs. "Trust me, man. Find another bathroom. That chili fucked up my stomach."

"Seriously, cap?"

"Get the fuck out of here, Auggie!"

A string of grumbled curses echoed from the other side of the door, and I had to press my hand down harder to hide my giggles. As soon as the footsteps faded in the distance, I reached up on my tiptoes and kissed Damien's cheek. "Thank you for covering for us."

He reached out and tugged me right against his chest. "Oh, trust me, Bri. You're going to make it up to me next time."

"Next time?"

"Fuck yes," Damien growled as he palmed my ass. "And you're going to be in my bed so I can hear all of your pretty screams."

TWENTY-TWO

Damien

Over the next two weeks, Brianna and I spent almost all our free time together. Whenever we got the chance, we holed up in my apartment, hiding away from the world. Most nights, we'd checked things off her list—*now that she'd reluctantly shared it with me*—and others, we'd stay up late talking, telling each other all about our lives.

She loved to regale me with tales from her school, of the children who stole her heart during the months they were in her class, of her life growing up with her strict parents and the minor acts of rebellion she'd committed over the years. Hell, she even told me all about the books lurking on her kindle, how they made her more confident in herself. No matter the topic, Brianna captivated me, leaving me hanging on to every word like a man obsessed.

One night before I had to travel to Toronto for our next series, she lay on my couch with her head on my lap. My fingers glided through her hair of their own accord, needing to have a part of us touching. Brianna sighed as she tapped through the pages of her latest obsession—a series of dark rom-coms about serial killers—while I watched tapes of our newest rivals, trying to find any weaknesses in their outfield game. Despite our shaky start to the season, we were on a hot streak. There was already chatter about us making a run for the championship in a few short months, but I pushed that into the back of my mind. Focusing on the big win could mess with your head, and I was determined not to let it.

"Why does he do that?" Brianna asked, placing her e-reader on her chest.

My fingers stilled in her hair, frowning at the screen. Grabbing the remote, I pressed pause. "What do you mean?"

"The pitcher." She nodded to the frozen image. "He's doing this thing with his foot." She reached over my lap and took the remote, pressing the play button. "Watch. He's digging in with his foot, but only on certain plays. Is that some sort of signal to the catcher?"

"Might be." I leaned forward, taking in more of his movements. "It's more subtle—head shakes and motions with his glove, things like that. I don't..." Pressing the forward key, I pushed through other key plays, trying to see what Brianna meant. After a few more innings, a pattern emerged, one I'd failed to notice during the first dozen times I watched him play.

"It's his tell," I whispered. Brianna shifted on the couch, coming to sit at my side. I took her hand, linking our fingers together. "Look..." I pressed play again, and the same movement was there, a subtle stub of his toe on the mound. In the past, I wrote it off, assuming he was just getting into position, but now that Brianna had pointed it out, there was no unseeing it. "Every time he's going to throw a fastball, he twists his foot into the mound. Shocked no one's pointed it out."

"So will that help you?"

I beamed over at her, almost leaning in to press my lips to hers. "Yeah, it just might. Shit, Bri; you might be my lucky charm."

She rolled her eyes and lifted her e-reader. "Let's not get carried away here, Damien. I just noticed a little twitch."

I shifted and pulled her onto my lap. As she shook her head, I took the e-reader and deposited on the couch, needing all her attention on me. I cupped her cheeks, forcing her eyes to meet mine. "Don't do that, Bri. Don't hide from me."

Brianna grimaced. "It's not that. I just don't do well with compliments. Makes me feel a little too exposed."

I tucked her into my side, the subtle scent of her floral shampoo rushing through my senses. As I kissed her temple, Brianna let out a content sigh, snuggling into me like we were a couple instead of only enjoying each other's bodies. It felt right. Real. I nuzzled my nose along her neck. "Well, better get used to it, angel, because I plan on showering you with them."

"ARE YOU OKAY, MAN?" Parker edged beside me at the bar, trying to find a place among all the guys from the team. "You're not usually this sulky after a big win."

I nodded, unable to say anything to contradict him. My mood had gone downhill over the past two nights, hating that I'd spent each one in a hotel room by myself. Ever since the team dinner, Brianna had been spending most nights at my place, giving up her arguments about keeping distance between us after the first couple of nights.

And over all those hours, when we thought we were just filling each other's time, I'd grown more attached. Being apart from Brianna was painful, and I hated waking up without her clutched to my chest. Phone calls and texts weren't the same, and I counted down the minutes until I was back in Erie City with my girl in my arms.

But I couldn't say any of that to Parker.

Instead, I exhaled and brought my beer to my mouth. The cold taste of the IPA soothed the unease in my chest, but it wasn't enough to clear it completely. Classical music pulsed through the speakers, barely audible over the hum of the bar patrons, but that did nothing to soothe me either. Instead, the sterile, high-end bar made me miss home even more. Our usual haunt, Foul Tip, was right across from the stadium, so on game nights, it filled up quickly with fans and players. Most of us were familiar with the owner, Henry, considering he was one of the first fans to buy season tickets when the Hawks came into town.

In thanks for his unwavering support, we'd made it our mission to drive more business to the bar, especially considering it predated the team. The Foul Tip had been a landmark in the city before it could even be called one, but it used to support the Rebels as their New York team. Now that Erie City had a hometown one, the entire bar became the Hawks' unofficial clubhouse, lending a bunch of signed photos and jerseys to help fill the space with team decor.

But being far from home, with more nights to kill, we didn't have many options, so we'd trekked to the hotel bar. It beat sitting alone in my room, pining over a girl who wanted to keep things casual.

As I downed the last dregs of my beer, the bartender slid over to us, nodding at my drink. "You want another?"

I shook my head. My arm and chest already ached after

a wonky throw earlier, and the team physical therapist wouldn't be able to fit me in until tomorrow afternoon, right before we had to go back out on the field. We might have won the first game, but we had to keep it up for two more games before we flew down to Florida for the next series.

Or was it Texas? Fuck, at this point, I couldn't even remember. We were only half-way through the season, and the travel was already getting tedious. What I wouldn't give for a full week in my bed, preferably with Brianna at my side.

With that thought, I glanced back at my phone. I'd sent her a couple of messages when we first got into town, but Brianna hadn't responded yet. Not that it surprised me. With Brianna, it always felt like one step forward, two steps back. While there was something more than casual between us, she rarely sought me out, instead relying on me being the one to initiate things.

And it had started to wear on me.

At first, the secrecy was fun—a secret we kept from the rest of the world. Brianna wasn't ready for her name to be splashed across social media, and I was still trying to keep my reputation clean. Keeping this between us was the best call.

But I wanted more. Every time we walked out of my apartment, the walls went up, and we reverted to pretending we were only acquaintances.

And I hated it.

Hated not being able to claim her right then and there. Hated that she looked at me like a stranger when I spent the entire night curled around her. That consuming need twisted into jealousy when she came to my games and had Parker's last name scrawled across her back.

Plenty of people wore my name every day. Plenty of

women came up to me and asked me to sign their backs, and as much as I liked it, I never craved it before now, never felt the need to see my name adorning someone else's body like I needed my next breath.

But I wanted it all with Brianna.

Parker sat silently by my side, watching but not forcing me to talk about what weighed me down. What could be the harm in talking to him? If I didn't say her name, he might give me some advice—although, in the years I'd known Drobrek, I'd never seen him with a girl. I'd never even saw him take someone home for the night. As much as he tried to deny it, we all knew why.

"I fucked up," I muttered. "Got involved with someone I shouldn't have."

"Does this have to do with you and Bri both disappearing during team dinner?" he asked, shifting to face me. When I narrowed my eyes at him, he shook his head. "Never mind. Forget I asked. Can't lie to Oleander if she asks me about it."

"Smart move," I sighed.

"So, is this a fatal attraction kind of situation, or did you catch feelings?"

"Fatal attraction?"

"Guy hooks up with a woman, and she becomes obsessed with him. And not in the fun, dark romance kind of way." He chuckled. "Don't tell me you've never seen it. You gotta go with the classic, though."

I shook my head. "Nah, not like that. The opposite. She wants to keep us casual, and I agreed with her, figured it was the best of both worlds. Got to be with this beautiful woman with no strings attached. But now, I'm spending more time with her—"

"And you want more..." Parker answered for me.

"Yeah..." I groaned. "And I'm not sure what the fuck I'm supposed to do with it."

Parker sighed as he leaned back on the bar stool, bringing his hands together on the rough bar top. He stayed silent for a few moments, studying the screen in front of him like it held all the answers. The media loved to portray him as a good-time guy, likening him to the mortal disguise of one of those superheroes. But once you dug a little deeper, there was a lot more lurking under the surface.

He huffed a breath then turned back toward me. "There are only two ways to play this. First, bow out now. Don't get any more attached."

"Fuck that," I growled.

Parker smirked. "Figured that would be your answer. Then the only other option is to fight for her."

I shook my head. "How am I supposed to do that? She doesn't want a relationship. I can't force her into one."

"Obviously," he said. "Show her you care. I'm assuming she might be wary of relationships because she got burned in the past?" My eyes narrowed in his direction. "I'll take that as a yes. So it might not be that she doesn't want a relationship ever, but she's worried about getting hurt again. Prove to her you're not her ex, that you'd never intentionally hurt her."

"I can't promise I won't, though." My head fell as I forced the words out. "Not on purpose, but you know this career, Park. It'll always come first. How can I promise I'll never let her down when there's hardly any time in my schedule for her?"

Parker shook his head as he turned back toward his drink. "Listen, D, I respect you more than you know. You're a damn good ball player and an even fucking better Captain. But that's a bunch of bullshit."

"What?"

He chuckled at my tone. "Yeah, our jobs get intense for most of the year, and you should be honest about that with her, but it's just a game. It could end tomorrow, and what would you do then?"

I swallowed, having no answer to his question. Truth be told, I had no fucking clue. Retirement was always in the back of my mind, but I never dwelled on it for too long, afraid I'd jinx myself if I put a lot of thought into what would happen after I hung up my bat.

And maybe it was too soon to think I'd want more with Brianna, but for the first time, the idea of a life after baseball didn't make me nauseous. Instead, a picture formed in the back of my mind, one of laughter, travel, and a life with someone at my side. Someone who looked a lot like Brianna.

Tipping back another sip of my drink, I sighed, turning back toward Parker. "Okay, Romeo. Tell me how I make her want more."

Parker smirked back at me. "Thought you'd never ask."

TWENTY-THREE

Brianna

Staring at the television, I watched as Damien sauntered off the field into the dugout. He'd been gone for almost a week, darting off around the country for back-to-back series. When he first mentioned leaving, I was relieved, needing space after spending so much time with him. Yet, from the moment I left his apartment, I wanted to go back, missing him more than I expected.

I tried to push the thought away, instead focusing on the schoolwork I'd been neglecting all summer. I immersed myself in the updated curriculum, crafting graphs and spreadsheets to track my students' progress, anything to help me get more prepared when I walked through the doors next month. September was always a time of transition, trying to get to know the new students and teach them the routines. There was also the matter of my co-teacher.

Don't get me wrong—I enjoyed my career. I'd worked with many incredible teachers over the years, but no matter how much you knew someone, there was always an adjustment period when you shared a classroom. Depending on the mix of personalities, it could be a rough transition, two people battling for shared power instead of coming together to best serve the students' needs.

And this year would be a harder one than most. As if I conjured him with my thoughts, an email pinged into my inbox, Brad's name plastered on the top. As I scanned his message, my blood boiled. No greeting. No perfunctory questions about my summer. Instead, he'd jumped into a list of documents he wanted me to create and his expectations for me when I stepped into *his* classroom.

As I scanned his words, my hands tensed. The man wanted me to be a body in the room, only managing behaviors, nothing else. In all caps, he wrote: I WILL LEAD ALL INSTRUCTION. YOU ARE THERE TO SUPPORT ONLY.

With a groan, I shot off a reply email, reminding him we were co-teachers and I wasn't his assistant. If he did not think he could handle the assignment, he was welcome to go to the principal. Then, I slammed the lid shut, not bothering to wait for a response. It was only for a year. I could do anything for a year. Ten months—185 days, if we were being technical.

As I debated exchanging my teaching license for any other career, Ollie crashed through the door, her hands filled with a large package. She plopped it on the table and grinned. "It's for you."

My brow furrowed. "It shouldn't be. I didn't order anything."

She nodded to the upper corner. "Check out the return address."

Damien Ramos.

"What did he send me?" I question aloud. Curiosity

tickled the back of my mind, but my hands didn't move, too nervous about what sat inside. "I—he didn't say anything."

"Duh," Ollie chuckled. "That's why it's a surprise. It's romantic. Oh!" She clapped her hands as she grinned. "What if it's a bunch of sex toys?"

"Not that I'm telling you anything about what's going on between us, but..." My eyes darted open as I took in the box's size. "If that's true, he's got way too much faith in my kinky side. There'd have to be a toy in it for every day of the month."

"Only one way to find out," Ollie mused as she walked over to a drawer and pulled a pair of scissors. "Better open it up."

I stared at the scissors in her hand, inhaling a steadying breath before taking them. Slicing open the tape, I pushed away the packing paper, revealing a bunch of books and other items from the Oakland area. As I pulled out each one, I chuckled, recognizing most of them from my online book wishlist. Thumbing through the pages, I gasped when I saw the author had signed the front cover. After I placed the first one down, I grabbed the other three from the package, finding them signed as well. I shook my head, reaching into the box to pull out a handwritten card.

Remembered how much you loved these ones. Saw them and had to grab the set for your shelves.

- D

Ollie's eyes widened as she read the note over my shoulder. "Wow. Gotta give it to the guy. He knows the way to your heart."

I shook my head. "It's not like that. He's just being nice."

"No, nice is grabbing someone a trinket or two from the

airport. Searching a bookstore for someone's comfort series and buying signed copies? That's a love language if I've ever heard one."

I thumbed the card, waiting for the usual unease to prickle my spine. This was not about love. At least, it wasn't supposed to be. But as each day passed without Damien, I found myself missing him, and not just for the sex. He was easy to talk to—to confide in. Besides Ollie, he was the only person I opened up to about my divorce, and never once did he make me feel like less because of it.

Ollie let out a loud laugh as she pulled the card from my hand, flipping it over.

Think this is worth at least two items from your list, angel...

"I'm on Team Damien with this one. You need to finish the whole damn list now." Ollie arched an eyebrow. "What have you crossed off with him?"

My cheeks flamed, and I tucked the note into my pocket. I was unsure why, but I wanted to keep it. My mouth opened, ready to tell Ollie all about the items we'd checked off together, but the words refused to come. It was one thing to talk about this stuff with Ollie when it was hypothetical, but now that Damien was involved, I had a harder time telling her about our time together. I wanted to hold it close, keep it tight to my chest, keep us unsullied by other's opinions and perspectives.

"Not telling," I mused, digging deeper into the package. There were a couple of snacks: chips I told him I could never find here, a few chocolate bars. But when I reached the bottom, my fingers snagged on some fabric. I pulled it out, holding the dark emerald jersey up. I knew what adorned the back before I even turned it around. But when

I did, I couldn't help but smile at *Ramos* etched into the fabric.

Ollie squealed as I held it up for her to see. "Girl, that man is gone for you! Wearing his jersey and sitting in the family area? He's practically peeing around you in a circle."

"Ew, Ol. Did not need that visual."

She rolled her eyes. "You know what I mean. Damien's making his intentions very well known." A sudden seriousness washed over her face. "Are you ready for that?"

My breath stuttered in my chest, unsure of what to do . Maybe Damien realized what he wanted, but my head and heart were speaking completely different languages. Past hurt and fear made me want to shove everything back into the box, pretending it'd gotten lost in the mail. However, Damien's face flashed in my mind, and I pictured his smile as he put together this package just for me. When was the last time someone took the time to show me they cared?

"I'm not sure," I muttered. "This was supposed to be safe—easy and no feelings involved. But Damien..."

"He's under your skin?"

"More than I ever thought." I sat on the stool next to the island. Shaking my head, I dropped the jersey on my lap. "It's like I'm standing in this crossroad, and I don't know which way to turn. Either I keep going down this path with Damien and he crushes me, or I stop it now..." My voice trailed off, unable to even finish the sentence. Because honestly—the idea of losing Damien now seemed like a worse fate than getting hurt down the line.

Ollie plopped down next to me, taking my free hand in hers. "Those aren't the only options."

"They're not?"

"No, dummy. Those are just the scariest ones. You

might do this for a bit, and it fizzles out, no hard feelings, no lingering doubts. Or..."

I glared at her as her voice trailed off. "Or?"

"Or you both take the leap and find out you have something here. A real chance at happiness, Bri. Sure, that thought might be terrifying, but you'll never know if you don't decide to jump."

Could I do that? Thumbing my free hand over the smooth fabric of the jersey, I pictured Damien's face—the soft smiles he saved only for me, the way he held me close in the midnight hours, the stolen moments that existed only between the two of us. For a moment, Todd's face flashed in my mind, as if trying to sully the moment. But for the first time in a long time, his presence didn't weigh me down, didn't make me feel as if I was trying to take a breath underwater. Instead, I was more annoyed, tired of focusing on my past when I might have so much more in the future.

My eyes flashed open at the thought. Ollie just shook her head with a knowing chuckle. "Go get your man, Bri. Stop overthinking and take what you want."

THE NEXT MORNING, I still hadn't decided what to do about Damien's gift. Despite Ollie's words, I couldn't bring myself to let go, to let down that last wall in my heart. After I'd gone to bed, I sent off a text thanking him for the gift, but when he tried to call, it went to voicemail, all because I was too much of a coward to talk to him with my head so jumbled. I might say something stupid like how much I missed him, or that I'd watched all his games while he was on the road.

After Ollie headed off to her makeshift office for the

day, I debated being productive. I even plotted a response to Brad's email in my mind. But instead of stopping at my laptop, I passed right by it without a second thought, instead grabbing my e-reader and a fresh cup of coffee to head to the balcony. The city noise met me as I slid open the glass door and took a seat at the bistro table tucked in the corner. Reaching out, I thumbed a few of the plants I'd brought back from the school, glad they were thriving in the fresh air.

As I slid into the seat and took a sip of my coffee, my phone dinged on the side table. I glanced at it just long enough to spot Todd's name at the top of a message but didn't bother to check it. It could live with the dozens of unanswered ones from the past month, ranging from a heart-felt apology to passive-aggressive messages when I refused to answer him.

If it kept going, I'd have to block him. I probably should have done that already, but guilt tugged in my gut. Todd might have changed throughout our marriage, but he'd been a major part of my life for so long, I couldn't imagine never contacting him again. When things were good, he was my best friend—my first true confidant outside of my family.

And now? He was practically a stranger to me.

When we first split up, I convinced myself we'd become friends again one day, when the hurt was less. After almost a decade together, we had a shared history, one no one else understood. Late nights in our college dorms, our first terrible apartment with mold in the walls, the joy of starting our careers—Todd filled the frame in each of those memories, and for the longest time, letting go of him seemed like flushing them away as well. But with some distance, I'd seen those moments would always be a part of my story, even if I closed the chapter on Todd and me for good.

With that realization, I grabbed my phone, crafting a short but to the point message to Todd.

Me: Please stop contacting me. We said everything during our divorce proceedings. I have no interest in continuing our friendship and only wish to move on from our marriage in peace. If you can't respect my wishes, I'll block your number.

Todd: Bri, please. I need to talk to you. It's important.

ME: Find someone else to talk to about it.

Three bubbles instantly popped up, followed by concurrent messages pleading for me to talk to him and hear him out. Instead of reading any more, I clicked the contact info bar in the corner of my messages and blocked his number. For a moment, I waited for a pang of regret or sadness to wash over me. Instead, a calmness washed over me, finally able to close the door on my past marriage for good. Instead of anger or betrayal, when I thought of Todd, only apathy remained.

"Better," I whispered to myself as I shifted the phone to the other side of the table. But as my fingers touched the screen, another message came through. This time, Damien's name sat at the top of my screen.

D

Are you avoiding me, angel?

My lip tucked between my teeth as I read the simple question. Was I avoiding him? Kind of. After his gift, my mind had been in a tailspin, but there was one universal truth in it all—I missed him. A groan left my throat at that realization. This was not what was supposed to happen. We were supposed to only be friends with benefits—sex was supposed to be the extent of our contact. Yet, the longer I stayed away from Damien, the more my stomach ached, desperate for him.

God, maybe I needed to end this thing.

My thumbs hovered over my phone, unsure what to even type. *Sorry, Damien, but my stupid little heart is developing feelings for you, and I'm too cowardly to face them?* The idea of saying that to him made my stomach lurch, twisting into a horrible knot. As much as my head told me to let him go, there was no way I'd be able to. Without trying, Damien had opened my heart, and walking away was no longer an option, not without crushing myself in the process.

As I debated what to say, my phone chimed again with another message.

D

I'm outside your place. Open the door, Bri.

"He's where?" I asked as I darted through the apartment, as if I could see him waiting on the other side of the threshold. Instead, all I saw was my reflection in the glass door. "Oh my God," I squealed as I took in my sloppy bun and stained pajamas.

Dashing through the apartment, I ignored the knocking, focusing instead on finding anything to wear other than my oversized teacher t-shirt with a dozen coffee stains all over it. I threw on some gym clothes and ran my fingers through my hair before walking over to the front door. When I placed my hand on the knob, I inhaled slowly, trying to calm my erratic heartbeat.

"You're being ridiculous," I muttered to myself, hating that the idea of seeing Damien again after only a few days apart made my heart patter so much faster. But even as I told myself those lies, it was hard to ignore my excitement.

"I can hear you overthinking from here, Bri." Damien chuckled from the other side. "C'mon, open up."

My hand twisted the knob and pulled the door open to reveal a smirking Damien leaning against the frame. "About time," he chuckled, looking all too casual as he toyed with the bundle of flowers in his fist. "Thought you were going to leave me out here all day."

TWENTY-FOUR

Damien

What the fuck did I normally do with my hands?

Staring at the bouquet clutched in my fist, I tried to make myself appear casual, even though it was the exact opposite of how I felt. I wasn't this guy—not the one who stood outside a girl's apartment after spending way too much time searching through rows of flowers at the market. Everything about being here seemed wrong, but after a week without Brianna, I couldn't force myself to stay away.

The moment I got off the plane, I dropped my stuff at my apartment and rushed over here. The only stop I made was at the flower shop down the block, grabbing a bouquet of roses for the girl who occupied my every waking thought.

So fucking stupid. I played professional ball in front of millions of people for the better part of the year, yet standing here, in front of Brianna, made my palms sweat like never before.

She arched a brow as she stared back at me, shock coloring all her features. Even in casual gym clothes with her hair tossed over her shoulder, she was the most beautiful woman I'd ever seen. Our time apart had only increased the need pulsing in my chest, making me crave her like no one else in the world.

Brianna continued to stare at me as my words settled between us. After the longest silence of my life, she finally smiled, leaning against the other side of the door. "And what if I did leave you out here?"

I held out the flowers and appraised them. *Fucking roses.* The woman at the stall insisted they were the best, but now, the gesture seemed like too much, especially given the casualness of our relationship. But the red color called to me, reminding me of the dress Brianna wore the last time I saw her.

Searching my memories, I tried to remember the last time I bought flowers for a woman. Outside of my sister and her wife, it had been a good five years. I smiled, trying to hide my anxiety under my cocky grin. "Then I wouldn't be able to give you these. Pity."

Brianna rolled her eyes, but took the flowers from my hand. She leaned forward, smelling the bouquet with a serene smile. I could only watch, too transfixed by her to consider doing anything else. "Thank you," she said. "They're beautiful."

You're beautiful.

I cleared my throat, trying to keep those words inside. "Saw them and thought of you. Figured if you were avoiding me, it might be a good first step to earning your forgiveness."

She shook her head. "I'm not avoiding you, Damien. I was just trying to clear my head a little..."

"Was the gift too much?" I asked, anxiety climbing through my chest. Fucking Drobrek. He'd made the trek to a little romance bookstore to look for a surprise for Ollie and dragged me along. But when I walked in and saw the set of books on display, I recognized the name from talking with Bri. She'd spent almost an hour explaining how she needed to move to Montana and find herself a family of hot, broody hockey players. I then spent the hour after reminding her why her baseball player was a better option. Without a second thought, I grabbed them and a bunch of other things that reminded me of Brianna. It hurt my soul a little to spend that much money on books about hockey players, not baseball, but it was worth it to make her smile.

The last thing I added to the box before sealing it—and what I was most nervous about—was the jersey.

Brianna reached out and gave me a tight hug. "Not at all. I loved every part, especially the books. I'm shocked you remembered."

"As if I'd ever forget that night." I smirked, pulling back to search her eyes. God, I fucking missed her. Just being around her melted away the tension, and my entire body relaxed.

She reached down and linked our fingers. "Why don't you come in?"

I glanced behind her, and my feet almost moved toward her, all too tempted knowing what might happen behind closed doors. But for the first time in a long time, that wasn't what I wanted. "I have a better idea," I said as I held my hand out for Brianna. "Let me treat you to lunch."

"Lunch?" Brianna asked, staring at my hand like it was poisonous. "We don't do stuff like that. Besides, I thought you weren't supposed to be photographed with anyone. What are you going to say if someone catches us?"

"The team wants me to stay away from clubs and too messy hook-ups, I think they'll be fine with us grabbing some food." I shrugged. "It's just lunch, Bri. You need to eat, I need to eat. Let's not overthink it."

She continued to stare at me, trying to decipher the hidden meaning in my offer. If the situation were reversed, I might do the same thing. But as much as I loved being with Brianna, today, I was taking Parker's advice to show her what a relationship between us might be like. Even more, I wanted to talk to her, to understand her better, to figure out why she had such a hold on me. Eventually, Brianna smiled. "Okay, lunch sounds nice. But careful, Damien. Between the flowers and the invitation, you're making this sound like a date."

A sourness coated the back of my tongue, but I swallowed it down, keeping up my sly smirk. "Wouldn't dream of it, angel."

As she walked inside, mentioning something about finding her purse and a vase for the flowers, I stood in the hall, contemplating her words. A date. Was that what this was? I couldn't remember the last time I'd gone on an actual date. It had to be with Talia, but even with her, it was always more like fancy dinners or a show. We'd spent a lot of time out of the house, enjoying the Manhattan nightlife a little too much. There weren't many quiet moments just the two of us. Realization washed over me as I looked back on our relationship, seeing it with fresh eyes. Even though I loved Talia—it might have been more about loving having someone as opposed to the woman at my side. I'd hardly taken the time to explore her beyond the surface, and yet it seemed like enough to build our lives around.

But as Brianna walked back out of the door to stand at my side, I couldn't help but think about how I wanted so much more.

"THIS MIGHT BE the best thing I've ever put in my mouth."

I snorted, sucking back a piece of my taco into my throat. My breath sputtered around the piece of food, desperate to breathe again. *God, please do not let me go out like this*—not by choking on a piece of carne asada because Brianna has no idea what she just said.

As I coughed up the remnants of my food, Brianna flew to my back, thumping between my shoulder blades. When the offending piece of meat came flying out, she pulled up my face, trying to hide her smirk as she looked me over.

"Are you okay?"

"Yeah," I said through rasped breaths. "Next time, save comments like that for after I'm finished. You tried to kill me, woman."

"Can't do that. Pretty sure that would make this the worst date ever."

The same delectable blush filled her cheeks, and I liked being the one to cause it. I swallowed the thought, trying to keep my head together. *This was not a date.* Despite the slip of her tongue, Brianna made that clear as we walked to the park by her apartment. She asked multiple times until I almost got offended.

Brianna shook her head as she sat down on her side of the picnic table. The rest of the park was quiet today, and we were the only ones close to where my favorite food truck loved to park. In less than an hour, the whole place would be swarmed with the lunch rush, but for now, I got to enjoy my time with Brianna uninterrupted.

And what if this were a date? Would she be against it if I pushed? At this point, we knew each other's bodies as well as our own, and I'd spent more time with her than anyone else in years. Fuck it. I replayed Parker's words in my head, and I stopped holding back.

I leaned forward on my elbows, leaning in toward her. "Thought this wasn't a date, Bri?" Her eyes widened and her mouth fell open. But before she could retract her statement, I reached out and took her hand. "But if you want to make this our first date, I'd be all for it."

She shook her head. "That's not what we do, Damien. We have rules—"

"That *we* made, Bri. They can change whenever we want. You want to go on a date? I'd drop everything to take you on one."

She studied me for a moment, and I waited for the rejection, waited for her to shut it down. Instead, her eyes just softened. "This can be our first date."

"Yeah?"

She blushed and ducked her head. "This is perfect for me. I'm not big on fancy meals or nights out. Just give me good food, nature, and great company, and I'm a lucky girl."

"Noted," I said, unable to hide my grin. With anyone else, this would seem like nothing, but getting Brianna to admit this was more than sex was like overcoming insurmountable odds, the same as winning a marathon or climbing a high peak. "So, now that we established this is a date, what should we talk about?"

Brianna shrugged. "What do you want to know?"

A familiar question tugged at the back of my mind, and I couldn't hold it back any longer. "Tell me about your ex."

The color drained from her face as she ducked her chin to her chest, the happiness fleeing her expression. "Why?"

"Call it curiosity," I said, trying to keep my tone as casual as possible. "Might explain more about you."

Brianna sighed, wiping the tips of her fingers on her

napkin. "We were together for a long time. We met right during freshman year of college, and everything seemed just...easy between us. I thought it was because we were so connected, but looking back, it was more because I gave in so much, molded my life around his. Now, when I think about our time together, sure, there were a lot of happy memories I want to hold on to, but there's also a lot more loneliness. He never saw the real me, and when I grew up and stood my ground, he didn't handle it well." She paused, tapping her fork on her plate. "When we first split, the idea of repeating that pattern with anyone else scared the hell out of me, of giving someone else the power to break me like that..." She shrugged her shoulders. "Honestly, it still scares me."

"I get that," I admitted, tucking my elbows onto the table. "I was engaged a few years ago."

Brianna's eyes widened as she stared at me. "I'm sorry, Damien."

"Don't be," I said. "Sure, it hurt like hell, and it's probably why I haven't wanted anything real since then. But lately, I've been wondering if she made the right move."

"Can I—" Brianna chewed on her lower lip. "Can I ask what happened?"

"Too devoted to the team, gone too often, all the things I should've noticed before she walked out the door. Talia, she's a good person, but we weren't right together. Instead of supporting each other, we got resentful, and instead of addressing the cracks in our relationship, we grew apart. Honestly, we would've ended no matter what, so I'm a little grateful Talia walked away when she did. I would've kept going, and who knows what might have happened."

"You could've walked down the aisle and then found

yourself in the same position, only now, you'd have wasted almost a decade of your life with nothing to show for it."

I reached out and took Brianna's hand. She stared at my hand on top of hers, and for a moment, I wondered if I'd crossed the line. Instead, she twisted her hand to intertwine our fingers. Shit, they fit together perfectly. Had we ever touched outside of our apartments? Probably not, but I liked it—too much. I liked holding her hand when she was hurting, liked to be the one offering her the support.

"You can't go back and erase the past, Bri. It hurts, and you need to let yourself feel that hurt, but don't let it define you." I squeezed her fingers. "You've got too much heart to hide it away."

The corners of her lips turned up. "You seem so sure. I might be a horrible person."

"Not a chance," I said, leaning closer to her. "Besides, we know each other a lot more than you realize."

"How so?"

"I know what you like in the bedroom, what you look like when you fall apart."

Brianna's cheeks flushed as she shook her head. "That doesn't mean anything, Damien. You don't know my middle name, or my favorite color, or anything else like that."

"Maybe not." I leaned back and started ticking things off on my fingers. "But I know you're smart, too damn smart, and it intimidates some people around you. I know how your face lights up when you read a spicy scene in one of your books, how you chew on your lower lip when something romantic happens. That you like to make others comfortable because you've been the one on the outside of the circle. I mean, hell, Auggie hasn't stopped talking about you for weeks. You connected more with the guy in one night than the rest of us have all season." I paused, searching her widening hazel eyes. "And look at the day we met. You busted your ass for weeks because you wanted to help your friend. You spent the entire day baking in the sun because it gave your students joy. I might not know the little details, Bri, but I see you, see your heart. So listen to me when I say when you decide to give it to someone, they're going to be the luckiest bastard on the planet."

TWENTY-FIVE

Brianna

I stared at Damien, trying to ignore my racing pulse. His dark eyes bore through me, as if he saw how quickly my heart fluttered in my chest. We'd spent less than a month together, and yet, with just a few words, he proved how well he knew me.

My eyes darted down to my plate, where my toppings had slipped off my tacos and into the cardboard box. Picking up my fork, I ignored the words flashing through my mind, questions about whether Damien wanted to be that guy for me. He'd gotten me to admit this was a date, and as much as it scared me, I was glad we were here. At least, until he turned my world around by pointing out everything I tried to hide close to my chest.

I shoved some of the pico de gallo into my mouth then turned back toward Damien, desperate to take the attention off me. "So how did you get all this insight? Are you secretly the relationship guru of the Hawks?"

"Not exactly," Damien chuckled. "I've spent a lot of time with the team psychologist, and he's helped me realize some things, like how I can't control other people's actions or let it define who I am."

"Wow," I said. "That's incredible."

"What? That I'm in therapy?"

"That you admit it so openly." The words came out of my mouth before I could stop them, and my hand flew up in embarrassment. "I'm sorry. I didn't mean it like that. It's just...I come from a very traditional Greek family, and many people in my family don't believe in mental health. They've been through a lot, but they'd rather bury those emotions down deep and ignore them. Even my ex-husband hated the idea of it. When things began going south with us, I suggested couples counseling, and he shot that right down. Said he had no interest in airing our dirty laundry to a stranger."

He smiled as he leaned back on the wooden bench. "Can't lie—I thought the same way for a while, but playing at this level, it can fuck with your head. The pressure can consume you if you let it, especially as a rookie. But in the last few years, there's been more talk of mental health, and the Hawks have been great about providing support."

"That's amazing."

"Yeah," Damien said. "As uncomfortable as it was at first, if I wanted the other guys to try it, I knew I had to lead by example. So, I talk about it a lot to take that stigma away."

I toyed with my fork, pushing the spare tomatoes around as I tried to put my thoughts into words. "I've been considering it lately. Going to therapy, I mean." Damien arched an eyebrow, and I dared to continue. "The last year has been hard, even harder than I assumed it would be. Not only was getting divorced a gut-punch, but the fallout seems never ending. The bills, the new housing, untying everything we'd built over the past ten years." I swallowed, trying to avert Damien's gaze as I unloaded my soul to the man. But despite the nagging voice in the back of my mind telling me he didn't want to hear my ramblings, I pushed on. "And while I'm ready, there's still a little voice in the back of my head, reminding me what's at stake."

Damien took my hand, rubbing his thumb over the ridge of my knuckles. His touch was warm, steady, and exactly what I needed at that moment. "Then you should do it. Not for anyone else, but for you. Fuck everyone else. It's your life, and if it'll help you get to a better place, try it out."

I chuckled as I still stared at Damien's hand on top of mine. That invisible knot around my stomach wasn't as tight when he held me; in fact, I enjoyed being here with him. As much as I'd tried to fight our connection, talking with him lifted a weight from my chest. "How do you know exactly what to say?"

He let out a loud laugh, and I couldn't help but smile. I did that. I brought a wide grin to his face. Damien shook his head. "I don't, not by a long shot. My sister says I have an innate need to take on the world's problems, but it's more than that. If someone I care about is hurting, I want to help any way I can, even if it's just being here to listen."

Someone he cares about. Did I count in that group now? Because despite my insistence to the contrary, he was at the top of my list. Over time, Damien had become more than a lover. He'd become my confidant, my biggest supporter, one of my closest friends. The idea of being the same for him melded the damaged pieces of my fragile little heart, and I tried to ignore the temptation to hand the whole thing over to him now.

I cleared my throat, needing to shift our conversation to

a safer territory. "I met your sister. Mari, right? She was sitting with us during the all-star game."

He chuckled. "Yup, that was her and her entire crew. Hopefully, she didn't give you too hard a time. She means well, but she mother hens everyone, including her big brother."

"Oh no, Mari was great," I said. "Angie too. I especially liked Cami; she was asking me all about what to expect in middle school."

His eyes widened. "Cami talked to you?"

"Yeah..." I drawled. "We bonded over our mutual love of math class and how much the social studies curriculum needs to be updated. Why?"

Damien shook his head. "Cami's always been the quietest of all the girls. She's great with family, but strangers are a different story, especially since the twins were born."

"Well, if she ever needs someone to talk to, I'm more than happy to do it. She seems like a bright kid—they all do."

"In that evil genius way, you mean." Damien laughed. "I swear, those girls are going to run a Fortune 500 company or take over the world . There's no in-between. The first time I babysat their middle two, Chloe and Cat, not only did they figure out how to undo all the child locks after I spent hours putting them on everything, they then turned them around and locked me out of my stuff."

"Oh my God." I laughed, relishing the mental image of Damien trying to corral two toddlers in his loft. "What did you do?"

"Nothing to do," he answered. "I refused to ask Mari for help, so I had to use the guest bathroom for a month until I swallowed my pride."

Heavy laughter poured out of me until tears pooled in

the corners of my eyes. As I went to wipe them away, Damien beat me to it, flicking them away with the pad of his thumb. It was the least intimate gesture he'd done to me, and yet, it seemed more monumental than any other. "You love being with them."

"I do," he admitted. "But I also like it when they head home, and I have some peace. Does that make me a bad person?"

I shook my head. "Pretty sure most people feel that way about their extended families. I do when my brother's kids come over."

"A brother, huh?"

"Yup; he's the older one too. Jason and his wife have two boys who I love more than life itself. But I also love being able to hand them back when they're upset."

Damien held up his drink in a toast. As I lifted mine to clink against his, he said, "To being the fun aunts and uncles for as long as possible."

"Cheers to that," I answered, grinning as we both sipped our margaritas.

But that delicious drink almost spluttered out of my nose when Damien asked, "Do you want kids?"

Quickly grabbing a napkin, I wiped away the remnants of my drink that had sneaked out. Familiar shame washed over me as I thought about my answer, knowing it could change everything. I didn't know what we were heading toward, but the next few words could snap everything in half. Despite the urge to hide it, I shook my head and forced out my truth. "Not biologically."

I debated holding back the rest—refusing to let Damien in any further than I already had. But as he stared at me, waiting for me to say more, my lips opened easily.

"I've always thought about fostering and adopting older kids, but that was something my ex wasn't open to trying. He was pretty insistent about trying for a baby, even though we both knew I didn't want one. He insisted it was just a phase for me, that once we settled down, I'd change my mind."

"That's bullshit," Damien snapped. "And he held that against you?"

My cheeks colored in shame, replaying so many arguments in my mind, when Todd made me question my mind, refusing to understand why I didn't want to have a baby. Not that I didn't want a family—but there were already so many kids in the world who needed a loving home. After working in schools for the past decade, I saw so many wonderful kids who were victims of their circumstances, so many children who needed a safe and loving home to land. Maybe it was naïve of me to assume Todd would feel the same way, but in my heart, I knew if I was going to become a parent, that would be the route I'd take.

Damien sighed and sat back. "I've never thought about kids, probably because the game has always been my focus. I've spent so much time being tied to someone else's schedule. I'd like to travel—do things on my own terms."

"Not easy when you have kids."

"Nah." Damien chuckled. "But I do like the idea of giving a good home to kids in need. And you'd make a great mom, Bri."

Heat filled my cheeks, and I broke our stare, instead focusing on the last bites on my plate. Damien said nothing; he just sat with me in the silence. It wasn't tense like I would've expected; instead, it was almost calming. He didn't need me to fill the void with empty words; Damien was content to sit with me as I worked through the fears in my mind.

And that was the scariest thought of all.

TWENTY-SIX

Brianna

As summer dwindled down, I found myself in a new routine. During the week, I'd head over to the school and meet up with Brad and the other teachers to plan for the first few weeks of instruction, leaving with blood on my tongue after biting it all day. Despite my years of experience, Brad seemed to enjoy undermining me at every turn, questioning everything I brought up during our grade-level meetings. Which was fine. I never minded having input from others. But with Brad, it was just constant negativity, because he was a lazy asshole who only cared about himself.

And that was where I drew the line.

When we wrapped up our meeting for the day, Brad didn't bother to say goodbye, claiming he had too much work back home. *Good riddance.* Before I did the same, my principal stopped me.

"Brianna, are you alright?"

No, not even a little. You've tied me to the world's biggest narcissist for the year, and I'm not sure how I'm going to survive the next ten days, much less the next ten months.

"Fine," I said, hiding my retort behind my most professional smile. "We'll make it work; we always do."

"That's true," Ethan answered, leaning back in one of the conference room chairs. Ethan Cutler had been my mentor for almost a decade, and above everyone else, I trusted his opinion. Over the years, he'd put me in some challenging positions, but it was always to help me grow as a teacher. This time, though, I failed to see the point of pairing me with Brad. It was a partnership destined to fail, and while it might bruise my ego, I only cared about the kids in our shared class. Discord between us would affect them the most, and I refused to be the one who let that happen.

As I stepped into the doorway, I paused, tapping my nails on the steel frame. "Why him?" I whispered as I turned to face Ethan. "Out of all the teachers in the school, why did you pair us together?"

Ethan sighed and steepled his fingers together. "Because I wanted to see if Brad would rise to the challenge. If anyone can help him pull his head out of his ass, it's you, Brianna."

I arched an eyebrow at him. "Are you supposed to tell me that?"

"Probably not," Ethan laughed. He paused then stood and shut the door behind me. "Between you and me, there are going to be some changes over the next few years in our district. The superintendent is planning on retiring, and he's been asking around about quality candidates to replace him."

"Are you...?"

"Perhaps." Ethan smiled. "I might toss my hat in the ring, but there's still time before anything happens, and who knows what might change before that day? However, if I were to leave, I want to make sure my school would be in the right hands." He gave me a pointed look. "Preferably yours."

"Mine?" I squeaked, bringing my hand up to my chest. "I don't even have my admin certification."

"You started taking the courses. What happened?"

I chewed my lower lip. "My life sort of spiraled downhill. Figured I should put those goals to bed until things got better." I let out a humorless laugh. "That ship seems to have sailed."

"I wouldn't go that far," Ethan answered. "Brianna, it's not my place to comment on your personal life, and I would never want to make you uncomfortable, but I will say you've seemed lighter since your divorce. Sure, there was that usual mourning period, but everyone could see Todd was weighing you down. Now, you have the chance to go for what you want. If it's admin, go for it. There aren't many people I'd want to see take my chair, and it would be an honor to pass this school over to you." Ethan shrugged, like he hadn't just upended my life with a few brief sentences. "I'd like you to consider it. If you decide it's not the route you'd like to take, then I support your choice."

I paused, only able to nod my head slightly. *Was this what I wanted?* Once upon a time, I'd applied for my school building leadership certification. Todd pushed me to so I could bring home more money, but my heart wasn't in it. Now, however, pursuing my admin degree held more appeal. I'd reached the end of what I could do as a teacher, and this might be the right step if I wanted to make a lasting change.

Before I turned to leave, I frowned at Ethan. "So this whole Brad thing, is it some kind of a test?"

"Not exactly," he said. "*But*, if you decide to pursue this route, there are many people who'll walk through that door without the right intentions. You still need to motivate them, help them become a teacher worthy of our students. Consider this a trial run."

"I CAN'T BELIEVE he might leave," Hadley said as she scooped a handful of popcorn. "Mr. Cutler is an institution at that place."

"Right?" I groaned as I dipped my head back, waiting impatiently for the commercials to end so we could get back to the game. *Wait, what? When did I become this person?* If someone had told me last year that I would spend my Friday nights with my friends watching a baseball game and yelling at the umpires on screen, I would have laughed.

Yet, here we all were.

Hadley and Victoria had come over earlier in the day with Emilia, all wearing their matching Seda jerseys for Cam. We'd made burgers and veggies on the grill, talking about the latest changes in our lives. Hadley was in full-on wedding planning mode and surprised Ollie and me with little gifts asking us to be her bridesmaids. Of course, we both said yes instantly, already looking forward to the wedding. Victoria was the maid of honor, and as Hadley helped prepare our dinner, she filled us in on her plans for the bachelorette party. While the flower girl, Emilia, tried to convince her mother to let her come to the party too, we all sat back, looking over the dozens of pictures Hadley saved on her online boards.

"So, what did you tell him?" Victoria asked from the other couch.

"That I'd think about it," I said. "As much as I love teaching, this seems like it might be the best next step. I've already completed half the coursework, so I'd be able to finish my certification in the next eighteen months or so."

"I say go for it," Hadley announced. "You're already helping run that school. Might as well get the paycheck too."

"Seconded!" Ollie yelled from the kitchen.

I shook my head and grabbed my empty cup. *Time for a refill.* As yet another medication commercial came on the screen, I stood and moved to the kitchen. At least, that was the plan until I turned, and all the voices in the apartment went silent.

"What?" I asked.

"Umm, are you going to tell us why you're wearing Damien's jersey?" Hadley yelled, jumping to my side and twisting me to see the back again. "I knew something was going on!"

"You did not," Victoria teased.

"Okay, I didn't like *know*, know, but I hoped it was!" Hadley clapped her hands together. "Okay, details, Bri. Need every single one."

"Good luck with that." Ollie snorted. "This one holds her secrets tight. She won't even tell me, and I'm pretty sure I orchestrated this whole thing."

"You did not. We got together weeks before that," I mumbled as I walked into the kitchen, keeping my words low so no one else heard them. At least, I thought I did.

"WHAT?" Ollie yelled. "You've been holding out on me, Brianna Sideris!"

"It's not that big of a deal," I said after I filled my glass and walked back over to the couch. "We might have... *connected* in Dallas during the all-star game, but it's not like we're dating. We're just spending time together."

"Uh huh," Hadley said, not believing a word that came

out of my mouth. Not that I blamed her; I didn't even believe them anymore. Over the past month, things between Damien and me had shifted. Some nights, when I went over, we didn't even sleep together, instead cooking or me learning little phrases in Spanish. It was still the most fun I'd had in years. There was much more to Damien than I'd ever realized, and I enjoyed being around him—not only because of the orgasms, but because of how alive he made me feel. Hadley narrowed her eyes at me. "If it's not a big deal, then why are you wearing his jersey? You know that's, like, a thing for these guys. Showing up in your man's number screams committed."

Internally, I knew the moment I slipped his jersey over my tank top, but the idea of not wearing it made my stomach sour. Even if he wasn't here to see it, watching Damien play in anything else seemed wrong. I shrugged, trying to imbue as much casualness as I could into the gesture. "It's just a jersey, Hads. Now that rock on your finger, that's a commitment."

"Oh, I know!" Hadley continued, ignoring my comment. "You should fly out with me and Ollie tomorrow! You can surprise Damien while we surprise Cam and Parker."

"What about me?" Emilia frowned.

"You get to come next time," Hadley said as she clutched her future stepdaughter against her thigh. "Besides, Mommy and Adam have something awesome planned for you."

"You do?" Emilia said as she looked at her mother.

"We might." Victoria smirked. "But only if you have a good week in school. No more threatening the boys if they say something."

"But they were being stupid," Emilia groaned. "It's not

my fault they didn't think before they opened their mouths."

Victoria shook her head but failed to hold back her grin. They were in for it when Emilia got older. At seven, she was already a spitfire and could hold her own with most adults. "That's true, but you need to rise above it, Em. Don't let them pull you down to their level."

"Fine." Emilia sighed as she plopped down on the couch. "This better be a good surprise."

As the game resumed and we found our spots for the next couple of innings, all talk of Damien and the other guys faded away. Instead, we focused on each play, dissecting every single call, Hadley most of all. You'd never know a couple of years ago, she knew nothing about base-ball. Apparently, love turned her into the biggest fan of us all.

"You should come," Ollie whispered as Hadley flipped off the ref for calling Cam out. "No matter what's going on with Damien, it'd be nice to show him you care." She plucked at my jersey. "Clearly, he does. It might be the push he needs, going into post-season."

"Does it come off desperate?" I asked. "He didn't invite me to go with him."

Ollie frowned, looking at the screen. "Have you given him a reason to ask?"

"What do you mean?"

"Every time you talk about what's happening with you guys, it seems like he's the one pursuing you. And you have your valid reasons, but it seems like you're still holding back a little. Maybe the reason he hasn't asked is because he didn't think you'd want to come." She took my hand and squeezed it. "Besides, it's almost the end of the summer, Bri. If you're going to do this for him, now is the time."

I pushed out a long breath, hating how her words struck true. Everything about our relationship had been a dance, Damien leading me forward while I kept throwing up reasons to push him away. And honestly, I was so tired of being afraid. Damien had given no reason not to trust him; in fact, he'd gone above and beyond to make sure I felt safe with him.

As Damien's name was called out on the screen, my eyes lifted, unable to look away from the man who'd turned my world upside down. For the longest time, I swore I wouldn't let anyone else in, keep my heart protected behind its walls. But with each moment I spent with Damien, he dismantled them—not with a sledgehammer but with gentle and methodical care. Somewhere along the line, our relationship had shifted, and now, I wanted everything with him.

He swung the bat over his shoulder, glaring at the pitcher with his usual intensity. When he connected with the ball and sent it careening into the outfield, I couldn't hold back my wide grin. I would've given anything to be there with him right now, to be screaming in the crowd as he raced along the bases. After he slid into home plate, Damien stood, brushing the dust off his white baseball pants. When the camera panned to him, he winked, and my insides lit up, as if it was a message just for me.

"Okay," I said. "I'm in."

TWENTY-SEVEN

Brianna

"I can't believe you talked me into this."

As I walked through the hotel lobby, I tugged on the ties of my overcoat, hoping it concealed what was hiding underneath. The whole thing felt ridiculous. After we'd dropped our stuff off in Ollie's room, she'd immediately dragged me out into the city in search of the perfect ensemble to surprise Damien.

While I wanted to blame Ollie, this was equally my fault. I might have let it slip that I'd never bothered with lingerie in the past, and a plan hatched in her mind. Now, only hours after landing, I stepped back into our hotel in a black trench coat, picked to conceal the matching black lace set, garters attached to my ridiculous thigh highs hidden underneath.

I had to admit, when I looked at myself in the mirror at the store, I barely recognized myself. Sensual confidence made my spine straighten, and a sly smirk formed on my lips as I imagined Damien's face. But that was before I had to walk through downtown Miami in ninety-degree heat with a thong riding up my ass.

"Please," Ollie teased. "You're about to show up and surprise the man in lingerie. In a few hours when you can't walk, you'll be thanking me."

"Only if he doesn't slam the door in my face," I grumbled, fixing my sunglasses. Despite it being mid-afternoon, tons of people filled the lobby. Just my luck. My steps quickened, and my hands reached down to cover the slit. No one's eyes seemed to be focused on me—their attention was on their phones or their companions, but I couldn't take the chance, not when one wrong move meant exposing my goods to the world.

"Never going to happen," Ollie answered as we stepped into the elevator. "Damien is literally obsessed with you. My money's on him coming in his pants the moment he sees you."

I snorted. "That doesn't happen in real life."

"It should. If the man doesn't attack you the moment he sees that outfit, send him my way. I'll knock some sense into him." She reached out, pressing the buttons for her floor and the ninth one above it. Parker slipped her Damien's room number when we got here, but after our excursion, I was on my own.

When the elevator landed on Ollie's floor, she squeezed my hand. "Go get 'em, tiger."

A laugh escaped my throat as she sauntered down the hall, ready to torment Parker for a few hours before he needed to get to bed. On the flight down here, Ollie spent hours filling me in on how the post-season worked in baseball. While the Hawks were already in the playoffs because they held the third-best record in their section, their opponents were desperate for a wild card slot, so the competition on the field tomorrow would be fierce.

My eyes darted up to the numbers above the door,

studying them as we climbed further into the sky. This was a bad idea. Damien needed his rest, and most nights before a big game, we just hung out, watching a movie on the couch, him needing to conserve his energy for the field. When this first started, I would have stayed away, not wanting to impede his pre-game rituals. Lately, though, his routine had become enmeshed in mine, and I liked being there for him, enjoyed ogling him as he stretched, making fun of the disgusting smoothies he guzzled down before darting out of his apartment.

I liked *him*.

Maybe even more than liked.

"Oh God," I chuffed to myself. "What are you? Twelve years old? Get a grip, Brianna."

By the time I reached Damien's floor, my pulse had to be in the high triple digits. The elevator doors opened, and I rushed out, searching through the plated room numbers as fast as my feet would let me. *Room 918.* This was it. If Parker was right, Damien sat on the other side, mentally preparing for their next series. My heart raced, imagining him lying on the bed, a sleepy grin on his face as he watched more tape from the other team. Suddenly, I couldn't wait to see him, couldn't wait to hold him in my arms.

But when I reached up to knock, my hand refused to move.

This was out of my comfort zone. Hell, it was so out of character for me, I felt like I was watching someone take over my body. Not only because of my outfit, but because I was putting myself on the line. Even though I'd talked to Damien a couple of times while he was out of town, never once had we discussed my coming out to visit him. Yet here I was, standing on the threshold of his hotel room after traveling hours to be by his side. The possibility of rejection crashed over me, and I was unsure if I'd ever be able to recover if Damien shot me down.

As I debated rushing back down to Ollie's room, the door yanked open, taking the choice away from me. Damien stood right in front of me, his phone in one hand and a bag of snacks in the other. My mouth gaped as I stared at him dressed casually in a vintage-style Hawks shirt and with his dark hair still damp from the shower. God, how did he get more attractive? It had only been five days since we last saw each other—not even a week—and yet, my mouth watered like I'd been drowning and he was the freshest water on Earth.

But when I met his gaze, Damien's eyes were wide, almost as if I was the last person he expected to see on the other side. Instead of the excitement I'd been fool-heartedly expecting, fear flooded his eyes. "Bri, what are you doing here?"

Tucking away my insecurities, I attempted to smile up at him, but it felt strained. "I came out to surprise you. Ollie and Hadley were heading down here for the series, and they asked me to tag along." As the words left my mouth, he peeked over his shoulder, pulling the door closed behind him. I followed the movement, my smile dropping at the grimace on his face. "Unless it's a bad time?"

"No," he said, dragging his hand over his face. "It's just...Bri—"

"D, who is it?"

The sound of a woman's voice inside his hotel room made my blood turn to ice. A familiar ache crushed through my chest, and my lungs refused to fill with air. Reality snapped back into focus. It all made sense—the shock on his face, the way he blocked the entrance with his body.

Someone else was in his hotel room.

Flashes of him in a stranger's embrace replaced the images of him in bed watching tape, of him claiming her as thoroughly as he did me. Did he whisper sweet words of adoration in her ear? Build up her confidence so she'd show him pieces of herself she'd hidden for years?

Tears pooled in the corners of my eyes. How had I been so foolish? I'd always known about Damien's reputation, seen the string of broken hearts he left wherever he went. And yet, for some reason, I convinced myself we were different, that even with no labels on our relationship, he'd keep his word that he'd only be with me.

So, I did the only thing I could.

I turned and ran.

TWENTY-EIGHT

Damien

The pain on Brianna's face was agony—her eyes twin daggers that cut to the deepest depths of my soul. Before I opened my mouth to explain, she darted down the hallway, frantically pressing the down button for the elevator. But I wouldn't let her go that easily, especially after almost a week of missing her. Despite keeping our calls and texts to a minimum, I thought about her constantly, wondering what she was doing at that exact moment. When I confided in Parker again about my situation, he told me to hold tight and let Brianna take the lead this time.

I was going to kill that fucker. Before we'd gone our separate ways earlier, he double-checked I planned on staying in for the night. I thought he was just being nosy, but he must have helped Brianna with this.

Brianna coming here unprompted was the best gift I could ask for, and yet, I'd ruined it before I even greeted her properly. Fuck.

My feet took off, dashing right after Bri as she snuck into the elevator. She tried to close the doors before I got there, but I shoved my hand between them, forcing them to stop. Her wide, hazel eyes stared daggers at me as I stood in front of her, both our chests heaving.

"Go away, Damien," she snapped.

"No," I said. "Not until you listen to me."

She rolled her eyes. "No thanks. Not interested in hearing your lies about the woman in your hotel room—"

"It's Mari."

Brianna froze, all the color draining from her face. Her posture softened, and the moment it did, I reached out and pulled her close. She dropped her forehead onto my chest. "Damien, I'm so sorry. I assumed—"

"I get it," I said, tipping her chin back to meet my eyes. "But I promised you, Bri. No one else." I chuckled, "Shit, there's no else I even want. Just you."

"Me?" she asked, vulnerability pouring out of her in waves.

"Yeah, angel," I said, letting my fingers linger along her cheekbones as I brushed some of her hair away. "Bri, I don't know what I'm doing here, and there's going to be a lot of times I fuck up, but one thing I can promise? I'd never hurt you like that. Please, trust me."

She exhaled before nodding, finally looking back up at me. "I do. At least, I'm trying to. After my divorce, it's been hard to let anyone in, to trust that someone would choose me." Brianna placed her hand on my chest. "But I want to try with you, Damien."

Joy lit me up from the inside, like I'd just walked away with the championship trophy in my arms. Brianna wasn't the type of woman to open up easily—it had to be earned. It might be a small step forward, but it was one in the right direction. A smug smile filled my face. "Admit it, Bri. You missed me."

Color filled her soft cheeks. "I—I might have."

"No might about it, baby. You missed me. There's no point denying it. But if it makes you feel better, I missed you like fucking crazy."

"You did?"

I rolled my eyes and pulled Brianna tight against me. "Woman, you've got no idea how much power you hold over me. Every time I wasn't playing ball, you were the first thing on my mind. Had to make Drobrek take my phone so I didn't text you non-stop."

She smiled, and all that earlier apprehension was gone. Thank God. I hated the look in her eyes and vowed never to be the one to cause it again. It was a sharp reminder of how much she'd been through at the hands of her ex, how many walls I'd have to climb if I wanted to earn Brianna's love.

Wait, love? Shit, was that the sensation burrowing deep in my chest? The realization crashed over me, and it was as clear as the blue in the sky. I loved her. Somehow, despite her attempts to push me away, to keep emotions out of our arrangement—I'd fallen for Brianna Sideris. I was in over my head with this woman, but I wouldn't have it any other way.

I'd always been up for a challenge, and she was worth all the effort.

Her hands drifted down my chest then slid around my hips, pulling me in for a loose hug. "I am sorry, Damien. I shouldn't have run before I even gave you a chance to explain. That was crappy of me."

"You're forgiven. Bri." I tipped her chin up to meet my gaze. "Can't believe you're here with me right now. I can't wrap my mind around it. Please tell me you're sticking around for the series."

She nodded. "If you want me to. We never talked about me going to one of your games—"

"Woman, I want you at every single one." My arm tightened around her waist. "But there's one rule."

Brianna rolled her eyes. "Thought we were doing away with those things."

"Nah, baby, we're just losing the ones that keep you away from me. But when you're at my games, I need you in my jersey, to find you in the stands, wearing my number."

"You'd like that?"

"You have no fucking idea how much."

She tucked her bottom lip between her teeth, and I reached up, loosening her grip. I was desperate to claim her, desperate to taste her lips on my own, desperate to consume every inch she'd give me.

But my phone dinged in my pocket, and I slid it out, seeing a text from Mari. "Fuck," I huffed, pressing my forehead against Brianna's. "Mari wants to go out to dinner. She's here for a work conference, and she's only here for the night. Otherwise, I'd cancel."

"No, no," Brianna insisted. "You go with your sister. I can hang out with Ollie and Parker."

I searched her eyes, hating the disappointment looking at me. *No fucking way.* It was only a couple of hours, but after days apart, I didn't want to leave Brianna's side until it was necessary. "Come with us."

Her hazel eyes widened. "Wi-with you and your sister?"

"Why not?" I asked. "She already likes you, and it'll help keep her interference to a minimum. She's probably got a laundry list of grievances to go over with me."

Brianna laughed. "Let me get this straight. You need me to keep you safe from your little sister?"

"Yes. Better stick close to me all night." I chuckled. As Brianna's laughter died out, I cupped her cheek. "If you're not comfortable, I won't push, but Bri, I want you to come with us. My sister's important to me, and I'd like it if you two could get to know each other better. It's up to you."

She exhaled, her eyes studying mine for the longest moment of my life. Slowly, she nodded. "Okay, I'll tag along."

I beamed, reaching behind her to hit the button for my floor. Somehow, we'd ended up down in the lobby, and I'd barely noticed the car move, too focused on Brianna and laying myself out for her. As we ascended, Brianna's eyes widened, and her hands fumbled onto her coat. "Actually, I'd like to change before we head out."

"We're not going anywhere fancy. You should be good."

She shook her head. "No, I'd really like to change. I have, uh...airplane germs on me."

I paused, taking in her outfit. When I was chasing Brianna earlier, the hurt in her expression distracted me from everything else. Now, my mouth watered as I spotted the black lace running up her thighs, the way it disappeared under the hem of her jacket. Her long black jacket. I might not be familiar with women's fashion, but even I knew that was an odd choice for summer in Miami.

"Bri..." I crooned. "What are you wearing under the coat?"

She sucked in a sharp breath. "Clothes?"

"Is that a question, angel?" I reached out, toying with the lapel of the coat. "Or did you wear something special to surprise me?"

Her cheeks flushed, and I waited for her to deny it. Instead, she reached up and opened the coat wider. My mouth went dry as sheer black lace came into view. My dick hardened in my pants, and I had to force my hands back, desperate to unwrap her like the best present.

"Fuck, angel. You might look like heaven, but you're tempting me right into hell."

"Good. Because that's all you're going to get until after dinner."

"Mari's lucky I love her," I groaned. "I'd give anything to be an only child right now."

"Don't worry, baby," Brianna said as the elevator doors opened onto Ollie's floor. "Be a good boy, and I will make it all worth your while."

TWENTY-NINE

Brianna

"How long have you been sleeping with my brother?"

My eyes widened as I met Mari's grin across the table. *So much for playing it cool.* I'd met up with Damien and Mari in the lobby after I'd changed, and as soon as I saw them, the urge to run overwhelmed me. All my earlier bravado with Damien washed away, and instead, fear gripped me like a vice. It took way too many calming breaths to force my feet to move forward instead of darting back into the elevator.

But as soon as Damien found me across the room, he offered me a slight smile, his eyes warm and understanding, as if he knew how desperately I wanted to bolt. I needed to do this. For him. He'd stuck by me through my fears, and I refused to let them win again. After all, it was just a dinner with his sister. How bad could it be?

When she followed her brother's gaze and spotted me on the other side of the room, she rushed forward and swept me into her arms. Despite her short frame, she held me tight, her arms wrapped around my stomach. Anxiety receded from my bones, and I let her hold me, needing it more than I realized, even if she was practically a stranger.

The first time I met Mari, it had been under very different circumstances. We'd been passing acquaintances, sitting by each other in the friends and family section at the all-star game. Little did I know, only hours later, her brother would be crashing into my bed.

Damien's groan broke me out of my memories, bringing me back into the present moment. Mari stared at me, waiting. *Oh right.* She wanted to know how long I'd been sleeping with her brother.

The entire restaurant seemed to go quiet as Mari waited for my answer. Suddenly, the bustling noise of the modernly designed room died out, and all I could hear was my heart beating heavily in my chest. God, did they suddenly spike the heat? Because my palms were not this sweaty seconds earlier.

Before I could splutter out an incoherent answer, a large hand moved over mine, tangling our fingers together. When I looked over at Damien, he kept his eyes on his sister but squeezed my hand once. *I got this.*

"Mari, boundaries."

She rolled her eyes with an amused smirk, not even a little upset about being called out. "Sorry, Damien. This is the first time you've willingly brought someone to meet me in years. Can't blame me for being a little curious."

"Curiosity is fine," he said. "Making Bri uncomfortable is not."

Mari's eyes softened and then turned toward me. "Sorry, Bri. That wasn't my intention. I've just never gotten to play the protective sister card, and maybe I overdid it." She twisted to glare at Damien. "And this one interrogated my wife for *hours* before he gave his blessing, so he deserves a bit of questioning."

My eyes widened at Damien. "You didn't."

His mouth fell open. "She came home with my baby sister. Of course I needed to make sure she was a good person—that she was worthy of her. Don't let the happy family routine fool you, this one had the *worst* taste in women before Angie came along."

"Pot, kettle, brother," Mari mumbled, hiding her words behind her wine glass.

Damien just rolled his eyes then dragged my hand over into his lap. With his thumb brushing over my knuckles and the easy rapport between the siblings, my guard lowered all on its own. Their relationship was so different from the one I had with Jason. Even though Damien and Mari had more years separating them, they were incredibly close. While my brother would drop everything if I needed him, we weren't friends. We never sat around and chatted about our lives, instead focusing on our mother and her demands.

Mari shoved her long dark hair over her shoulder then offered me a genuine smile. Despite her brash demeanor, I liked her. She didn't mince words but with the most caring intentions. Her fierce protectiveness of Damien only made me like her more, happy he had her by his side. "So, Bri. Damien tells me you're a Special Education teacher. How do you like it?"

I snuck a peek at the man at my side, arching my eyebrow as if to ask, *you've been talking about me?*

He just smirked in response. *Can't help it.*

I cleared my throat and faced Mari. "I love it. Seeing the kids' confidence grow, watching them master their goals, it's everything to me." My smile faltered, my conversation with my principal flashing in my mind.

"But?" Mari asked, not missing a beat. The woman had missed her calling as a therapist. Then again, working as a vet, especially at an emergency care center, required a high level of empathy.

"It's my co-teacher this year." I sighed. "He's a bit...difficult. My principal wants to challenge me to work with different personalities, but I'm not sure it's a good idea." I shook my hands in front of my face. "It's fine. I'll make it work."

Mari's eyes narrowed at me. "Don't do that."

"Do what?"

"Swallow down your annoyance to make others feel comfortable. If this teacher isn't pulling their weight, it's on them, not you. You shouldn't have to make things work." She shook her head. "And honestly, shame on your principal for putting you in this position. Has he done anything to fix the problem?"

"Well, I don't know—"

"That's enough of an answer," Mari said. My throat constricted, hating how true her words struck. It gave voice to all my feelings since my conversation with Ethan. He'd worked with Brad for years and hadn't done anything to correct his poor behavior. Yet he expected me to swoop in and magically fix it all in one year? Even if this was a sort of test to see if I could be a worthy administrator, it wasn't one I was prepared to pass.

My job was hard enough most days; adding my co-worker's failings seemed like a cruel ask.

I took a breath, not wanting to sully this evening with rage over my job. The impulse to back down was deep in my bones, and it took everything I could to hold on to those frustrations for another day, to not pass it off with a dismissive comment. "Thank you, Mari. I needed to hear that."

She raised her glass to me. "If you ever need to vent, call me. Can't promise to keep my mouth closed, but I'm always here to channel some additional female rage."

I chuckled, and the last dredges of anxiety slipped off my shoulders. Damien's hand released mine, probably noticing the shift in my demeanor. But the moment his fingers slipped away, I reached out, pulling his hand back to mine—not because I needed it, but I wanted to hold him, wanted the connection between us.

Damien smiled softly and pulled our joined hands over the table, kissing the back of my knuckles. The gesture was so simple—one that spoke of endless support and care. I never wanted to let go.

Never wanted to let *him* go.

The realization snapped the band in my chest, the one that held my heart together after Todd ripped it to shreds. But with each touch, each laugh, Damien had slowly knitted it back together. It was in his patience with me, how he encouraged me to own my pleasure and my strength. He saw me, even when I had trouble seeing myself. During our time together, he'd been by my side, never letting me drown in the tempting darkness.

Damien brought the light back into my world.

And I loved him for it.

No, that wasn't right. Sure, I'd started falling for Damien because he pulled me out into the world again, but it was so much more than that. I loved him because of his humor, the way his eyes danced when he spoke passionately about baseball. I loved his protectiveness over his family, how much his sister and nieces meant to him, the way he commanded the field as if he owned it.

So many reasons flashed through my mind. All the small moments that had tied my heart to Damien, making it impossible to keep up with our rules. Against his kindness, his empathy, his understanding, it never stood a chance.

Somehow, despite my fear and apprehension, he'd captured my heart.

And I had no intention of getting it back.

THIRTY

Damien

Hours later, we remained at the restaurant, one of the few tables left after the dinner rush cleared out. We'd traded our plates for glasses of wine and spent hours laughing, reliving different moments from my childhood with Mari. There was an ease between the three of us, one I hadn't expected but loved nonetheless. Brianna slid right in between me and Mari, cracking jokes and ribbing me with my little sister. You'd never know that, hours earlier, she'd been stiff as a board, terrified of saying the wrong thing.

Turning to sneak a look at the woman by my side, I couldn't help but smile. This was all I ever wanted. Someone who fit right in with my family. Someone to bring me out of my baseball-induced haze and make me spend more time living my life outside the game.

I never expected that woman to be Brianna, but the more time I spent with her, the more I was sure we were perfect for each other, the balance the other one needed. She tried to hide her soft heart behind reinforced walls, but it was impossible for her to turn it off completely. She cared more than most people bothered. For hours, she let Mari talk about her girls, sharing different stories from their time in school and their messes at home. Her focus never wavered; it never seemed like she was asking just to ask. Brianna wanted to get to know my family, and that meant more than I could put into words.

As if she knew my thoughts were only of her, Brianna turned toward me, her hazel eyes softening when they met mine. She stole my breath, stole the beat of my heart, and claimed it for herself.

She was becoming my everything, even surpassing my team.

With a shake of her head, Brianna turned toward Mari. "Excuse me for a moment."

Brianna stood from the table, and I watched every step until she moved out of sight. A snicker broke me out of my staring contest. My head snapped back toward my sister. "What, Mari?"

"Oh, nothing," she mused. "This is just so much fun to watch."

"What are you talking about?"

"You love her."

I blinked slowly, unable to open my mouth to contradict her. Sure, I'd admitted to myself—this was love—but only to myself. Hearing someone else point it out—*Mari, no less*—cemented it in my mind. Shaking my head, I forced myself to meet my sister's knowing smirk. "I might be."

Mari snorted so loudly, the remaining tables turned to stare. "There's no might about it, Damien. I've never seen you look at anyone the way you do Bri, not even when you were engaged. You are hopelessly in love with that girl."

"Keep your voice down." I turned to look over my shoulder, making sure Brianna couldn't overhear. "Maybe I do. But Bri's not ready, so let's keep it between us."

"Why isn't she ready?"

"Nasty divorce. Her ex was a cheating bastard, and she's skittish about relationships. It's taken a long time to admit that she likes me, not just my—"

"Do not finish that sentence," Mari said, holding her hand up, her smile down-turned as she weighed my words.

The sudden silence between us made my chest tighten. Mari wasn't one to mince words, so her keeping her thoughts to herself made me worry. The longer the silence stretched on, the more my anxiety built until I snapped. "What, Mari?"

"I'm worried about you." Mari sat back, staring at me with a knowing expression. "I like Bri, I really do, but I don't want your heart to get broken again. After Talia, you changed, D. You became colder, more shut off from the rest of us."

Was that true? Sure, I'd sworn off dating for a while, but I hadn't realized it affected my other relationships as well. Looking back over the past couple of years, it became clear. My distance. My resistance to anyone getting too close. The obsession with my career. All of it pointed to my hiding away from the world, happy to mask the aching loneliness with a placating smile.

Mari sighed. "Brianna seems great, don't get me wrong, but if she's not in the same place as you..." Her voice trailed off as her eyes filled with empathy. "I'm worried it'll destroy you."

My throat tightened, unable to hide the fear racing through my veins. She was right. Brianna never being able to fully commit to this—*to us*—was an actual possibility. Sure, her walls were steadily coming down, but each time we crossed a line, she pulled back, fear taking over as soon as we parted.

However, she'd taken the first step this time. She'd come to me. Hell, Brianna even willingly came to dinner with my sister, knowing it would out our secret for the very first time. Maybe I was reading too much into it, but I had to believe that meant something.

I meant something to her.

I sat back. "Then that's the risk I'm going to take. Brianna deserves it. She deserves someone willing to fight for her. I can't back down now, Mari. And I love you for worrying about me, but even if this all falls apart, it was worth it. Bri's worth the risk."

NORMALLY, I loved spending time with my sister. Mari and I could sit around a table for hours, filling the room with laughter and shared memories. But tonight, with the picture of Brianna in her lingerie and Mari's words still in my mind, I counted the minutes until we left for the hotel.

After my fourth not-so-subtle suggestion we call it a night, Mari finally relented, but not before she told me how much she loved Brianna, warning me to tread carefully. She wanted me to protect my heart, but it was too late. Brianna owned its every beat.

After we headed back to the hotel, Brianna made a comment about going to Ollie's room, but I wouldn't hear it. All night, the image of her skin lingered in my mind, teasing me to the point of madness. My dick had been semi-hard since she showed me a preview earlier, and if I didn't get my hands on her soon, I'd combust in my jeans like a teenager.

When we opened the door to my hotel room, I moved behind her, wrapping my hands around her waist. As my fingers toyed with the hem of her sweater, Brianna chuckled, dropping her head onto my chest. "Impatient, are we?"

My lips dusted along her shoulder. "You have no idea, Bri. Almost fucked you right at the table, but I didn't want to scar my sister for life."

"Not to mention the other people at the restaurant," she laughed.

"Don't care about them," I said, my lips continuing their path up to her ear. "I want to show the world you're mine, Bri. I'm tired of hiding it from everyone."

A sharp breath pressed out of her lips as she turned in my arms. Instinct made me shut my eyes, waiting for her rejection. *Too much.* Mari's words rushed through me—the warning Brianna may not want the same as me. My pulse pounded in my ears, and time seemed to still as her breath slowly washed over me.

But as I waited for the inevitable end, the opposite happened. Brianna's hands cupped my cheeks, and she softly brushed her lips over the corner of my mouth. My eyes burst open, unable to believe the sight in front of me. She wasn't running. She didn't seem afraid. Instead, Brianna stood in front of me with a wide smile, her thumbs running over my cheeks.

"I don't want to hide this either."

I blinked, unsure if I believed her. I waited for her to take back the words, to retreat into the safety of Ollie's room, but the woman kept surprising me. "Kiss me, Damien."

THIRTY-ONE

Damien

"Kiss me, Damien."

I almost growled, needing her mouth on mine. The urge to surge forward was strong, but I wouldn't do it unless she really wanted me too. My hands found her hips and dragged her flush against me. "You sure about this, Bri? Because I mean it. I'm done hiding us. You're mine, and I want everyone to know it."

She nodded, her eyes darting down to my parted lips. "Yes, Damien. I'm sure. Pretty sure I've wanted this since the night at Parker's."

"Thank fuck."

I didn't waste another breath before claiming her lips. It was a furious claiming, filled with all the missed moments her lips had been forbidden territory. Teeth and tongues clashed, each of us desperately searching for more of the other's taste. Brianna's lips were what I dreamt about—sweetness in the most tempting package. If this were to be my downfall, I'd happily go, letting her lead me into the abyss.

We remained in the doorway, and that wouldn't do. I

needed her, needed her laid out against the sheets, to see every reaction reflecting at me in her hazel irises, already blown wide from our lust.

I lifted Brianna, and she wrapped her legs around my waist, encircling me tight. I almost combusted when she rubbed herself against my hard cock, and it took every ounce of mental willpower not to blow my load right then and there.

When I dropped her onto the bed, I took a moment to study her, thanking every one of my lucky stars we'd stumbled together. I couldn't even imagine what my life would have been like if our paths hadn't crossed, if I'd never gotten to have Brianna like this. My mouth watered as my hands wrapped around her jean-clad calves, ravenous for a taste of her. I needed her release on my tongue. Brianna seemed just as eager, tossing off her shirt and pulling her jeans down her toned legs.

As soon as she was bare in front of me, I sucked in a sharp breath, taking in the sight. Her long, tanned legs folded onto the comforter, made all the longer by the high cut of the opaque thong covering her core. Lace lined the bustier that pushed up her breasts, small pearls and other details making Brianna look like an image pulled from my darkest desires. As I traced the seams with my fingers, Brianna smirked up at me. "Do you like it?"

"Like it?" I chuckled. "Not even close. You look like a fallen angel, Brianna."

"And that's a good thing?"

"It's fucking perfect," I hissed as my finger stroked the center of her panties. The dampness made me smile, knowing I wasn't the only one suffering tonight. "But you don't need to dress up for me, Bri. I want you just as you are."

"I know," she quietly admitted, her voice barely over a whisper, "which made me want to do it even more. I like being sexy for you, Damien. Like the way your eyes light up when I'm bare in front of you. Like that you're in awe of me."

"I am," I growled, crawling over her. "But it has nothing to do with your body. I'm blown away by your heart, how fucking kind you are. And your brain, Bri. It fucking turns me on so much..."

"Damien..." Brianna said, her hand reaching up to cup my cheek.

As her hazel eyes met mine, it flayed all my senses, and I couldn't hold back anymore. "Every day, I wake up so fucking grateful I walked into that Dallas bar, that you asked me into your room—into your life. Maybe it's too soon to tell you all this, but I don't want to hold back with you, Bri. Make whatever rules you want; I'll follow them all. But I'm done pretending you don't mean the world to me."

Brianna stared up at me, a mixture of fear and excitement reflecting in her eyes. She traced my lower lip with her thumb. I shivered under her touch, wanting so much more from her. "You mean the world to me too," she quietly admitted, her voice straining to get the words out.

With no further thought, I surged forward, capturing her lips again. As her tongue brushed against mine, I hated myself for denying this for so long. Brianna's lips were heaven, a place a sinner like me had no right to enter. I took it anyway.

Despite the force it took, I pulled away, searching Brianna's gaze. But she reached up, cupping my neck to pull my lips back to hers. It was no longer the desperate ones we'd shared when we walked into this room. Now, they were slower, savoring instead of dominating, like a quiet submission of what we'd been to something new.

My lips trailed down her jaw, nipping at her neck. "Tell me what you want, Bri. Anything, and it's yours."

"I want you inside me," she sighed, her legs opening so I could settle between her hips.

"I should make you wait," I teased as I toyed with her nipples through the sheer fabric. "After all, you tormented me all night, being so close and not letting me touch you."

"Please, Damien," Brianna pleaded, arching her back to deepen my touch. "I need you."

"You have me."

I reached up, sliding my hands around her back. As I pulled her to my chest, Brianna's finger traced my jaw, smiling softly as she took me in. The tender gesture made me lean in and capture her lips in a searing kiss, needing more of her flavor on my tongue. Reaching down, I slid the flimsy panties off her legs and tossed them over my shoulder.

I toyed with the seams of the top. "Tell me how to get this off you, Bri. Need it gone, and it's taking everything in me not to rip it."

She chuckled as she sat up and toyed with the clasps behind her. As soon as the fabric fell away, I sucked in a sharp breath, still not used to seeing her like this—bare, bold, and so fucking perfect for me. I climbed over her, letting my hands explore every inch of her silken skin. She tugged at the hem of my shirt, silently begging me to remove it. I smirked as I pulled it away, leaving us chest to chest.

Unlike in the past, when we both rushed toward bliss, we stayed there for a moment, our hands exploring, unhurried with our languid touches. I leaned down and kissed her lips, unable to stop. As Brianna shifted underneath me, my tip prodded her entrance, desperate to push inside her warmth.

"Shit," I hissed. "Need a condom."

As I pulled away from her, Brianna's hands gripped my arms. "Are you okay if we don't use one?" My eyes widened as I took her in. Brianna paled, mistaking the look on my face for anything other than excitement. "Never mind. I was just thinking, I'm on birth control and got tested after Todd left. There's been no one else since you—"

My mouth sealed over Brianna's, cutting off her nervous ramblings. "Fuck, angel. I'd give anything to be bare inside you. They have us run a full panel before every season, and my results came back clear." I lowered my forehead down to hers. "I've never gone without one before."

She searched my gaze. "Not even with your ex?"

I shook my head. "She never offered, and I didn't want to force her into anything, but I want to do this with you, Bri. I want you to strangle my cock with nothing between us."

Brianna smiled up at me. "Then what are you waiting for?"

Her legs wrapped around my waist, urging me forward. I shifted to get closer to her, testing her with my fingers to make sure she was ready to take me. Dampness soaked my hand as I explored her; she was as desperate for me as she claimed. I moved my hands away, but not before sucking her essence off my fingers. I lined up my cock with her entrance and used my fingers to brush her hair from her face. "Last chance to change your mind, angel."

"Fuck me, Damien," Brianna pleaded. "I need you so much. Make me yours."

As soon as the words left her lips, I surged forward, trying to get most of my length inside her tight heat. Brianna's nails gripped my back as I pushed forward, slowly finding a pace that suited both of us. But like our shared kisses, there was nothing rushed about my movements. Instead, I savored each thrust, studying Brianna as I moved against her, cataloged her noises, which angle made her eyes roll into the back of her head, what made her walls clench around my cock.

I committed all of her to memory.

"Damien," Brianna moaned, her eyes shutting tight as she climbed closer to the edge. I reached up, placing my hand around the delicate curve of her neck. Without adding too much pressure, I directed her gaze back to mine. "Eyes on me, angel. Need you to remember who's making you feel this way."

"It's you," she gasped, twisting her hips as my movements slowed, trying to chase her high. "God, it's only ever been you."

"Damn straight," I said, nipping at the curve of her lower lip. "And don't you dare forget it. You're mine, Bri."

Her hazel eyes went wild at my words, a sharp contrast to the way her pussy gripped me. She tried to shut her eyes, but I refused to let her, instead capturing her lips and stealing the moan off her tongue. "Are you mine, angel?"

Brianna nodded. "Fuck. Yes. I'm yours, Damien. Please, please make me come."

"Anything for you."

I leaned back on my haunches, dragging her hips to meet mine and slamming inside her. As Brianna's back bowed off the bed, my thumb found her swollen clit, pressing deep circles to match my frantic thrusts. She gasped and stared up at me, her pouty mouth forming a perfect circle. "Say it, Damien. I need to hear it."

"I'm yours, angel," I said as I kept up my brutal pace. "And you're so fucking mine."

My truth sent her hurtling over the edge, crashing into her orgasm with a vicious roar. Brianna's nails raked down my back, pulling me closer than ever before. But I hardly felt the pain, too busy surrendering to the sensations surrounding me. As she relaxed against the pillows, my release poured out of me, coating Brianna's walls with my cum. When it finally slowed, I inched back, loving the way it spilled out of her onto the pale sheets surrounding us.

After I flopped back onto the pillows, I pulled Brianna against my chest. We were both slick with sweat, but I couldn't bring myself to care, not when she'd just destroyed all my brain cells. Instead, I just held her, running my fingers through her brunette waves.

"That was incredible," Brianna said, exhaustion making her words mumbled.

"Yeah, it was."

There was so much more I wanted to say—so many more words I wanted to give Brianna. Truth be told, every moment I spent with her was better than the last. Since we'd met, she'd climbed under my skin, and I had no interest in digging her out. This woman owned me, and for the first time in my life, I was happy to hand over control.

The past decade of my life had been amazing. Getting to play ball in the major leagues was a gift—one I was determined to keep every single day—but spending this time with Brianna made me realize how much I'd forsaken in the name of the game. And while I might have made mistakes in my past, ones that cost me more than I even thought possible, I refused to lose this woman in front of me.

Because she was quickly becoming my everything.

A bunch of words rushed through my mind, ones I had

no right to say to her just yet, emotions that had started to build but didn't dare bring up to her. But they repeated in my brain like an anthem. *Mi amor, mi vida, mi alma.* All names that would have flown off my tongue if Brianna was ready to hear them.

Brianna drifted off to sleep in my arms, and I stayed up to watch her, unable to close my eyes just yet.

THIRTY-TWO

Brianna

As I stood in the stadium in Miami, the heat beat down along my spine. The sun glared above us, almost as antagonistic as the guys on the field. The tension was thick, muttered curses breaking out into a screaming match as they kept pace with one another.

Even up in the stands, the surge of adrenaline from both teams overwhelmed us. Both Erie City and Miami wanted to come out the winners in this series. With the playoffs starting next week, everyone wanted that edge, but only one team could walk away the winner. With most of the fans decked out in Miami's color, we were the lone patch of dark green in a sea of aqua blue.

I gripped the edge of my jersey, still trusting my instinct to wear it. Damien left for the stadium long before I woke up, so my wearing it would be a surprise to him. Sure, he'd asked me to, but it was different to actually have it on me.

During a normal game back home, he would have already spotted me, gifting me a cocky smirk that made my eyes roll and my thighs clench simultaneously. But tonight, gone was that arrogant man strutting across the field, playing up his skills for the crowd. Damien stayed focused, so focused, he'd barely had time to glance up here; he only offered me a slight smile when he saw me waving.

I tucked my lip between my teeth, imagining the spark in his eyes when he saw me wearing it, his rough hands running underneath the fabric, reminding me what it meant to be his. Because me in his colors, with his name embroidered along my shoulders, the number twelve boldly displayed along my spine, told the world I was his, just as much as Damien was mine.

Ollie practically squealed when I showed up at her hotel room, all dressed and ready for the game in her Drobrek jersey. I tried to push in to tell her all about my night, but she ushered me out too quickly, making up some excuse about the room being a disaster.

That was no surprise. The girl practically lived every day like it was a challenge to cover most of the floor with clothes, papers, and everything else she owned. But this was the first time she had ever hidden it from me.

"They need to get ahead of these guys," Ollie muttered from my side, her thumbnail jammed between her teeth. "Next inning. They're going to get so many hits during the next one."

Ollie kept muttering, her words more for herself than for me. As she whispered prayers to anyone who would listen, I zoned out, focusing on the field. While the opposing team worked through their batting lineup, the surrounding group chatted. A lot of the wives didn't travel for away games, but some other family members showed up and sat with us in the outfield. Most of them didn't travel for regular away games, but a couple made the trip down to Miami before the winter months took over upstate New York.

In fact, some seemed more interested in the nightlife

downtown than in the game in front of them, but I tuned them out. While baseball had never been high on my list of interests, knowing someone I cared about was playing his heart out on that field made things shift for me.

"Fuck," Ollie muttered as another player snuck past Parker, making a break for home while he rushed to grab the ball. Her eyes darted up to the scoreboard, frowning as Miami surpassed the Hawks in runs.

"Is Parker okay?" I quietly asked. That was the third ball Parker had let slip through his fingers. "He's having an off day."

Ollie's mouth opened and promptly slammed closed. Eventually, she sighed. "Something's going on with him, but he won't talk to me about it. I thought it was just the pressure of the season but..."

"But?"

Her face fell, more solemn than I'd ever seen. "We've always been open with each other, even at our worst. And if he's throwing up walls between us now..." She gave me a humorless smile. "I'm probably overthinking everything."

Before I could respond, a crack slammed through the air, and my eyes focused on the batter in front of us. He had barely moved, watching the ball to see what would happen next. As if he had predicted it, Cam rushed forward and caught the pop-up in his glove, holding it up to mark the out. The Miami fans groaned as the innings switched and our guys headed back into the dugout.

I reached out and took Ollie's hand. "Hey, we're only in the fourth inning. Still a lot of game left to play. He's going to be okay."

"I hope so," she answered, her eyes not leaving the dugout. As if he sensed her stare, Parker looked up, making a signal with his fingers. The tension instantly faded from

Ollie's shoulders, and for the first time all day, a genuine smile graced her lips.

The Hawks started going through their lineup, and we held our breaths every time the ball sailed through the air—mostly singles, one double, and the Hawks had resumed their close lead.

As Damien jumped out of the dugout and walked toward home plate, my breath caught in my throat. He'd had a great game so far, which I might have taken a little credit for in my mind. After all, was it such a leap to think our openness with each other led to him performing well on the field? Okay, it might have been, but in my lust-addled mind, it made complete sense.

When he stepped closer, his eyes scanned the outfield, stopping when he found me waving wildly at him. Without another thought, I leapt up, turning around to show him the back of my jersey. I peeked over my shoulder fast enough to catch his wide smile. My heart almost imploded, loving the look on his face. It made me feel loved, seen.

"Umm, Bri," Ollie whispered, tugging on my sleeve.

Apparently, I wasn't the only one who caught Damien's wave. On the large scoreboard, where the numbers for the game had sat only seconds earlier, was now my face, broadcast to the entire stadium. My knees wanted to buckle so I could hide back in my seat, but I refused to let it shake me. Instead, I just stared back at Damien and winked. The attention dug holes through my skin, but it was worth it. I'd never hide this again.

As the cameras turned away from me to focus back on Damien, I found my seat, clutching Ollie's hand. He had this. As he sauntered up to the base, his presence filled the entire stadium, all of us on edge as we waited for him to make his play. The first ball flew, and Damien hardly moved, only smirking when the ump called it in his favor. But the second pitch was perfect, careening toward Damien with precision. My eyes slammed shut when I heard the bat and ball collide, unable to take a breath until I heard the roar of the crowd.

"RUN!" Ollie screamed from my side, jumping out of her seat and pulling me with her. The Miami fans grumbled and jeered as their players tried to catch the ball, screaming the exact opposite of Ollie and me, but I didn't care. Not as Damien rounded the bases, hurtling toward second base with impressive speed.

With the other Hawks on the bases rushing through home, the scoreboard lit up with runs, giving their team the lead they'd been seeking all night. But just as Damien passed through second base, he hesitated before dashing toward third. Action caught my focus out of the corner of my eye, and I spotted the outfielder chucking the ball toward the baseman with all his might.

Damien would make it.

He had to make it.

He must have spotted the throw at the same time as me, because his legs pounded the dirt with renewed vigor, shaking the ground as he passed. Just as the ball reached the baseman's glove, he stepped off the base to catch it, giving Damien an opening. He rushed toward the bag, and his legs stumbled. One bent over the other as he collided with the ground, his arm landing right across the bag.

When the ump called out 'safe', Ollie and I sent up twin cheers of joy, elated he'd actually made it to third. But as the crowd died out, I glanced back at the field and saw Damien hadn't gotten up. He still lay on the ground, slamming his fist into the ground as he cried out in pain.

"Ollie..." I said, my voice trembling as my heart pounded in my chest.

She pulled me into a sideways hug, but my eyes never left the field, watching as the other players and Coach Weber rushed to Damien's side. I kept waiting for him to get up, to shoot me his usual smirk.

Instead, all I could do was watch as people gathered around the man I loved, trying to sort out what had happened. I clenched my hands in front of my face, unable to look away for even a moment. *Get up. Get up.* But when the stretcher rolled out onto the field, dread overtook me.

"Ollie, I have to go," I said, frantically searching the crowd for help. My best friend pulled me up the stairs, darting toward the elevators to the players' level. As she slammed her thumb onto the down button, I pulled back. "You should go back out there. I have a pass—"

"Don't even think about it," Ollie snapped, pulling me inside the opening doors. "We're family, Bri. When one of us goes down, we all do. There's no way I'm letting you handle this on your own."

And as the doors closed, my best friend's hand clenched in mine, the tears finally came as I muttered the words, "He has to be okay."

"He will be," Ollie said. "Even if it takes time, we'll be there, every step of the way."

Damien

When I opened my eyes, my entire body screamed in pain. Not only my leg, though that was where most of it radiated from, but all my muscles seemed like they'd taken a beating.

The last thing I recalled was trying to land on the base, hungry for the win. Miami was putting up a hell of a fight, but we refused to back down. So when I saw my chance to gain another base, I took it.

And then, the world went black.

"D?" My name broke through the aura of pain, forcing me to open my eyes reluctantly. Gone was the green of the field, replaced with the sterile white walls of a hospital room. The thousands of fans had dwindled down to one—my sister sitting at my side.

"Oh, thank God," Mari breathed as I turned my head, finding her waiting there, clutching my hand.

"What happened?" I asked, my voice gruffer than normal.

Mari's face paled, holding my hand a little tighter. "You had a nasty fall on the field. They brought you here for some tests, but you've been in and out for a while. How are you feeling?"

"Like shit," I said, running my hand over my face. I tried to shift in the bed, but the lower half of my body was in a sort of sling, my right leg suspended slightly above the bed, completely immobilized. Panic seized my chest, and all I could do was stare, wondering how I'd injured myself so badly. I'd slid like that a thousand times, made the same move more times than I could count, and I'd never come close to injuring myself, especially not like that.

"Don't move too much," Mari said, standing to help me get comfortable. "The doctor should be here soon to check in on you."

I sighed, dropping my head back on the pillow. Mari tried to head back to the chair, but I grabbed her hand, needing her close. My throat tightened as I stared down at my leg, a thousand questions filling my mind. How long would I be out? How my team must hate me right now. I was the captain—the man on the field they could count on. Now, I didn't know where I stood. Instead of facing that cold reality, I forced a bitter smile. "Thought you were supposed to be home by now."

She shook her head. "Not happening, big brother. I was heading to the airport when Brianna called. Came right here instead and met you in the ER."

My heart cracked a little at her words. My sister had a family and a thriving career, and she came here when I needed her the most. Thank fuck Brianna called her. Without a word, she knew I'd want my sister right now, and she made it happen. But as much as I loved having Mari here, I needed my girl just as much.

"Where is she?"

Mari's face softened, nodding to a chair in the corner. I

hadn't noticed it before, too distracted by the reality of my situation. But there she was, sleeping soundly. She'd curled up in the armchair and passed out like it was a queen sized-bed. She'd even tugged my jersey across her chest, using it like a makeshift blanket.

Mari sighed, leaning in closer to me. "She came in the ambulance with you. Hasn't left for longer than ten minutes. We tried to get her to go back to the hotel to get some rest, but she refused. Finally passed out about an hour ago."

She stayed.

I stared at her, and Brianna's eyes slowly flickered, awareness trickling in as she took in the room. When she saw me staring back at her, she hopped up instantly, moving to my side. She paused at the edge of the bed, her hands fumbling as if she were unsure if she should touch me. I reached out and took her hand, tugging her closer until her chest pressed against mine. As we hugged, she let out a shuddered breath, running her hands along my face, searching for any signs of distress.

"I'm good, angel." My words might not be true, but I needed them to be—needed to erase the worry lining her delicate features. Brianna had always been expressive, unable to hide much once I'd gotten past her walls. Fear and concern filled her hazel eyes, and I hated being the one who put it there. She clutched my hand, holding it between hers like a lifeline, and it took everything in me not to offer her empty platitudes.

Because as much as I wanted to assure her I was okay—I wasn't.

A woman with long dark hair rushed into the room, smiling when she spotted me. "Oh good, you're awake." She moved over, checking the machines before turning back to face me. "My name is Dr. Cooper, and I'll be monitoring you while you're with us. How are you feeling, Mr. Ramos?"

"Fine," I bit out, already tired of that question. "What's going on with my leg?"

She smiled, not at all fazed by my sour attitude. "You did some damage with that landing. Ruptured your patellar tendon." She turned her attention to her tablet, pulled up some images, and showed them to me. "If you look here, you can see it's almost a complete tear, which means we're going to need to operate to repair the damage."

"And that will fix it?" Brianna asked from my side.

"It should. With surgery and physical therapy, most patients regain almost full function of their knee within 12 months."

"A year?" Mari gasped, echoing the thoughts inside my mind.

Fuck. The color drained from my face. Twelve months? I didn't have twelve fucking months. I didn't have twelve *days*. The playoffs were starting next week, and I needed to be on that field with my teammates.

Dr. Cooper's face softened as she placed her hand on my shoulder. "I know this is a lot to take in, but we need to figure out next steps, Mr. Ramos. With an injury like this, the longer we wait, the more we're risking long-term damage."

Words sat on the tip of my tongue, but they refused to come out. The word *surgery* rang out in my mind as my breathing became more labored. This was not how my day was supposed to go. We were supposed to take home the win and then I was supposed to celebrate with the team and spend the night with Brianna wrapped in my arms.

But that wasn't my life anymore.

And it wouldn't be for at least a year.

Fuck.

Shame and frustration crept back through me, making it hard to breathe. No one said a word, instead watching me as if I were about to break. Maybe I was. After more than a decade of playing baseball, my future was a giant question mark. It would be different if I'd retired. At least then, the decision would have been in my hands. But this? One wrong move, and everything I'd worked for was gone.

No playoffs. No championship. Nothing but pain and hard work ahead of me.

Brianna leaned down and cupped my chin. "You're going to get through this, Damien."

I chuffed, "Not so sure about that."

Her hold tightened, and she lifted my chin to meet her gaze. "One step at a time. That's all you can do. Let's get you home, and you can tackle the next one."

"Can I even fly?"

Brianna winced and looked over at the doctor. She hummed for a minute and peered at the images again. "I have to advise against it. Not only because time is of the essence, but also, with an injury like this, you're more susceptible to blood clots, especially when flying. My advice—have the surgery first. The quicker we can repair the damage, the better it will be for your recovery."

I ground my teeth, not liking the answer one bit. As much as I wanted to get better, the idea of being trapped in Florida sounded even worse. My life was back in Erie City. My team, my home—my girl. "Is there any way to lower that risk? No offense, Doc, but I want to go home."

Dr. Cooper grimaced. "Not really, Mr. Ramos. The risk of continued damage is too high. Between the turbulence and the altitude, it could set back your recovery by months, if not years. You might never regain full function of your knee."

I shook my head, refusing to hear her. "It should be fine."

"Should?" Brianna bit out, turning to face me with malice in her eyes. "We're not risking any more damage for a *should*."

My mouth dropped open. "Bri, I can't stay here. My team—"

"Needs you *better*, Damien."

"She's right," Mari added as she stood at Brianna's side, reaching to take her hand. She glared at me, taking Brianna's side. "They can handle a few games without you. But if you end your career because you're being stubborn? No one will forgive you. Especially not me. You've sacrificed too much for that."

Their concern meant a lot to me, and a part of me knew they were right. But right now, all I could focus on was the anger coursing through my veins—anger at the doctor for giving me that news, anger at myself for making such a stupid play, anger at the women in front of me for not listening to what I needed.

My entire world had shifted in less than twenty-four hours, and I needed some semblance of normalcy, to feel like my life hadn't been completely upended. It was bad enough I couldn't play ball right now—I'd fucked over my team so badly. Now, they expected me to stay in Florida while the rest of them returned home?

I shook my head, needing a moment to breathe without everyone's waiting stares. "Give me a minute?" I asked the room. Mari ushered the doctor outside, giving me one last frown before shutting the door behind her.

Brianna stood at my side, fidgeting with her fingers. "Damien, I—"

"You too, Brianna."

Her mouth fell open. "What?"

"I need a minute." I forced my eyes up to meet hers, hating the shock and pain written across her delicate features. "Alone."

Brianna swallowed and then nodded. Each of her steps toward the door tore at my heart, as if she was dragging it out of the room with her. When she reached the doorway, she turned back to face me. "Take all the time you need, Damien, but you're not alone in this. We're all here with you."

When the door closed behind her, silence finally filled the room, leaving me to wonder if that was true.

THIRTY-FOUR

Brianna

"I'm going to kill him."

The sound of scissors slicing through tape only amplified Ollie's threat. She shook her head as she attempted to break down one of my boxes, only to give up and slam it on the floor instead. I arched a brow at her, and Ollie smiled innocently back at me. "What? I have some aggression to work out, and it refused to cooperate."

"I get it," I bit out as I opened another box, digging out some of my teacher manuals. Even though I'd had the same office space for years, every summer, I had to pack everything up, spending the last week of my vacation trying to recreate the room from memory. Most years, I loved this reset, getting to build up my excitement for the incoming students.

But this year, my mood was rotten.

My phone chimed in my purse, and I leaped across the room to grab it, only for the last of my hope to drain away when I saw it was a message from my mother. She wanted a reason for why I missed church this week, but I couldn't quite tell her the truth, especially knowing the accompanying judgment. Thank goodness I skipped it. My mother never mentioned it, but, my brother, Jason, texted me, letting me know Todd and his fiancée had shown up as well. When his fiancée left the room, Todd cornered Jason, asking him about my whereabouts. Luckily, my brother never cared for my ex-husband and told him to mind his own business.

"Be careful, Bri," Jason warned in his last message. "There's something off about him."

I shook my head, pushing away any thoughts about Todd. With everything going on with Damien, I was already struggling with self-doubt, and I didn't want the memories of Todd to drag me down even deeper. His voice was already the one in my head, making me feel like I'd never be enough for anyone. Only now, it was so much worse, because Damien was the one who'd walked away.

Reading the disappointment in my expression, Ollie tried to smile at me, but it came out flat. "Anything?"

"Nope." Returning to my desk, I dumped some papers inside before slamming it closed. "My mother again. She's pissed I haven't returned any of her phone calls since Sunday."

"Still nothing from Damien?"

"Nope," I said, popping the 'p'. The mention of his name soured my mood even more, and I darted my eyes back to the bookcase, looking for anything to distract me.

Ollie cursed under her breath. "How long has it been?"

"Almost two weeks."

Two fucking weeks since Damien last messaged me, insisting once again that he needed space. When they scheduled his surgery in Miami, I planned on sticking around, even contacting the school to let them know I might not be there for the first few days. It pained me to miss out on those crucial moments with my students, but Damien's health and well-being came first. There was no question in my mind. However, when I told him of my plans, Damien insisted I head back. Hurt lanced through me. It was so tempting to fight him, but how could I? He was the one who'd gotten hurt, the one facing a career-ending injury. All I wanted was to support him as much as possible. If he asked for space, that was the only thing I could do.

Leaving him behind physically hurt, as though I'd left a piece of myself with him in Miami, but I couldn't imagine what he must be going through. Baseball was Damien's life, and he'd just learned that he'd be out of the game for the rest of the season, if not longer. Even if the surgery was a success, there was a good possibility he might never play baseball again. That would jar anyone, but I couldn't imagine the strain for a professional athlete.

So I made excuses, forgave every unanswered text, let go of every ignored phone call, told myself it was just a part of his processing, that he needed time to come to terms with his injury.

But with each passing day, my empathy turned to annoyance.

He'd never explicitly said we were over, but everything pointed to that being the case. I mean, I had to find out his surgery went well from Parker, and that was only because Ollie needled him until he gave it up. All my hope that this was only temporary died then. As much as I wanted to be with Damien, that was the last straw, making me face the harsh truth: Damien didn't want to be with me.

Over the past couple of days, anger and sadness had become familiar friends. After spending most of the summer with Damien, I'd gotten used to his company, even craved it. During our time together, he'd made me feel safe, convinced me I could trust him by always following through and never giving me empty promises. He made me fall for him, and now, when I was ready to catch him, Damien wouldn't let me.

"It's just his stupid male pride," Ollie said as she shuffled through the rest of my belongings. She pulled out an entire package of color labels and stared at me. "We need to discuss your obsessive need to color code everything."

I glared at her before snatching them out of her hand. "As soon as we discuss your refusal to use a laundry basket. Most grown adults do not keep all their clothes on their floor."

"Okay, valid." Ollie paused, her hands on her hips. "So, what do you want to do about Damien?"

"What am I supposed to do? He's in a lot of pain and in recovery. I'm not about to add to his troubles by reaching out to him again. He has my number. If he wanted to talk to me, he would."

"You're not complaining, Bri. Damien got dealt a shitty hand, that's for sure, but he doesn't get to treat you badly because of it."

I opened my mouth, ready to argue in Damien's defense, when my office door swung open. Brad stepped inside, his nose wrinkling as he took in my pastel-colored posters and impeccably labeled supplies. Narrowing my eyes, I steeled my spine, meeting his glare with one of my own. "Can I help you, Brad?"

"Did you get that paperwork on the new student? They're going over our allotted numbers."

I sighed, rubbing my hand over the bridge of my nose. "The district got a variance from the state. As long as the student doesn't start on the very first day, we're allowed to exceed the number of students with IEPs."

"It's bullshit," Brad scoffed.

Rage bubbled on my tongue, but I kept my mouth shut, needing to keep the peace between us. I forgot Ollie stood only a couple of feet away from me, though, and she did not have the same compulsion. "What the hell did you just say to her?"

Brad's eyes widened, taking in Ollie with a sneer on his lips. "Who are you?"

"I don't matter," Ollie said, stepping around me to get in Brad's face. "What matters is that you came into my friend's office and started barking orders at her. She's not your assistant, she's your co-teacher, and you're damn lucky to have her in the classroom with you. You better treat her with some respect."

Brad's eyes darted to me, and some of the arrogance deflated from his shoulders. "Sorry, Sideris. Didn't mean to come at you like that. The district keeps pulling these stunts —piling on our class when we've already got a lot of students with high needs. It's ridiculous."

I swallowed, unable to hide my shock at Brad's apology. "I hate it too."

Brad stepped further into my office, dropping into the chair opposite my kidney table. It was almost comically small, used for my students, not full-grown adults. Ollie bit her lip, obviously noticing the same thing. As he sat down, Brad stayed quiet for a long moment, fidgeting with the now-bare strip on his finger. Oh, hell. That patch was a familiar sight. My ring finger had the same band for far too long. It took ages for it to fade, and I hated that almost as much, as if my decade of marriage never existed at all.

Brad's eyes followed mine as he tucked his bare ring finger under the other. He cleared his throat. "I don't like to broadcast this, but if we're going to work together, you should know. I'm going through some stuff at home. My wife asked for some time apart, and it's lasting a lot longer than I hoped."

"I get it," I said, taking the spot next to him. "Went through my divorce last year. It fucking sucks."

"Yeah, it really does." Brad turned to look at me, less guarded than he'd ever been. "I want this to work, Bri. Not just for the kids, but I need this too. It's no secret you don't like me—"

"I like you." Brad and Ollie both stared at me, like my lie was clear for the world to see. "You're a good guy, Brad. We just have different teaching styles. I don't know how we're going to mesh, but we need to figure something out if we want to survive the year."

"Agree," Brad said.

"However," I added, "I'm not going to sit back and let you take over everything. This is my class too, and I want equal say in what happens with our students."

He paused, taking in my words, before nodding. "This whole co-teaching thing, it's new for me. Ethan's been up my ass the past few years, and this seemed like some sort of punishment." He flinched and faced me. "Not because of you, but the level of scrutiny I'm under. You might not think I do, but I care about this job, about the kids, no matter what everyone else says." He ran his hand over his face. "The past couple of years have been tough at home, and that's where I've had to focus."

Now it was my turn to flinch. *Guilty.* Many times over the past couple of years, I'd questioned why Brad didn't just quit. He didn't seem to care too much about the kids, never going above and beyond like so many of us. Looking at him now, how he absentmindedly rubbed his empty ring finger, made me realize how unfair it'd been to hold him to the same standards I held myself. Time would tell if he meant it when he said he cared about this job, but for the first time, I wanted to look past my assumptions and see the person hiding underneath.

So, I offered him a truth of my own.

"Here is the only place I can focus. For a long time, my life seemed like it was out of my control, and this was the only place that was all mine. So the organizing? The need to keep everything together? That's me over-compensating for my life outside of school."

Shock colored Brad's face, and he stared at me, as if expecting me to take the words back. I shrugged. "We're all fighting our battles, Brad, and I'm not here to judge how you handle yours. But maybe we can help each other."

He nodded. "I'd like that."

I held out my hand to Brad. "It'll never be perfect, but we can try to make this work. Help the other out when things get tough."

Brad smiled at me before putting his hand in mine. "You offering me a truce, Sideris?"

I smirked. "I'm down with that."

After we released our hands, Brad got up from the chair. Ollie stood only a few feet away from him, her arms crossed over her chest like a sentinel. She waited until the door closed behind him before dropping the act. "Okay, I'm glad you two made peace, but I gotta be honest—I wish I took a picture of him in that chair. My stomach hurts from holding in that laugh."

"Thank goodness you didn't," I said, dropping my head to my table. "It's a start, right?"

"Better than what you had before," Ollie muttered as she turned back toward the bookshelf. She hummed something to herself, and my eyes narrowed.

"What was that?"

"Oh, nothing." Ollie smirked. "Just saying how you'd never have had the confidence to confront Brad before a certain someone dick-matized you."

"Dick-matized?"

"Oh please. It's true. Damien brought down your walls one orgasm at a time, and now, you're becoming the boss bitch you were always meant to be. Now, if only you'd turn those powers toward him."

"Ol—"

She held up her hand. "He's going through a lot, and I feel for him, I really do. But Damien's also a grown man. He signed up to be in a relationship with you, and he doesn't get to walk away without a conversation. After everything you two shared, he owes you that much. And if he doesn't reach out soon, he's going to hear from me."

"Don't, Ollie," I said, exasperation leaking into my tone. "You don't have to get involved. This is between the two of us."

Ollie stared at me. "That's where you're wrong. He's hurting someone I love. The best woman I know. And after everything you've been through, no one gets to mess with my girl. Not even Damien Ramos."

THIRTY-FIVE

"You can give me five more, Damien."

Fuck that. My leg throbbed and sweat covered my brow. Every fiber of my being fought against my physical therapist's command, wanting nothing more than to slink back into my bed and sleep away the rest of the day.

But worse than the pain? The fucking shame that covered me like a second skin.

Chase, our team's physical therapist, stood in my guest bedroom, staring as I laid out on the floor. The room had transformed over the past couple of weeks, going from an extra bedroom to a home gym designed for my recovery. Mats lined the floor, resistance bands hung from the wall—there was even a set of parallel bars sitting on the other side of the room.

Not that I'd gotten there yet.

No, I was still working on basic fucking functions, like lifting my damn leg off the ground and putting slight weight on my knee. Last month, I would have pushed through these exercises without a thought. I pushed my body to the brink daily, running the bases and hitting a ball at almost 90 miles per hour. The knowledge of how far I'd fallen almost hurt more than the actual injury. Knowing what I'd been capable of—the limited mobility I had now—filled me with rage.

With a scoff, I dropped my leg back to the floor. "I'm fucking tapped, man."

Chase sighed as he moved to my side. He dropped beside me, helping me to sit up. "You're getting there, Damien."

"Right," I said sardonically. "Can't lift my leg more than an inch. Real fucking victory there."

"Healing takes time," he said, not for the first time. In the three weeks since my surgery, he'd reminded me of it every step of the way and celebrated even the smallest of victories. His energy was infectious, but it wasn't enough to push through the clouds shrouding my mind.

The little progress wasn't enough.

It'd never be enough to get me back on the field, back to playing ball at a professional level, in time. Weber and the rest of management stood by me during my recovery, but a player at my age, with an injury like this? They were just waiting for me to call it, to tell them I was stepping into retirement.

The end had always been on the horizon, especially as my muscles fatigued more after every season. But this injury had opened my eyes, made me realize I wasn't ready to call it, though I might not have a choice. I itched to get back on the field, wishing more than anything to be back with my team, help them gain another victory. Since I got injured, I hadn't even been able to watch a game, too fucking angry to see them out there without me.

"Have you thought about telling your family more about your recovery?" Chase said as he put the resistance bands away. I grimaced, unsure what to say. I'd flown home the week after the surgery with Chase by my side but hadn't bothered to tell everyone I was back. In fact, in the weeks since my injury, I'd barely talked to any of my friends. As much as they wanted to help, their pitying stares and empty reassurances only made me angrier. No, it was easier to keep everyone away, at least until I could face them without bitterness overwhelming me. The guys all gave me space.

Mari and Angie came around every couple of days to check in and help me tidy up around the house. They'd even brought the girls around a few times. My family tried to lift my spirits, tried to tell me how far I'd already come. But their hope was like an anchor around my neck, reminding me how far I'd fallen.

And then, there was Brianna.

Her last text sat on my phone, waiting for a response, but I couldn't bring myself to do it. I couldn't show her this new version of myself. She'd liked me because I was strong, because I'd helped to lift her up when her world seemed like it was crumbling. To bring her down into my darkness was a step back, like I was dragging her into this pit with me after all the progress she'd made. No way I'd ever do that.

I loved her too much for that.

Every day, I woke up and reached out, hoping I'd imagined the past month, that she was in the bed next to me. When my fingers stretched and found her space empty, the disappointment dragged me right back to that hospital room, after I told her I needed space. Her hazel eyes were filled with so much hurt, I almost pulled the words right back. An ache ripped through my chest, and it had only grown bigger each day.

But despite the pain, I refused to drag her down with me.

Chase leaned down, helping me get back into my knee brace, and held out his hand. Another thing I couldn't fucking do on my own: get up off my damn floor. After he helped me lower into a chair, he rubbed the back of his neck. "You should think about it, Damien. Check out the research on recovery. Having people in your corner, having that support you need? It's going to make the entire process a lot more manageable."

I just grunted, unable to voice my fears aloud. Luckily, a knock came from the door of my apartment. "Get that, would you?"

Chase just nodded, not sparing a second glance my way. He was getting frustrated? Join the fucking club. My hands clenched; I hated that this was my life. I slammed my palm against the arm of the chair, needing that jolt of pain to feel anything other than the throbbing of my knee.

"Shit, D. What the hell did that chair do to you?"

My head popped up, finding my former teammate, Jace, standing in the doorway with a smirk on his face. A duffel bag hung from his shoulder, and he'd dressed casually, like he'd just popped by after hitting the gym. I cleared my throat. "What are you doing here, Lyons?"

"Checking on your grumpy ass." He smirked. "Seda and Drobrek called, told me you've been hiding out, keeping Chase captive." He stepped inside the room, pausing when he got close to me. "It smells like the damn locker room in here."

"Yeah, fucking leg raises almost knocked me out. Pretty pathetic, right?"

"Three weeks after major surgery? That sounds like progress to me."

"Right." I scoffed. "That's what Chase keeps telling me."

When I finally looked over at Jace, I sucked in a sharp breath. It'd been months since we'd stood in the same room, and the time had been good to him. He'd put on weight, looking more like when he first joined the team. That lingering tiredness was gone from his eyes, replaced by the same cocky smile.

I shook my head. "Still haven't said what you're doing here."

"I'm here to help," Jace said, dropping his bag in the doorway and taking a seat on the floor across from me. "You want to get better? I'm here to make sure that happens. Might not have a degree, but I've been through enough PT to know how to do basic stretches."

"Got Chase for that."

"You and I both know the team needs him more." Jace leaned forward. "Besides, even if Chase was here all day, he'd never get to the real problem."

I shook my head. "What about your team?"

"Our season's over, so I'm off for a bit. Told them I needed to go visit some old friends."

"Well, as good as it is to see you, I don't need a babysitter. Tell Seda and Drobrek to fuck off, would you?"

I huffed, pushing myself out of the chair and grabbing my crutches to stabilize me. Before I got too far, Jace stepped in front of me, blocking my path. "Get out of my way, Jace."

"Nope."

I cursed under my breath. "Jace, just fucking move. I don't need this shit. Get out of my way."

"No," Jace said, more sternly this time. "When my world fell apart, you were the only one who stood by my side, the one who forced me to take a hard look at my life. Without you, fuck, I don't know where I'd be right now. So, no. I'm not going anywhere, D."

All the bravado poured out of me as I stared up at my friend, not knowing how much I needed someone before this moment. As the fight left me, I lowered myself back to the chair and dropped my head into my hands, letting my crutches fall to the floor.

"I don't know how to do this." The quiet admission broke something in me, something I'd barely had the strength to admit to anyone but myself. "Baseball's been my life for so long, and now, it's just gone. In one moment, I lost everything, and there's a chance I may never get it back."

Jace leaned forward. "I get it, man. I know it's not the same, but when I got cut from the team, it put me in a dark place, like I'd fucked up my one chance, and I'd spend the rest of my life chasing that high." He shook his head. "But it took leaving to realize it's only a part of my life. It can't define the whole thing."

"How did you do it?" I asked. "How did you move on from the game, knowing you had a lot more left to play?"

"I didn't." Jace shrugged. "I just embraced that I needed more outside of it, learned to turn off the noise and focus on the parts of it I enjoyed, left the rest behind me." He shifted forward, forcing me to meet his eyes. "You've always been a killer out on the field, D. The legend who never gave up. And now, you're going to let one setback fuck everything up? Let this injury decide you're done?" He smirked. "Not my captain, oh captain."

"Swear, if you quote that fucking movie, I'm walking out this room."

"Like to see you try, man." He pulled my crutches away. "And that movie is a classic."

"It's depressing as shit."

"Maybe, but it's also true. So you need to decide, D. Are you going to let this injury kick you in the dirt and stay down? Or are you going to fight like hell?"

I sighed, pulling my hair back from my face. He made it sound so easy, like this fight was just something I could easily overcome. Sure, I'd made progress in the week since I'd been home, but every step was almost microscopic. By the time I got better enough to walk out on the field, would the team even want me? Or would I be just another relic pulled off the reserve list for sentimental reasons?

Jace shook his head. "I can already see the gears turning in your head, convincing you not to fight. If that's the case, I'll get out of here. Don't need to get sucked into some male version of Gray Gardens."

Despite myself, I grinner. "Fuck, man. When did you become the insightful one? Last time you were here, you tried to sleep with half the women in the city, convinced you were some kind of sex god."

Jace's smile dropped away, and he shuffled on the floor. "Started talking to someone after I went back down to the minors. I'd never get back to the team if I couldn't get my head right. There's still a lot to unpack, but it's helping me look at everything differently."

My throat caught at his admission, knowing how much it took to get Jace to admit that. When I suggested therapy last year, he shut me down, refusing to even think about spilling his problems to a stranger. But the man in front of me was a far cry from the one who'd left our clubhouse without a look back. It might not have seemed like it at the time, but going back down to the minors had been the best thing to happen to Jace.

And it might be time I took his advice.

"If I promise to stop being a dick to Chase, can I have my crutches back?"

"Not yet," Jace said. "First, you're going to tell me all about the girl Seda and Drobrek warned me about, and then you're going to explain how badly you fucked that up."

THIRTY-SIX

Damien

"Man, you are so fucked."

After Chase left for the day, Jace and I moved into my living room, my leg propped up on a cushion. Jace had tried to sit in the chair opposite the couch, but I told him no. No one had sat there, not since Brianna bared herself to me, showing me how beautiful she was when she owned her pleasure. Now, I refused to let anyone else sully that memory.

In fact, she'd etched herself into every inch of my apartment. Her shampoo sat on the shelf in my shower, her favorite sweater curled up on the bench at the edge of my bed. One of her favorite romance books was still on my end table, and I hadn't moved it an inch.

Despite our insistence that our relationship had been casual, every piece was evidence to the contrary. Never had I let a woman step foot into my apartment. Talia and I had a place together in Manhattan when we were engaged, but that had never felt like home. It still hurt like hell when we boxed up all her stuff, leaving me with nothing more than the memories. After that, when I moved up here, I swore I'd never let another woman into my home, not wanting to deal with that emptiness ever again.

But just like everything else with Brianna, she'd crept into my world, leaving pieces of herself with me. And even though I'd given her every reason not to, I wasn't ready to let go of the hope she'd come back and claim them just yet.

We spent the next hour catching up. Jace filled me in on his life up in Portland. While he missed the rush of the major leagues, he'd been doing well out of the spotlight. Without the constant pressure and scrutiny, he'd kicked a lot of his darker habits, focusing instead on becoming a better ball player. And it had paid off. When Jace left, he'd dropped a ton of weight and had dark circles under his eyes, but now, there was a new life in his gaze, a lightness that had dimmed over his time on the team.

Being here with him now loosened the guilt that had plagued me since the day he left. While you never wanted anyone to get knocked back down to the minors, in Jace's case, it was the right call.

Just as I was about to say as much, a knock pounded on my door, and I stared at Jace. He stood, shaking his head as he walked over. "Don't give me that look. You're lucky they waited this long."

When he pulled the door open, Cam, Parker, and a bunch of the other guys trickled into my apartment. Even Benny joined them, holding a crock pot or something in his arms. Grabbing my crutches, I stood and moved toward them. "What the hell are you guys doing here?"

"Better question," Cam said as he smacked my shoulder, "is why the hell didn't you call us? We've had to stalk Chase to get any information about you."

I shook my head as Parker, August, and Benny came over, also patting me on the back. "Didn't want to fuck up your season with my shitty mood. Figured I'd see you guys after."

"Don't give us that shit," Parker said, throwing a bunch of bags on my counter and pulling out snacks. "We're a fucking team, cap. One of us goes down, we help him stand back up."

"Besides," Gray, our pitching coach, called out after he made his way into the kitchen, "it's team dinner. No way we were letting you miss another one." He moved closer to me. "The team needs you, captain. Needs to see you're doing okay."

"And if I'm not?"

Gray smirked at me, just as he'd done millions of times when we played together. Of everyone in the room, he'd known me the longest, considering we'd moved through the majors together for almost ten years. "You will be. No one keeps Damien Ramos off the field for long."

My smile faltered; I wished I had the same faith Gray did. But seeing my team in the same room made my resolve harden, lifting away the fog that had plagued me since I woke up in the hospital.

I nodded to Benny as he set up the crock pot. "Is that Ollie's chili? Please say yes."

"Nah," Parker answered for him. "She's too pissed to cook you anything. I even got my head bit off for coming over here."

"Ollie's pissed at me?"

Cam grimaced. "All the girls are. They're all on Team Brianna right now."

I shuffled over to the kitchen, taking a seat on the stool next to my island. The rest of the guys came over and greeted me then wandered off to find food and entertainment. The hum of the conversation didn't soften the blow of Cam's words though. "What do you mean, Team Brianna?"

Parker scoffed. "C'mon, man. You ghosting us is one thing. We all get it. But Bri? She's trying to hide it, but she's fucking hurt. The rest of the girls are just as pissed on her behalf."

I muttered a curse then ran my hand over my face. "How the hell do you guys even know about me and Bri?"

This time, it was Benny who scoffed. "Any idiot with two eyes can see you're crazy about that girl."

"Not you too, Weber," I groaned.

He shrugged as he grabbed a drink from my fridge. "Not my fault you got those heart eyes every time she came around. And when she came to the hospital, she refused to leave your side. No hiding that kind of love, Ramos."

Love. The word pinged around in my mind, a beacon in the darkness. Did Brianna love me? God, I'd hoped she felt the same, but I'd convinced myself she'd never let her walls down enough to fully fall for me. Now that Weber planted the seed in my mind, I wanted nothing more, and I hated myself for backing away before I could find out.

I swallowed, forcing my eyes back down to the counter. "Doesn't matter. I fucked up, and I doubt she wants to hear from me. Hell, I might be Team Bri at this point too."

Cam shook his head. "Nah, man. Brianna's pissed, and that's a good sign. If she didn't care, she wouldn't be so upset, and the other girls wouldn't be waging war against you."

"You need to grovel," Jace said when he came over to join the rest of us. "If you want Brianna back, you need to do some serious fucking groveling."

"What does that even mean?" I sighed, dropping my head to the back of the couch.

"You need to own that you messed up and prove you'll never do it again." Parker snapped his fingers. "Read one of those romance books she loves. Ollie's always talking about Bri's book boyfriends and how perfect they are. Beg—on your hands and knees if you have to."

I motioned to my leg. "And how the fuck am I going to do that?"

"Metaphorically, dumbass," Jace said. "Show her how much you love her. Show her you're not going anywhere."

I sat with that for a moment, trying to ignore the dark thoughts rushing through my mind. Looking down at my ruined knee, I couldn't help but wonder if she'd even want to take me back, much less if I deserved it or not. I shook my head. "Can't bring her into this mess right now, not until I get my head together."

"Is that what you think?"

I looked up, and Cam had leaned forward, resting his elbows on the counter. "You got hurt, D. And yeah, that fucking sucks. No way around that. But let me ask you something: what would hurt you more? Never stepping back on that field again or losing Brianna?"

"Losing Bri." The words left my mouth quickly, almost too quickly for me to realize them. But as I thought about it, the answer was just as clear. I'd gotten a decade of playing baseball on a professional level. That was more than most people could ever dream of. If that was it for me, I could walk away, happy I'd gotten to spend the time I had on the field.

But with Brianna, our future had only just begun. My future flashed through my mind, and for the first time, it didn't revolve around a baseball team. It was all tangled up with her.

Mornings cuddled together on the couch.

Nights spent in each other's arms.

Standing at her side as she took on the world.

I wanted more than a few hurried weeks.

I wanted *everything* with her.

"Fuck," I hissed, dropping my head into my hands. "Tell me more about this groveling."

Jace smirked, looking around at the rest of the group. They all smiled, and apprehension seized my chest. He nodded at me. "Alright, D. If you want to get your girl back, we're here to help. Just tell us where to start."

THIRTY-SEVEN

Brianna

"No, Mom, I told you—I'm fine. It's just been a long week," I groaned into the phone as I slid the key into the lock, twisting the doorknob to my apartment. After eight hours on my feet, every step seemed heavier than the last. We were two weeks into the school year, but it seemed like so much more. September was always hectic, even more so when working a new co-teacher. Thank goodness Brad and I reached that tentative truce before the year started, because otherwise, the past couple of weeks would have been unbearable.

Even with it, we'd had a few bumps, and there'd be a lot more throughout the year. Hopefully, we'd continue to work through them together and help our students grow.

"Are you sure? I could bring dinner over?"

My whole body stiffened at her offer. Sure, it was great that she wanted to take care of me for once, but her smothering, intrusive kind of care wasn't what I needed right now. Quiet. Peace. All the things that called to me from inside my apartment.

For the past month, I'd been avoiding her, not even attending church on Sunday. While I missed the community, I didn't miss the judgmental looks and whispers about my former marriage. Todd had been attending, which only added to the reasons I refused to go. Despite my brother telling him to back off, he continued to ask about me, wondering how I'd been. Jason tried to intervene, but Todd insisted he was just curious. I had no idea why he was suddenly so invested in my well-being, but I didn't like it.

As I shoved the door open, I continued the conversation with my mother, "Tonight's not a great night for me to come over. Can we do something next weekend?"

"Fine." She sighed. "Let me know what works for your schedule, and I'll cook something you like."

"Thanks, Mom."

"Don't need to thank me," she answered, muttering something to my niece and nephew in the background. "Anything else new with you? Everything good in the city?"

I tensed, wanting to tell her how much my life had changed in a few short weeks. Brad and I were finding our footing together, and I felt more confident at work than ever before. While I'd always let my work speak for itself in the past, now, I'd become more vocal, only taking on tasks I wanted to instead of letting the guilt force me into it.

But outside of work, my world was bleak. Between Todd showing up at my church, and the blocked number that had been calling me, I was having a hard time sleeping, unable to shake the feeling that something was off with him. And then there was the loneliness and heartache that Damien had left behind. Every day, I hoped it would get a little better, but it only got worse. Time was supposed to heal all wounds, but this one was still festering and raw. No matter what I tried, it never seemed like it would get better. I missed him—missed everything about him. Missed his touch, missed his laugh, missed seeing him, just talking about everything and anything under the sun.

The only sign of life had been the wilting bouquet by my door, the ones he'd sent on the first day of school. Even though the mere sight of his name annoyed me, I couldn't bring myself to throw them away, wanting to believe this subtle sign meant he might miss me too.

However, with my mother's reaction to my divorce, I refused to tell her anything about Damien. Those memories were too precious to me to be sullied by her judgment. Instead, I forced on my fakest cheery voice and smiled into the phone.

"All good here, Mom. Just getting back into my routine after the summer. You know how it goes."

We exchanged a little more small talk as I shucked off my layers and dropped my overloaded teacher bag by the door, in desperate need of couch therapy. My pajamas, a deliciously smutty romance novel, and a pile of snacks were calling my name. After my mother ended the call, I turned around and walked through the entryway, scrolling through my emails, not bothering to look up. "Hey Ol, you home? I'm thinking about ordering something for dinner."

"Yes," Ollie groaned as she walked into the living room, dressed in her favorite kitten pajamas. "But only if you promise nothing healthy. I've been going through growth reports all afternoon, and I desperately need some grease to cut through the brain fog."

"I'm on it." I chuckled as I pulled up the delivery app, scanning through our options. But before I could click the first item, a knock came from the door.

Ollie arched her brow. "Okay, either that's the best service ever, or I blanked and ordered a pound of fries already."

"Or someone else is here," I mused as I walked back down the entry hallway, stopping to check the peephole. When I glanced through it, my heart stuttered in my chest. I pushed off the door, unsure if I believed the sight in front of me. *Damien.*

Ollie joined me at the door. "Well, who is it?" She pushed me to the side, gasping when she saw Damien standing there. Without waiting for me to say anything, she ripped the door open, glaring at the man in front of us. Like a coward, I tucked behind her where I could see them but he couldn't see me, trying to catch my breath. "You have a lot of fucking nerve, showing up here."

"Good to see you, too, Ollie," he chuckled, shuffling on his feet. "Can I talk to Bri?"

"Why?" My roommate crossed her arms across her chest. "Finally decided to give her the time of day? Must be a fucking miracle."

"Ollie..."

"Don't," she said, holding up her hand. "Save your charming smile for someone who still likes you, Ramos. You've put yourself on the top of my shit list."

"Trust me, no one hates me more than myself right now. But please, Ol. Let me in. I need to talk to her." He swallowed. "I need to explain myself."

Ollie glanced over her shoulder at me, and in that moment, I knew she'd kick him out if I asked. If I hadn't loved Ollie before, I definitely did now. She'd been at my side for the past month, my constant shoulder to cry on. No judgment, just unwavering support. As she studied my face,

I nodded, needing to talk to him just as much. I couldn't keep living in limbo, unsure of where we stood.

She stepped to the side, letting him into our home, but before he spotted me, she held up her hand. "This is your last chance, Damien. You mess this up, and I'll make your life a living hell."

He smiled sadly at her. "It already is."

As Damien crossed over the threshold, his dark eyes met mine. My heart pounded in my chest, so loud, I was sure everyone else in the room could pick up on it. It felt like just yesterday we'd shared this space, since he'd crawled into my bed and held me through the night.

But time had taken its toll on him.

Damien seemed more disheveled than the last time I saw him, his dark hair now curled at the edges, brushing the tops of his shoulders. His facial hair had gone from a dusting to almost a full beard, and I had to admit—I liked it. It was a rawer version of him, one without the shiny veneer of the Erie Hawks on his shoulders.

The last time we'd seen each other, it had been in the hospital room almost a month ago, when he asked me for space. The words had cracked open all my barely-healed wounds, sending me to a dark place. Heading back to New York was one of the hardest moments of my life, every mile away from him tugging at the ties in my heart. But even as I sobbed into my pillow, my naïve heart convinced me it was temporary, that Damien needed me to be strong—to hold out hope until he was ready to face his new reality.

However, with every passing day, that hope dwindled until all that remained were embers, painful memories of empty promises in the dark. It had become clear that while I'd clung to Damien in my darkest hours, he didn't trust me enough to do the same.

Sometime over the past week, I'd made peace with his choice. After all, I'd spent so much time fighting this— fighting us. Why would he think I wanted to stick around? And why would he even want to? Our arrangement had been born out of convenience, a way for him to spend time with someone without affecting his baseball schedule.

Now, that wasn't as much of an issue. Damien wouldn't be traveling for a while, and maybe he'd realized he wanted someone more, someone to build a life with. While even I could see my growth over the past few months, it was no secret my divorce damaged my heart. Maybe after his injury, with everything else in upheaval, Damien had decided I wasn't worth the fight.

These thoughts had plagued me ever since I came home, since the first unanswered message to Damien. The longer the silence stretched, the more I'd convinced myself of those dark truths until I could barely breathe at all, sure I'd never see Damien again.

And now, he stood in my home, in my city. I desperately wanted to crawl to him, wanted to hold him tight, to beg him never to let me go. I wanted his touch, his taste, his love, wanted him to overwhelm me in the best way, especially after so much time apart.

The anger in my chest ebbed and flowed, unable to handle the discrepancy between my brain and the rest of my body. Why did he have to look so good? It would have been so much easier to stay mad at him if he'd just let himself go.

I crossed my arms over my chest to stop myself from reaching out for him. "What are you doing here, Damien?"

"I came to see you."

He stepped closer, and I finally noticed the contraption on his knee. It looked like a smaller brace than the one he'd had at the hospital, which had to be a good sign. My heart ached at the sight, knowing how much the injury had cost him. But in the aftermath, he'd used his pain to break us apart, forcing me away to fight his battles all alone.

I swallowed, keeping my face as neutral as possible. "That was kind of you, but it was unnecessary. How's your leg healing?"

Damien's dark eyes met mine, and the longing etched in them almost knocked me to the ground. "It's fine. Still throbs and aches, but I'm getting better. PT's been kicking my ass, but I'm getting there. Healing takes time."

"Glad to hear it," I said, stepping toward the entry hallway. "But if you don't mind, I have a lot to do."

"Just a few minutes, please." Damien swallowed and ran his hand through his hair. "Five minutes, and then you don't ever have to talk to me again."

Ollie glanced over at me, arching a brow—*do you want me to kick him out?* I subtly shook my head. *Not yet.* As hard as it was, I needed to hear him out.

"I'm going into my room. Let me know if you need anything." She stopped in front of Damien. "Don't pull any more stunts, Ramos. You have no idea what I'm capable of. No one hurts my girl and gets away with it, not even you."

I grimaced, waiting for Damien to bite back a reply to Ollie's harsh words. Instead, he placed his hand on her shoulder. "Glad she has you, Ol."

Her grimace fell away, and she stared at him as if she wanted to say something, but he'd killed every comeback. She turned around, squeezing my hand before walking back into her bedroom and shutting the door.

Once we were alone, I turned and walked into the living room, already overwhelmed by the growing tension. Space. I needed space. Otherwise, I didn't know if I'd fall apart or fall into Damien's arms. Neither seemed like the right option.

As soon as I got to the other side of the living room, I turned to face Damien. "Okay, you have five minutes. What do you have to say?"

"I'm sorry, Bri."

THIRTY-EIGHT

Brianna

"I'm sorry, Bri."

Damien's quiet words cut through my defenses, striking me in the heart. Tears tickled the corners of my eyes, but I forced them back down, determined to keep up my unflappable exterior. Even though inside, I was crumbling.

"Thank you for the apology, but like I said, it's unnecessary." I smiled tightly. "You needed to focus on getting better, and you needed space for that. I understand."

Damien cursed under his breath then stepped forward, holding onto the edge of my couch for support. "Brianna, come on. Talk to me. Yell at me. Fuck, scream at me about what a fuck-up I've been. God knows I deserve it. But don't stand there, acting like...."

"I'm not acting like anything, Damien." I sighed, rubbing the bridge of my nose. Frustration nipped at me, wishing he would just let this go, because standing here was killing me. Being around him but keeping this wall between us? It physically hurt, and every moment he stood in front of me, demanding something I couldn't give, only hurt more.

It would have been so easy to accept his apology and go back to the way things had been between us, to let his words soothe the ache burrowing in my chest. But I'd been here before, heard too many pretty lies to cover up the hurt. While I knew Damien was nothing like my ex-husband, he'd hurt me all the same. Worse, honestly. When my marriage to Todd fell apart, the pain came from the fear of failure, from the number of years I'd invested, only to walk away with nothing.

But if these past few weeks showed me anything, Todd never had the power to truly break my heart. My spirit? My confidence? Yeah, he'd splintered those. While I'd loved him once, it had never been that soul-consuming, all-encompassing kind of love. It was born of quiet moments, shared experiences, and the right timing.

Nothing like what I shared with Damien.

From the start, the odds were stacked against us because of my bitter divorce and his commitment-phobic ways, all signs we should never have lasted beyond that first night. Yet, somehow, my damaged heart had latched on to him, letting him in deeper than anyone else had ever gone before.

Damien alone had the power to break me.

As if he could read the break in my resolve, he made his way over to me. His nearness was too much, too consuming. So, I took the coward's way out and tucked into the kitchen, using the island to keep the distance between us. But it wasn't enough. Damien's eyes darkened as he followed me, standing on the other side of the kitchen with a determination I'd only seen when he was on the field.

"What are you doing?" My hands wobbled, and I steadied them on the counter, forcing myself to meet his eyes. "You apologized, I accepted. I don't know what else there is to say. You should go, Damien."

"No."

I huffed out an annoyed breath. "You asked for five minutes, and I gave them to you. But let's not draw this out any more. I'll ask the girls to back off, and you can go back to normal, like what it was before this whole mess started."

"Sorry, angel, but I can't do that. There's no going back to a life without you, not for me."

I shook my head, frustration lighting me up inside. "This was only supposed to be casual, remember? No feelings, no promises. And now it's over, Damien."

"Is that what you think?"

I pressed my hands further into the stone. "It doesn't matter. You need to heal and get back to work. That should be your only priority right now."

He lifted his dark eyes to meet mine. There was so much written in his expression. Pain, longing—*regret*, all the emotions I didn't want to see. This whole situation would have been easier if I could vilify him. But as I stood close enough to pick up the subtle, masculine scent of his body wash, his pain fused with my own, telling me his heart was just as broken as mine.

My chin wobbled. "I can't do this, Damien."

He reached out, straining to take my hand in his. Just a slight touch made my thighs clench. The rush of longing made my knees weaken, and all I wanted was to collapse into his arms, but my pride refused to let me.

"Why?" I asked, my voice hardly over a whisper. "Five weeks, Damien. I'm trying to understand, trying to put myself in your situation, but I can't. Didn't you trust me to be there for you? Because damn it, Damien." I squeezed my eyes shut, trying to keep my hardened walls. But as it always seemed to be with Damien, they crumbled into dust, letting the weeks of heartache come straight to the surface. "You should have trusted me. I would have been there for you, every step of the way, and you just shut me out like I didn't matter to you."

"You are the *only* thing who matters, Bri." Damien's words made my head snap up, watching as he rounded the island and came into my space. "Look, angel, I don't have a good reason. I wish I did, but when I shut you out, I shut everyone out. It had nothing to do with trusting you. Because I do, more than anything."

I scoffed, turning away from him. "You have a terrible way of showing it."

"Tell me about it," Damien muttered. "But it was never about you, Bri. It was me and the dark places I went to in my mind. Baseball's been my world ever since I was a kid. For thirty-five years, it's been the reason I got out of bed in the morning, and with one stupid move, I threw my career away, all because I wanted to show up the other team. It fucked me up."

"I get that," I said. "And I don't want to hold your recovery against you, Damien. I can't even imagine what that was like, your entire world being ripped out from under you."

He stepped closer and took my elbow, turning me slowly to face him. I sucked in a breath at the determined expression on his face. "That's the thing, Bri. I thought baseball was my reason for living, but that was before you literally crashed into my arms. Now, if I never walked out on that field again, yeah, it'd be disappointing, but I'd be grateful for the time I'd had on the team. And the biggest reason for that?" I stared up at him, watching as the corners of his lips curled up. "It led me to you."

My mouth dropped open, trying to process his words, but all that came out was a squeaky, "Me?"

He chuckled as he brushed his knuckles along my cheekbone. "Yeah, Bri. You. You're the most important person in my life, and I'm so sorry I lost sight of that for a little while."

"But we made rules," I spluttered. My brain couldn't take the abrupt shift. It latched on to those words, needing something to keep me stable under the weight of his declaration.

Damien chuckled. "And we bulldozed right through them, didn't we?" His dark eyes held mine, and all the humor died in his expression. "Because you are everything to me, angel. I love you, Brianna. Pretty sure you've had my heart in your hands since the moment we met."

He loved *me?* My heart pumped furiously in my chest—overwhelmed by his admission. God, I wanted to believe him, wanted to trust in what we'd shared. Despite the doubts, despite the anxiety—what we'd shared had been real, one of the most real experiences of my life.

But fear held me back.

"I want to believe you, Damien. I really do. But if I've learned anything from my past, it's that words are easy. Your actions matter more." I stood up straighter and placed my hand on his chest, forcing him to step away from me. "And right now, I don't trust you."

Damien's skin paled. "Don't say that, angel."

"You should go, Damien. I promise, I won't make things weird between us. Maybe we can eventually be friends again, but right now, that's all I can handle."

Damien's eyes searched mine, looking for any sign of hesitancy. If he'd looked hard enough, he would have found it, but I'd let my heart guide me for far too long, and it had only led to pain. Now, I had to be more rational—put my well-being over the fickle organ in my chest. Right now, it was screaming for me to get some space from Damien.

He reached out, brushing his thumb along my jaw. "I'll take you in any way I can have you, Bri. But I'm not done fighting for you—for us. I spent five weeks without you, and that's enough to know I want a lifetime with you."

I slammed my eyes shut. "Damien, you need to stop saying things like that."

"Never, angel. I'll give you time, but I'm not going far. I'm gonna prove to you that you can trust me again."

THIRTY-NINE

Damien

"What are you doing here?"

Brianna's hazel eyes met mine, and I held my breath, still getting used to being close to her again. It had been only two days since our talk in her apartment, and I was done waiting for her to come to me. I'd messaged her a bunch of times since she insisted I leave, but they all sat unanswered, and as much as it stung, I deserved it.

But I'd never been good at standing on the sidelines.

As Brianna stepped out into the autumn air, her eyes lit up, either from annoyance or confusion, I wasn't sure. Her hazel eyes were wide, and I found myself lost in them. God, I missed her. When we were apart, I'd convinced myself I played up our connection in my mind, that it couldn't have been as powerful as I remembered.

I was wrong.

Even with ten feet between us, she called out to me, igniting a hurricane of lust and longing in my veins. Desperation clawed through me, missing the way she felt against my chest, needing to feel her nails tracing my spine. I hated that I'd only gotten to make love to her once—to taste her lips and know I owned her heart as much as she owned mine. But then, the next day, my world shattered, and like a fool, I let it ruin what had taken months to build between us.

Everything else in my life had returned to normal. I spent my nights with the team, rebuilding the bonds that had fractured when I left without a word. The PT sessions were grueling, but I pushed through them, determined to get myself back to peak condition. A week ago, I'd finally gotten clearance from the doctor to lose the crutches, and it seemed like the biggest victory so far. The brace would have to stick around for a while longer, but I wasn't about to take it for granted. Just being able to stand on my own brought tears to my eyes—finally proof I'd made progress.

And while that had seemed like the greatest fight of my life, none of that progress mattered without Brianna at my side. I could handle anything—the PT, not being able to play baseball, all of it. None of it compared to the pain of losing her, especially knowing it was all my fault.

But I'd meant what I said the last time we spoke. I wasn't done fighting for her. I'd never be done fighting for her. She might not want me right now, but I was a stubborn bastard. For most of my life, I applied that determination to baseball, letting it fuel me as I walked onto the field.

After I left Brianna's that night, I'd met up with the team and made a game plan to help me win back her trust. Although her words might have said we were done, I knew her better than I knew myself. She was hiding behind the hurt, letting that protect her heart when I'd broken it. While I hated myself for putting those thoughts in her mind, I was determined to prove it was a mistake, not a pattern.

I pushed off my car, walking to the entrance of Brianna's apartment building. Her steps had faltered when she spotted me, and now, she stood there, almost frozen in place. As I moved toward her, I took in her outfit. It was a far cry from the athletic gear she usually wore on the weekend, trading it in for a sleek black pencil skirt and a dark green silk shirt, topped off with a charcoal peacoat. The color played up the greens in her eyes, and once again, I found myself lost in them.

Clearing my throat, I moved in front of her, handing out the coffee I'd picked up earlier. "It's Sunday morning."

She stared down at the coffee before taking it with a long sigh. "Yes, Damien, I know that, but you still haven't answered my question."

"On Sundays, you meet up with your family for service. Thought I'd go with you."

Brianna's eyes flared. "What? How did you even—"

"Angel, you'd leave my bed at the same time every Sunday, telling me you had to go to church or your mother would disown you. Did you think I didn't listen?"

She chewed her lower lip. That was exactly what she'd thought, but as I talked with the guys, I realized I knew so much about Brianna's world, though I was yet to be an actual part of it. She'd gotten used to doing everything on her own, and while I'd never stand in her way to fight her own battles, I sure as hell would stand at her side.

Brianna snapped herself out of her daze then shook her head. "You are not coming with me."

I shrugged as I turned back toward my car. "Says online everyone's welcome. I think that includes me." Her mouth dropped open, and she spluttered some sounds, none coherent enough to form a word. I pulled open the passenger-side door and motioned for her to get in. "Are you coming or what, angel?"

"What is this, Damien?" she hissed as she stepped closer, her eyes darting between me and the offered ride.

"This is me fighting for you, angel. Told you I wouldn't let you go that easily. Besides, I'm selfish when it comes to you, and I'll take any time I can get, even if it's just a ride to your church."

She stared at me, and I hated the uncertainty in her eyes. As much as I wanted to reach out to her, it needed to be her choice. I waited with bated breath as she stood on the curb, praying she'd take the step toward me. With a beep of her phone, she groaned and climbed into my car. "You're *not* staying. This is just a ride because I can't be late."

"Whatever you say, angel."

"THIS COUNTS AS STALKING. You realize that, right?"

Brianna's eyes reached a new fever pitch as I dropped into the seat next to her. While the rest of the room hummed with conversation, she'd found a seat at the furthest table in the back, not engaging with anyone else. Without another thought, I shifted my chair closer to her and dug into the breakfast spread I'd gathered from the buffet. I groaned as I bit into the eggs. "Damn, these are pretty good. Usually, the eggs at these things are trash."

Brianna reached out and snatched my fork away. "No. You shouldn't be here, Damien. These brunches are for members only."

"That's not what they told me." I pointed the knife over

to the group of women I'd befriended during the service. Brianna thought I'd left after I'd dropped her off, but I'd snuck in, determined to be there for her, even when she didn't ask for it. While she darted up to the front row to sit with her family, I'd tucked into the back, among a group of women in their eighties. They'd latched on to me almost immediately. Their congregation suffered from a lack of young men among their parishioners, with way too many eligible women. I'd laughed off their matchmaking attempts, telling them I was already in love with someone.

Even though she seemed to hate me right now.

Brianna followed my line of sight and sucked in a sharp breath. "Did they say anything about me?"

"What?" I said, narrowing my gaze. "No, but have they said something *to* you?"

She shook her head. "Nothing important."

"If it matters to you, Bri, it's fucking important. Now, tell me what they said."

"First—don't curse so loudly. Not here." She sighed, turning away so her eyes could avoid mine. Anger clenched my heart at the sight, knowing shame when I spotted it. Brianna continued, but her voice shook with each word. "Divorce might be pretty common now, but people around here still act like it's a cardinal sin. When I left my husband, even though *he* cheated on *me*, they treated me like a pariah. As much as I try to ignore them—it hurts."

My hands clenched in my lap. "I'll kill them."

Brianna chuckled. "I shouldn't have said anything. Bad enough to be divorced and over thirty. Now I brought someone threatening murder into our church."

Despite the humor in her words, I could sense the hurt lingering underneath. For too long, the world had forced its judgments onto Brianna's lap. But now that I was here, I refused to let it happen again. I reached out and took her hand. "I'm glad you told me, Bri. Promise, no bloodshed today, but I can't promise to keep my cool if they say anything like that to you in front of me."

"You don't have to defend me, Damien."

I reached out, shifting her chair so she faced me. Her hazel eyes met mine, and the same familiar spark ignited between us. She tucked her lower lip between her teeth. She felt it too. I sighed, trying to force down the lust building in my veins. "You've had to fight your own battles for long enough, angel. Let me stand at your side."

She sucked in a sharp breath then shook her head. "Stop saying things like that, Damien. It's making me forget why I was mad at you in the first place."

"Kinda the plan, angel," I chuckled, bringing her hand up to my lips. As I kissed her knuckles, I said, "But I mean every word, Bri. When you give me back your heart, I'm going to protect it like my own."

"When?"

I chuckled as I pulled back. "Yeah, angel. *When.* Because you might not be ready to admit it just yet, but you loved me once, before I fu—messed everything up. And if it's the last thing I do, I'm going to prove to you I'm worthy of your love."

Brianna's hazel eyes shimmered as she looked back at me. "You've always been worthy of it, Damien. That was never the problem."

But before I could respond, her gaze darted over my shoulder, and her entire body tensed. She dropped my hand and shoved her chair away from me. I would've been offended if it weren't for her expression. She'd pulled back those walls I'd spent so much time dismantling, schooling her features into an impenetrable mask. It took me back to when we first met, when Brianna guarded her joy and kept everything close to the vest.

"Are they coming over?" I asked, referring to the group of women I'd befriended earlier but who were now at the top of my shit list.

"No, worse," Brianna whispered. "It's my family."

FORTY

Brianna

As soon as my mother's footsteps faltered, my stomach sank. Her eyes narrowed on Damien, taking in his imposing frame and the tattoos that stuck out under the sleeve of his shirt. Her lip curled before her dark eyes turned toward me. Even with half a foot between us, her confusion and disappointment were palpable. *Please let the floor swallow me up right now.*

Damien didn't bother to turn around, simply keeping his eyes on me. As he searched my expression, he whispered, "Do you want me to go, Bri?"

I paused, unsure how to answer. The answer should have been easy—yes, please go, before my mother makes you rethink everything between us. My mother was notorious for her invasive questions and judgmental stares, which was nothing I wanted to subject Damien to right now. But the words refused to come. As confusing as it was to be around Damien, I didn't want him to leave. Somehow, having him here was like pulling on my favorite worn blanket, keeping me from spiraling.

"No," I whispered, offering him an apologetic grin. "But you might want to after you meet my mother."

He smiled at me, some of the earlier tension melting from his shoulders. "You're not getting rid of me that easily, angel. Gonna have to meet her eventually."

His words made my cheeks flush, and I stood to greet my mother and brother. Jason's wife and kids had left right after the service ended, needing to run errands to get ready for the week. But he'd stuck around, and a small part of me wondered if it was because of Todd's recent appearances. As Damien turned around to greet them, my brother sucked in a sharp breath. "Holy fuck, that's Damien Ramos."

"Jason," my mother chastised, but her words held a little mirth, "don't talk like that."

"Sorry, Ma," he spluttered, shooting his arm out toward us. "But do you know who this guy is?"

"No," she said, slowly perusing Damien. "Should I?"

"Mom, Jason, this is my friend, Damien. He had some free time this morning and joined us for worship."

He stood and held out his hand to greet my family. My mother took it reluctantly, barely touching him with the tips of her fingers. My brother was another story—he clasped Damien's hand with both hands, shaking it vigorously. "Mr. Ramos, I'm a huge fan. I've been following you for years."

"Thanks, man. I appreciate it, but it's just Damien." He leaned down to meet my eyes. "You should come out for a game sometime."

"Are you serious? Yeah, Mr. Ram—I mean, Damien. I'd love that."

As my mother asked Damien his thoughts on the service, Jason continued to stare at him with stars in his eyes, in complete disbelief that one of his favorite baseball players stood in our church's community room.

I nudged him in the side. "You okay over there?"

"No," Jason answered. "I'm freaking the fuck out. How on Earth do you know *the* Damien Ramos?"

I rolled my eyes. "My roommate is friends with Parker Drobrek. I've become friends with a lot of guys on the team."

"Yeah, but this is different. It's one thing to hang out with them after a game. But he's here...meeting Mom." My brother's eyes widened impossibly larger as he stared down at me. "Are you dating Damien Ramos? Please say yes. Actually, no, I don't really want to picture my favorite player with my sister, even if it means tickets for life."

I smacked my hand against his shoulder, and he let out a little oomph. "First, stop calling him by his full name. He doesn't need any help in the ego department." My head turned, and I caught Damien smirking at me. My cheeks heated at the unspoken words in his gaze. "And second, we're just friends."

"Right," Jason chuffed. "Hate to break it to you, Bri, but friends don't look at each other like that."

I tried to argue, but the words refused to come out. Damien's dark eyes had pinned me to the spot; even if I could've broken away, I didn't know if I would. Being here with him, having him in my life, seemed right, more than it had ever been before. I'd always been on the outside, the member who never quite fit in with everyone else. But with Damien beside me, I didn't care about anyone else's comments or judgments. As long as he kept looking at me like I was special to him, no one else in the room mattered.

"So," my mother's accented voice carried over our conversation, "Ramos doesn't sound Greek."

Damien shook his head. "It's not, Mrs. Sideris. I was

born in Puerto Rico, but I've been living here for almost fifteen years."

She nodded, but her eyes held no warmth. "Then what exactly are you doing at our church?"

"I'm here to support, Bri," Damien said. "It's nice to meet you both. Brianna has told me a lot about you."

She scoffed at his comment, judgment written across the faded lines of her face. It twisted something deep within me—shame my mother took everything at such face value. After all, she'd done the same thing with Todd. She saw his style, took in his family, and decided he was worthy. And yet, he'd turned out to be one of the biggest mistakes of my life. Damien might not seem like her ideal man for her daughter, but he had the biggest heart out of everyone I knew, and I hated her a little for not being able to see that.

My mother arched her brow, looking over at me. "You never answered your brother's question, Brianna. Are you dating this man?"

I squeaked out a lackluster "no" at the same time as Damien said, "yes". I turned and glared at him, finding nothing but humor reflected at me. Swallowing my pride, I turned back to my mother. "It's complicated, but right now, we're just friends."

"That's enough." She held up her hand. "This is not the time or place to discuss the complications in your love life."

"Of course, Mom."

Damien and Jason started talking about the Hawks, and my mother came right over to me, taking my arm in her hand. She twisted me away from the rest of the crowd and lowered her voice. "This is highly inappropriate. What would you have done if Todd had been here? You can't drag some stranger into our lives just because you're upset about his wedding. Be more mature than that, Brianna."

Her tone was properly chastising, and I tucked my chin, hating that it just took a few words to pull me right back into my childhood. I was about to offer a muttered apology when Damien stepped in front of me. "Don't speak to her like that."

My mother's mouth dropped open. "Excuse me?"

"Do not speak to Brianna like that. She did nothing wrong. If she wants me here, this is where I'll be, even if you think it's inappropriate." He lowered his voice. "As for that idiot ex-husband of hers, I wish he'd come. I wish I had a chance to look him in the eyes and thank him for making the biggest mistake of his life."

"How dare you—"

"I wasn't done," Damien bit out. "Because the real question is, how dare *you*? Your daughter works so damn hard to make everyone around her happy, and do you ever stop to think about what makes her happy? Or are you too busy judging her choices to even consider it?"

My mother's mouth dropped open, and she turned, perhaps seeing me for the very first time. But before she could say anything that might ease the tension between us, her eyes darted around the room. While we were tucked far enough away from any prying ears, I should have known she'd never let down her defenses in public.

"As I said, this is neither the time nor place for this conversation." She narrowed her eyes at Damien before turning back toward me. "We will discuss this later. I expect you to be ready by five on Friday."

I couldn't speak, so all I did was nod, hating that the words I wanted to say stalled on my tongue. As they walked away, Damien's hand engulfed mine, pulling me out of the room. Once we broke out into the gardens, he twisted me to face him.

"I'm so sorry, Bri. I didn't think—"

I cut off his words with my kiss. He let out a sharp breath before relaxing into my embrace, and his hands found my waist. His touch soothed the broken pieces inside my heart, clicking back together, just needing him close to feel whole again. But the reality of our situation crashed to the forefront of my mind. I leaned back, needing to get my head together. God, being around this man was turning me into the queen of mixed signals.

The sudden thought caused me to push him back, needing some space to get my thoughts together. I shook my head. "I'm sorry. I shouldn't have done that, not until—"

"Don't." Damien silenced me with his forefinger on my chin, tilting it up so I had no choice but to meet his eyes. "I'm trying here, Bri. I really am. And you know I'll keep fighting for you, as long as it takes. But I can't keep fighting you."

"Me?" I asked, snapping out of his grip.

Damien sighed and placed his hands on his hips. "I fucked up, Bri. I own that. But when are you going to stop pushing me away? I told you I love you, told you I'm not going anywhere. But at some point, I need you to meet me halfway."

"Do you..." My voice trailed off, unable to finish the thought. "What are you saying?"

"I need something, Bri. A sign, something to show me you're in this too. That you're fighting for us just as much as I am. I can't keep standing here, begging for you to give me a chance. It hurts too fucking much." His dark eyes met mine, and the pain lurking in them knocked the air from my lungs. "Tell me you don't love me. Tell me I'm wasting my time. Because I'd do anything for you, Bri, but I can't keep going without something."

I clutched my hand to my chest, hating how his words cut so deep. All I wanted was to forgive him, to lay down my walls and let him back in. Although he'd lowered them, they were still standing strong, keeping me from laying my heart in his hands. "You're not wasting your time," I whispered, averting my eyes. "I want to be with you, Damien, I really do. I'm struggling to trust you right now, but that doesn't mean..." My voice cut off, unable to complete the sentence.

That doesn't mean I don't love you.

I shifted closer to him and placed my hands on his chest. His heart pounded against the fabric of his shirt, so hard, I could feel it in my fingers. He was here, being open, laying his heart out for me, unsure if I would protect or crush it. "Please don't give up on me, Damien. I just need time."

Damien searched my gaze, and I prayed he could see the emotions behind my words, how hard it was for me to admit them, though I felt them all the same. Eventually, his eyes shuttered closed, and he dropped his forehead against mine. "Then I'll keep waiting."

I let out a choked sob, relief like I'd never known overcoming me. My fingers dug into his shirt, and we held each other for a long moment. Eventually, others started to pour into the garden, so we broke apart. But before Damien could leave, I grabbed his hand. "Thank you for waiting for me. I'm trying. I promise."

"No need to thank me for that," Damien sighed. "There's no timeline when it comes to you, Bri."

FORTY-ONE

Brianna

"There's no timeline when it comes to you, Bri."

Damien's words played through my mind like an anthem, and no matter how hard I tried, they refused to leave. All day, even as I tried to focus on teaching, I kept picturing his expression, the resigned hope I'd get over my fears and come back to him.

The Hawks game droned on in the background, coming from Ollie's laptop perched on the edge of my bed. I had no interest in watching, but she insisted, claiming she needed moral support as she watched Parker. Honestly, she surprised me when she announced she wouldn't be going to the game, even though it was at home. She claimed to have a big meeting in the morning, but I felt it had more to do with my plans for the night and her being a great friend than anything work-related.

"For the record, I still think this is a terrible idea." The clothes in my closet muffled the sound of Ollie's voice. She'd been in there for almost ten minutes, trying to find something for me to wear to Todd's wedding. "But if you're sure about going, we need to find the hottest dress you own."

"Ol, trust me, there's nothing that impressive in my closet." I thumbed the fabric of my black sheath dress. "This is probably the nicest thing I own."

She pouted as she pulled her head out, and then she snapped her fingers. "Then it's a good thing shopping is my greatest stress relief. I've got a bunch of dresses you can try on."

"Have I mentioned you're the best?"

"Not today." Ollie smirked as she walked out the door. But before she got too far, she stopped, tapping her nails on the frame. "Before I go, I'm calling in the bestie card right now, and I need you to do me a favor."

"Okay..." I drawled, frowning as I turned to face her.

She sighed and shook her head. "Tell me why you're going tonight."

"Ol, I already told you. I promised my mom I'd go and at least show my face for a little bit, prove to everyone I haven't turned into a bitter spinster. Besides—she made some good points. It'll be a good olive branch between our families. We might not be together anymore, but our families run in the same circles. In the end, I can sacrifice one night if it makes them happy."

"Yeah, but is it going to make you happy?"

My eyes darted down to my toes. *No, not even a little.* Tonight was not about me—nor should it be. I didn't even truly understand why Todd had invited me. We were the past, and tonight should be about him moving into the future with his new wife. I'd love to say he invited me to keep the peace, but at this point, it felt more like a dig, as if he wanted to show how quickly he'd rebuilt his world while I was still finding my footing in mine.

Ollie sighed at my non-answer. "If you really want to go, I'll support you. Hell, I'll throw on my dancing shoes and walk into that reception, zero fucks given. But at some point, Bri, you're going to have to stop doing what everyone expects from you and do what you actually want to do." She stepped closer, taking my hand in hers. "So tell me, if you could be anywhere right now, where would it be?"

With Damien.

But I was too much of a coward.

Which was the same reason I was about to go to my ex-husband's wedding instead of running into the arms of the man I loved.

Staring back at the mirror, I took in the sleek lines of the classic black dress. I used to love it, but now, it was all wrong. It looked like I was in mourning, as if I still clung to that last vestige of my old world. But like everything else from that time period, it no longer fit, too tight in some areas and loose in others. It fit the girl my parents wanted me to be—the one who desperately wished for their approval, even giving up my happiness to keep the peace.

Over the last few months, there'd been a shift within me, but those past desires had teeth, and it wasn't as easy as I had hoped to ignore my family's wishes.

I turned back toward Ollie, running my damp palms along the lines of my dress. "You know what my answer would be, Ollie, but it's not that easy."

"Why not?"

"You *know* why, Ol." I shook my head. "Remember when Damien was enemy number one? Don't think I didn't notice your search history. Laxatives? Really? Remind me not to get on your bad side."

Ollie smiled evilly, shrugging without a hint of shame. "Oh, I think he still has some work to do. But then again, he comes here every night, with dinner for both of us, and you know food is my love language. More than that—I see the two of you together. You spend hours talking, and it's like no one else is in the room." She leaned closer toward me. "Let me ask you this: ever since he came back around—has he seemed like he's holding back?"

My brow furrowed. "No, not at all."

"And has he been honest and open about everything?"

"Yeah..."

"He's not holding anything back, Bri," Ollie sighed. "And I don't know if you could see it through your heartbreak goggles, but that man fell to pieces without you. He looked like hell when he came here. And now, even though his heart's been broken, he's right back at it, fighting for you. He's not afraid of going through that pain again."

She took in my expression then grabbed my hand and led me over to the bed. "I'm not one to believe men, because, well, they're men, but Damien's kept all his other promises to you, Bri. When he messed up, he owned it. He didn't hide or try to pass the blame. He's been there for you every step of the way, no matter how much you try to push him away. But the question is—how long do you want to keep punishing him?"

"That's not what I'm doing," I snapped, shifting to face her. "At least, I don't think I'm trying to punish him."

"I know you don't," Ollie said. "And that's why you're getting the kid gloves right now. If I thought you were doing it on purpose, we'd be having a very different conversation. It's okay to be scared of love, Bri, but you're letting that fear hold you back, punishing him while protecting yourself." Her brown eyes searched mine. "You're not afraid of trusting, Damien. You're afraid of trusting yourself."

Before I could answer, the screen panned to the Hawks' dugout, and my mouth fell open. "Is that?"

"Wow, look at that," Ollie mused, sitting back on the

couch with an amused smirk. "Guess it's a good thing we turned on the game."

But I barely heard her, too focused on how Damien's wide smile filled the screen. For the first time since he'd gotten injured, he was back at a game. My smile came out, so proud he'd taken that step. It had to be hard for him to be so close to the field but unable to play. Yet, there he sat, his knee propped up while the rest of the guys joked with him. The media was clearly just as excited to see him back with the Hawks, because they rushed into the dugout while the rest of the players warmed up.

A cute brunette reporter I recognized from earlier in the season got there first, shoving a microphone in Damien's face. "It's good to see you back with your team, Damien, even if you're only here to support them. Tell us, how's your recovery going?"

"Good." He smirked, nodding along with the reporter. "PT's a lot of work, and we're making slow but steady progress. My trainer's hopeful I'll be back on the field next season."

"That's great to hear," she answered. "How's it been, being away from the game, especially while your team is battling it out in the playoffs?"

"It's hard, that's for sure. Even though I'm not on the field with them, they know I have their backs. We're still a team—still a family—and I'm honored to be a part of the Hawks family."

"I'm sure they're just as honored to have you be a part of it. Any parting words before the game gets started?"

Damien turned to the camera with the same devious sparkle in his eyes. Anxiety bubbled up in my chest as I watched him, loving that the spark had returned to his eyes. It was like he was coming back to life right in front of all of us, coming back from the darkness. He grabbed the microphone. "Just want to say to my girl watching at home—I love you, angel, no matter how long it takes."

My eyes searched Damien's face, and the truth in them made my knees wobble. Was Ollie right? Had I held on to my anger with Damien because I was letting fear win? And how was I able to hold on to that anger with him, yet it slipped through my fingers with everyone else?

I'd made excuses for so many people in my life. Blamed my mother's upbringing for her strictness and conditional love. Gave Brad a break when I found out that his marriage was falling apart. And yet, I couldn't do the same thing for Damien. He'd been open about how badly he handled his injury, and I told him I understood—but did I? Or did I just see that as an out, a convenient excuse to hold on to when fear threatened to overwhelm me?

"Oh my God," I said, covering my mouth with my fingers. I could still feel Damien there, the gentleness of his kiss. He never hid how much he wanted me—and not just in the bedroom. He'd fought for us for so long, and yet, when things got challenging, I was the one who ran away without giving him a chance. "I really messed up."

"Nah." She smiled as she moved to my side, slinging her arm around my shoulders. "Nothing you can't fix now. But Bri?" She turned us so we faced each other. "Be sure this is what you want. One time is forgivable, but people won't wait forever for you to get over your fears. It's not fair to ask them to. So if you're going to be with Damien, *be with him.* Don't constantly look over your shoulder, waiting for him to fail."

"I won't." I pulled Ollie into a tight hug, ignoring the tears clinging to the corners of my eyes. When I pulled back, I wiped them away with the pads of my thumbs. "I want forever with him, Ol."

"Duh." She snorted. "That guy's had your heart since day one. Glad you're finally owning it."

"I need to go," I muttered, searching around the room for my purse and phone. "I need to talk to him."

"Agree." Ollie glared at my dress. "But not wearing that thing. We can do so much better."

FORTY-TWO

Brianna

My feet moved as fast as possible as I rushed through the parking garage, desperate to get to the stadium. Now that I'd decided to tell Damien I wanted to be with him, I wasn't about to waste a single moment. We'd already missed out on too much time because of my stubbornness.

As I pulled my keys out of my purse, I ran my shaking hands down the lines of Damien's jersey, hopeful he'd still want to see me in it. The last time I'd worn it, it was before his injury, and I hadn't touched it since. Ollie tried to loan me one of her sleek designer dresses, but this seemed the most fitting thing to wear when I admitted I loved him.

Even if Damien never wore his jersey again, I wanted to stand by his side, to be the one to make him smile. He'd spent so much time proving his love to me, and now, it was my turn. He'd gone through so much, but his love for me never wavered, and he'd spent all his free time showing me how much he cared. If it took the rest of my life, I'd make it up to him, prove I loved him just as much.

As I walked up to my car, I unlocked the doors. But before I could climb in, my name echoed across the parking garage. Turning around, I frowned, finding Todd walking toward me. Despite his immaculate tuxedo, his demeanor seemed off. His dark blond hair was disheveled, his eyes bloodshot and rimmed red. Concern made my stomach drop as I walked closer to him.

"Todd?" I asked, my voice echoing off the concrete walls. "What's wrong?"

"What's wrong?" He scoffed, swaying a little on his feet. When he came closer, the heavy scent of tequila clogged my senses, making my eyes water. "Everything, Bri."

I stepped back, holding out my hands to keep the distance between us. Todd wasn't like this. He'd drink socially when we were together, but he seldom drank at home and never to this level. It made anxiety twist through my gut, and I glanced over my shoulder, hoping to see anyone else around. But it was a Friday night, and most people were out or already tucked away at home. We were the only ones around.

I shook my head. "You should go, Todd. Get cleaned up. You're getting married in an hour."

He chuckled, but the sound held little humor. "No, I'm not. The wedding is off."

"What are you talking about?"

He stepped closer and tried to place his hands on my neck, but I stepped back, glad I'd exchanged my heels for sneakers. Being around Todd right now was like being trapped with a stranger, one who reeked of anger and despair. His eyes narrowed at me. "I called the fucking wedding off, Bri. Because of you."

"Me?" I sucked in a labored breath. "What does any of this have to do with me?"

Todd shook his head. "I fucked up, Bri. Our marriage—

you—were perfect. And then I got bored and thought Emily was better for me." He leaned down, flicking my hair over my shoulder. "But she could never be you."

"Don't say that."

"Why not?" Todd hissed. "You and I both know we belong together. Fuck, even your family knows. Why do you think your mother kept inviting me around? It was only a matter of time."

I shook my head and took a large step away from him. My back collided with the trunk of my car, and panic made my heart jump. I tucked the keys into my hand, wishing I'd gotten out here a few minutes earlier. I should have been with Damien, safely tucked against his chest. Instead, I was stuck here, trying to get away from my drunk ex-husband while he waxed on about our 'perfect' marriage.

When Todd tried to touch me again, I slapped his hand away. "Don't. We're done, our marriage is over. If there's anyone you should talk to, it's Emily, not me."

"Don't say that," he whined. "It's you and me, Bri. Always and forever."

He leaned forward and took my hips in his hands, dragging me against his wobbling frame. Nausea rushed through me, and I fought back, pushing and shoving to get away.

"Is that how you like it?" he whispered in my ear. "You want to fight me? Want me to work for it? I'll do it—I'll do anything to have you again."

"Todd, stop," I shrieked, trying to get his hands off me. Every place he touched stung, and I twisted, trying to get away, but he dug in harder, to the point of pain. I clawed at him. "Get off me."

"Not until you admit it. Not until you say you want me back. We both know you do. You're mine, Brianna. My wife."

"No," I cried out, pushing him away with all my might. Todd stumbled back, anger replacing the sadness in his eyes. My chest pounded with fear, hating the unease that slithered through me under his glare. I fought past it, steadying my breath. "We're done, Todd. You need to move on."

"Like you did?" He menacingly inched forward. "Yeah, I heard all about you and Damien Ramos." Todd's hand snapped out, gripping my chin between his fingers. "Did you fuck him, Bri? Did you let him touch you?"

"That's none of your business," I bit back, baring my teeth. After everything Todd put me through, he had the nerve to question me? That made the fear sharpen into anger, something darker and more dangerous rushing through my system.

But Todd's gaze held the same fury. "You are my fucking business."

"Not anymore."

A shout came from the other side of the lot, and Todd turned, loosening his grip enough for me to shift slightly. I twisted quickly, lifting my knee so it collided with his balls. Todd let out a pained groan as his hands fell away, clutching himself as he crumpled to the ground. A security guard from the building rushed over, holding out his flashlight. He walked over to me first, checking me over. "Ma'am, are you alright?"

"No," I wheezed. "That's my ex-husband, and he attacked me. Please call someone for help."

He muttered something into his radio, and I turned back toward my car. I'd probably need to talk to someone about what happened, but I couldn't bring myself to do it right now, not when I could still feel Todd's fingers digging into my flesh. I didn't spare him a second glance as I darted around my car and wrenched the door open. Once I got inside, I glanced at the rearview mirror, checking to make sure Todd was out of my way before shifting the car into reverse and speeding out of the lot.

It took five blocks for my breathing to level out, for my heart to stop hammering in my chest. Flashing blue and red lights passed me, and I had to wonder if they were going after Todd. My hands shook on the steering wheel, but I kept moving, not wanting to see my ex-husband ever again.

As I rushed through the city, my phone rang through the car's radio, and Ollie's name flashed across the dashboard. My fingers shook as I pressed answer. My best friend's voice instantly rushed out, "Brianna, tell me you're okay. The security guard just called, said there was an issue in the parking lot."

"I'm okay," I said, trying to keep my voice steady. "Todd came to talk to me, and it didn't go well. He tried to grab me—"

"That motherfucker," she hissed. "I hope you knocked him on his ass."

"I did," I answered. "The last I saw, he was rolling around the ground, clutching his pathetic balls."

"That's my girl," Ollie said. "The guard said they were calling the police to take care of the situation, but just in case, find somewhere else to stay tonight."

"Already on it." I sighed. "I'm heading to Damien's. He..." I exhaled slowly, letting the thought of him soothe me. "He makes me feel safe, Ol."

"Then that's where you should go. I'm going to call Hadley and Cam. Emilia's with her mom this weekend, so maybe I can crash in her room."

For a moment, I wondered why she wasn't going to Parker's house, especially when she usually spent a couple of nights with him each week. Lately, it had seemed like they'd been spending more time apart than together. I made a mental note to ask about it once the dust settled after Todd's visit.

Right now, all I could think about was Damien and how much I wanted to be with him. Not just for the night, but forever.

Just a few minutes in Todd's presence made me realize how much I'd changed since our divorce. While he'd stewed on his regrets and mistakes, I'd carved a better path for myself, one filled with good friends and a lot of love.

Something I never would have experienced without Damien.

And it was time I told him as much.

FORTY-THREE

Damien

Bile churned through my gut as I shuffled down the hall of the stadium, my gait somewhere between a jog and a quick walk. No matter how much my anxiety raged, I couldn't move any faster. As I glared down the door at the end of the hall, Ollie's words in my ears, driving me to the point of desperation. *Todd went after Brianna.* No other details, nothing to tell me what the bastard had done to her, just that I needed to get to her as soon as possible.

All questions about our damaged relationship stuttered to a stop; I didn't care if she'd figured out what she wanted from me. I'd tried to give her space over the past week, to let her know I was there for her, but I wouldn't push her more than I already had. If Brianna wanted me, she'd come to me.

But all those ideas ground to a halt when Ollie called, worried about Brianna. Nothing else mattered. Pride be damned—I needed to get to her.

I'd hung out after the game, celebrating the win with the rest of the team. We were just about to head out for the night when my phone rang out, and Ollie's voice broke through the hum of the clubhouse. Her voice was uncharacteristically calm—too calm. That only caused the panic to rise, unsure if I'd ever heard Ollie so serious.

As soon as she hung up, I took off for the exit, ignoring the throb in my knee as I kept moving down the concrete hallway. She had to be okay. While Todd had never raised a hand to her before, desperation made people stupid. I'd had a bad feeling in my gut for a while now. Between him showing up at her church and her blocking his messages and phone calls, he seemed to be fixated on her, despite the end of their marriage.

But he couldn't have her, not anymore. He'd fucked that up, and I refused to let him continue messing with her head. Even if she never wanted to be with me again, that was a promise I intended to keep. Brianna deserved so much more than that.

Security called after me as I reached the exterior doors, asking if everything was okay. Not even fucking close, but I didn't have time to talk to them, didn't have time to do anything but get to my girl. I grabbed the keys out of my pocket and headed toward my car.

However, once I reached it, the air heaved out of my lungs. Brianna. She stood at my passenger-side door, her arms wrapped around her chest. Her dark hazel eyes looked far away, as if she was lost in her own mind, but as soon as I stepped closer, her gaze snapped up to meet mine. Relief and concern flashed through my system, and I dropped my bag on the pavement, holding out my arms. "Angel."

She crumbled as she raced to me, her arms wrapping tightly around my neck. Her muffled sobs soaked my shirt, but I didn't care, too relieved to have her safe in my arms. As her breathing slowed, I leaned back, tucking up her chin to search her face. There were a couple of red marks on her neck, and that only fueled the fire inside me. I brushed them with my fingertips. "Did he do this?"

Brianna inhaled sharply then nodded. Fury exploded in my chest, and I had to clench my fists, trying to quell the beast inside me. He was a fucking dead man. I didn't care about the consequences; I only listened to the bloodlust racing through my mind, obliterating any other thoughts. Brianna's hand snaked up, pressing into my cheek.

"I'm okay, Damien."

"You're not okay," I whispered. "He put his hands on you. I'm going to fucking kill him."

Brianna shuddered against me. "Don't. He's not worth it."

"It is to me. No one hurts you and gets away with it." Taking her hand, I kissed her knuckles before placing it back at her side. I turned, already plotting out a map in my mind, but before I pulled the car door open, Brianna slid in front of me. Her fingertips directed my eyes back down to meet hers.

"Don't leave me, Damien." Her hands shook as she clung to my shirt. Letting go of the door handle, I surged forward, holding her tight against me. Sweet relief doused some of the anger, happy to have her safe in my arms. Brianna nestled against me, her fingers digging in as if I'd take off if she loosened them. She glanced up, her hazel eyes filled with so much adoration. "He's being dealt with. Right now, I need you, Damien. Please, stay here with me."

"Always," I sighed, leaning forward to run my lips over her forehead. "Tell me you're okay."

"I am now," Brianna sighed.

We held each other for a long moment, not needing any words to pass between us. I didn't want to think too much about why she'd come here, why she'd sought me out during one of the scariest moments of her life, but a small tendril of hope grew anyway, hoping that meant she was ready to try again. I ran my hands down her back, but I suddenly stopped when they met the raised number along her spine. My eyes widened as I leaned back, taking in her shirt. My jersey.

As if she read the question in my eyes, Brianna let out a watery chuckle. "Before Todd stopped me, I was coming here. I needed to talk to you."

I swallowed, trying to temper the anxiety swirling inside me. "Why?"

"Even before everything happened, I made a choice. About us. But tonight showed me that anything could happen, and I don't want to waste another moment living in fear." Her striking eyes met mine, and the breath rushed out of my lungs. "I love you, Damien, and I'm so sorry for fighting it for so long. Truth be told, you terrify me. You have since the moment we collided in Dallas. Inside, I knew —knew that if I let you into my heart, you'd never let me go. I'm done being afraid, done second guessing us. So if you'll have me, I'm all yours. I've always been yours, Damien."

Joy like I'd never known rushed through my veins, pushing out all the rage and anger. I ran the back of my fingers along her cheek. "You love me, angel?"

Tears clung to the corners of her eyes as she nodded. "More than anything. You're the best man I've ever known, and I'm sorry I lost sight of that for a while. But if you'll still have me, I want to be with you."

"You never lost me."

I pulled her against my chest, needing to hold her to believe this was real. For weeks, I'd dreamt of this moment, to hear those precious words fall from Brianna's lips. While I wanted to give her as much time as she needed, there was a small part of me that feared she'd never get there, that she'd never be able to forgive me for doubting us—*doubting her*—after I got injured.

"Tell me again."

Brianna smiled up at me. "Damien Ramos, I love you. I am hopelessly, wonderfully in love with you, and if you're willing to put up with my flaws, I'll be yours as long as you'll have me."

"I love your flaws, Brianna Sideris. I love you when you're stubborn, when you're overthinking everything, and everything in between." He pressed his lips to my forehead. "I love every part of you, angel. There's no one else in this world I want to spend my life with."

"I like the sound of that."

DESPITE MY INSISTENCE that Brianna should get checked out by a doctor, she refused, only wanting to be with me right now. Maybe I should have fought her harder, but truth be told, I wanted to be alone with her just as much. We came straight back to my apartment from the stadium, and I led Brianna upstairs. Once she walked inside, peace clicked inside my chest. When she was gone, this place lost the comfort I'd spent so long curating. Now that she was back, it returned as if it had been waiting for her, just like me.

She glanced at the couch, then frowned at me. "Is it okay if I take a shower? I can still feel—"

Her words cut off, but I picked up on her meaning. She wanted to wash the night off her, erase every place Todd had touched her without her permission. I nodded. "Make yourself at home, angel. Whatever you need; you don't have to ask."

Brianna gave me a grateful smile as she walked through my home and into the bedroom. As she disappeared behind the door, my hand flexed, wanting to go in there and claim her, to show my love with my mouth, my tongue, and every other part of me. But Brianna had been through too much tonight, and I wouldn't push, letting her guide our pace. Until she was ready, I'd be here in every other way possible.

Realizing she was probably hungry, I pulled out my phone, going through different delivery options. But before I could get too far, Brianna called out, "What did you do?"

I smirked, walking through the primary bedroom and into the bathroom. Brianna stood in the middle of the room, gaping at the newest addition. She whipped her head around, her eyes wide with surprise. "When did you get a clawfoot tub?"

"About a week ago." I stepped forward to lead her closer to it. Taking her hand, I ran it over the surface. The tub had been a bitch to install, especially because I only gave the crew a couple days to get it done. Luckily, I'd made great money throughout my career, and I couldn't think of a better use of it than by giving Brianna everything she ever wanted. "I remember you saying you always wanted one."

Her mouth dropped open, and her words came out stuttered. "Wh—what? How? I mentioned that months ago. You remembered?"

I shifted closer to her, running my fingers along her back. She shivered under my touch, and I couldn't help but smile. "I've had a lot of time to think over the past month, replayed all our conversations, especially about what you've always wanted. Might not be able to give you everything, Bri, but I thought this would be a good start."

"I love it. It means more than I can even say." She beamed up at me and pressed her lips to mine. It was just a hint of a kiss, but there was something so honest and consuming about it. She pulled back and searched my gaze. "But you know none of this compares to you, right? You're everything to me. This is just a bonus."

"Good answer, angel," I chuckled. "But I'm going to spoil you, Bri, show you everything you deserve. So get ready, because this is just the beginning." I pressed another kiss to her forehead. "Go ahead, take a bath. I'm going to be in the other room, figuring out dinner. Take as much time as you need."

Before I could get too far, Brianna's finger clasped around my hand. "Wait...I want you to stay."

A growl built in my chest. "Are you sure, angel? Because I've spent a long time without you, and I don't know if I can keep myself from touching you."

Her hazel eyes twinkled with amusement. "Who said I want you to?"

FORTY-FOUR

Brianna

Damien's eyes blazed with unrestrained lust as my words fell between us. He sucked in a sharp breath, and for a moment, it seemed like he would refuse me. But I meant what I said. I didn't want him to hold back—didn't want to wait to have him again. Todd might have tried to control me, to take away my choice, but with Damien, it was the opposite. He was my safety, the person I trusted most in this world.

As he stood there, completely still, I turned around and twisted the handles on the tub. The sound of the rushing water broke the silence between us, and I shifted back to face him. With sure fingers, I unbuttoned his jersey, letting it fall to my feet. Damien's eyes darkened, watching as my fingers toyed with the hem of my cami. He didn't move, didn't speak as I undressed myself and, after checking the temperature of the water, climbed into the tub. The water enveloped me, warmth and comfort I didn't know I needed, but it wasn't enough.

"Join me," I said, holding out my hand to Damien. "Please, I need you."

That was enough to break whatever argument brewed in his mind. Damien quickly shed his sweatshirt and jeans, leaving him naked in front of me. I sucked in a sharp breath, taking in his perfect form. His cock jutted out toward me, and it was so tempting to touch him, I reached out to run my fingers along his shaft.

"Fuck," he muttered as my hand encircled him. "Not yet, angel. Not like that. It's been too long, and I need to get inside you."

"Then what are you waiting for?"

I leaned forward, turning off the water as he climbed into the tub, bending to settle in behind me. The tub was larger, much more than the antique ones I'd seen online, enough that both of us could fit comfortably. As Damien's hands directed me against him, images of many more nights like this flashed in my mind, and I smiled. Damien's nose trailed along my shoulder while his arms wrapped around my waist. "I missed this, Bri. Missed you."

"I missed you too," I said as my head dropped against him. "Touch me. Please, Damien."

"Are you sure?" He swallowed as his fingers timidly shifted against me. "You went through a lot tonight."

I shifted, twisting so I could face him. "Someone tried to take my power away, and in a past life, I would have let him. But not now, not when I had so much more to fight for." I cupped his cheeks. "It's you, Damien. I fought to get back here, to be with you. So please, touch me. Hold me and make love to me. Remind me what it means to be yours."

Damien didn't waste another second, pulling me into his lap. His thick cock jutted between us, and my hips shifted, desperate to have him. His lips claimed mine, brutal and tender all at once, as if he needed me like I needed him. Damien's fingers dropped to my core, carefully but expertly exploring me. "Fuck," he muttered as his lips trailed along my jaw. "You're so wet, angel. Is that all for me?"

"Only for you," I said, my words breathless. "It's only ever for you."

His fingers teased and probed, my skin alight with desire. It was too much yet not enough. As if sensing my increasing need, Damien pulled them away then lifted me to line up my entrance with his cock. He searched my eyes, and I just smiled, leaning forward to kiss him. As I worked my way down his length, his fingers dug into my hips, anchoring me to him. My body moved of its own volition, taking another inch each time. My mouth fell open when he was fully inside me, and I mewled needily. Damien smirked, lifting one hand to play with my breasts. My hips moved of their own volition, seeking more of him. Damien chuckled against my neck. "You feel that, angel? How your tight little pussy smothers my cock?"

"Yes," I groaned. "It's so good."

"Fucking perfection," he bit out. "You're fucking made for me, Brianna. Made to take my cock like it's always been yours."

The water splashed around us as we claimed each other, barely noticing how it splashed over the edges onto the floor. All too soon, pleasure crested through my veins, and heady need took over my movements. I tried to hold out, tried to fight off my orgasm for a little longer, but when Damien's thumb circled my clit, there was nothing I could do. A loud moan escaped my lips, echoing off the marble walls of the bathroom. Damien continued to work me through my high, and then his grip turned almost bruising as he chased his own release. He came with a similarly loud groan and dropped his forehead to my shoulder. My hands traced his back, trying to remind myself this was real. We were real—solid.

As I shifted again, he winced, and a sour taste filled my tongue. I turned to face his injured leg. "Did I hurt your knee?" I shook my head. "I didn't even think, I just—"

But Damien cut off my rambling concerns when he pulled me back against his chest, and he nuzzled into my neck. "It's good, angel. Doc cleared me last week."

I rested against him, relishing our post-coital bliss. As the water grew cold, I shivered, and Damien nudged me. "Come on; let's get you into bed. But fair warning..." he said as we stood together and dried off, "once I get you in there, I may never let you leave."

THE NEXT MORNING, the sound of my phone ringing pulled me from a deep slumber. I groaned as my eyes reluctantly opened, staring at the end table like it was my worst enemy. With an annoyed sigh, I shifted closer to it, trying to reach out and find it without moving too much.

But before I could get very far, the arm wrapped around my center tightened, bringing my back to his chest. "Leave it," Damien grumbled into my shoulder.

"I can't," I chuckled as I pushed him off me. "It might be Ollie. I don't want her to worry about me."

Damien just groaned, flopping onto his back and draping his arm over his eyes. Before I sat up, I stole a glance at him, unable to hold back my smile. True to his word, Damien refused to let me leave his bed last night, even ordering food and eating on top of the bedding. We spent hours wrapped up in each other, reacquainting ourselves with every inch of the other's body. But between bouts of sex, we'd also talked, mapping out how to communicate. While our relationship had started off in secret, we agreed to always be open and honest now, no longer willing to hide what we meant to each other.

It was as if a weight lifted off my shoulders, shedding away the last binds of my anxiety. Speaking openly and honestly about my feelings was hard, especially seeing how Damien's face darkened when we talked about my past, but it helped. It made me think about talking to a therapist, an impartial person who could work with me to let go of my fears.

"If you keep staring at me like that, I'm going to pull you over my face and eat you until you scream."

I smirked as I shook my head. "Promises, promises."

"Just come over here and test me, angel." Damien smirked, even though his eyes remained closed.

I reached out and grabbed my phone, sure it was Ollie calling to check in. I'd sent her a message before we got to Damien's apartment last night, just to let her know I'd made it here safely and would stay with him. She'd also left the apartment; until the coast was clear, she was staying with Cam and Hadley. Hopefully, we'd both be able to go home soon, but as I glanced over at Damien, who'd fallen back to sleep, I couldn't help but think about staying. It was too soon, but I hated the idea of leaving him. I was greedy for his time, especially with him hopefully returning to the Hawks next season.

When I looked down at my phone screen, my smile twisted into a grimace. Three missed calls from my mother. Anxiety flared in my chest, but I forced myself to call her back.

She answered with a relieved sigh. "Brianna, thank goodness. I've been worried sick about you."

"I'm okay, Mom. I promise."

"Todd's mother called—she said he got arrested last night for harassing you," she said. "What did he do? What happened?"

I shook my head. "I'm sorry, Mom, but I'm not ready to talk about it. Last night was a lot, and I need some time."

"Of course, Brianna," she cooed. "I'll reach out to Todd, make sure there's no bad feelings with his family. We can figure out how to move forward—after he apologizes, of course."

"Move forward?" I asked, my finger biting into the phone. "Why would I want to do that?"

"Brianna, please." My mother sighed. "Todd made a mistake, one I'm sure he deeply regrets. We've had a long history with his family, he's involved with the church—"

"He *attacked* me," I snapped. "Showed up at my home and put his hands on me. Tried to hurt me. There are still bruises on my arm."

"Oh, honey, I'm sure that was an accident. His mother said he'd been drinking. His fiancée had just called off the wedding—"

"Mom, stop. Stop making excuses for him." I laughed. "Todd is not a child who broke something by accident. He *hurt* me. Put his hands on me. Maybe you can forgive that, but I'm never going to. I want nothing to do with him ever again. If you insist on having him around, then I'm going to have to take some space from you too."

"What are you saying?"

"I'm saying we need boundaries, Mom. You're made your opinions about Todd very well known, but it stops today." As my anger continued to rise, a hand rubbed along my spine. I turned and gave Damien a grateful smile over my shoulder, finding my strength now that he was here with me. "I need some space from you."

"Space?" she snapped. "Is this because of that boy—"

"Don't you dare talk about him. Damien is the love of my life and has been more supportive than you have ever been. If you say another bad word about him, I will cut you completely out of my life."

"Brianna," she gasped. "How could you say that?"

"Because he matters to me. You don't get to say anything about him ever again. If you want to be a part of my life, you need to accept him, because he's not going anywhere. Actually, if you don't like *any* of my choices, you're going to keep it to yourself unless I ask for your advice. But for now, I need space from you. I'll reach out if I want to speak to you, but until then, please respect my wishes."

I hung up the call without another word, not wanting to hear another word out of my mother's mouth. I expected her to keep calling until I answered, but it never came.

With an uneasy smile, I crawled back into bed and snuggled against Damien's side. His arm held me close as he kissed my temple. "Proud of you, angel."

"It needed to be done. I've wasted enough time letting her be the voice in my head. If she can't be happy for me, she has no place in my life."

Before I said another word, Damien shifted me onto my back and nestled between my thighs. He smiled down at me, his eyes filled with adoration and lust. "You're amazing, Bri."

"You only say that because you love me," I teased, running my nails along his back.

"Nah." He brushed his lips along my chest. "Never

been a gambling man, Bri, but if I had to bet on you, I'd double down every time."

"I want to bet on us," I said, pulling back to meet his eyes, "and the family we've created. I'm not letting anyone else try to take that away from us."

"Good," Damien said as he claimed my lips. "Because I'm planning on loving you for the rest of my life."

EPILOGUE

NINE MONTHS LATER

"And you're sure your knee is okay? No tightness or twinges?"

Brianna chewed on her lower lip as Chase continued to check out my leg, testing my reflexes. The movements were still a little stiffer than before my injury, but the doctors warned me that might happen. All that mattered was getting back out on the field.

Today was going to decide my fate, and I'd asked Brianna to come along for moral support. My girlfriend stood by my side, but her eyes never left Chase's hands, trying to keep perfectly still as she watched him work. I reached out, taking her hand in mine.

"I'm good. Ready to get out there and play," I said, speaking more to Brianna than my physical therapist.

Brianna smiled at me, but it was a little strained. She'd never said anything out loud, but her nervous energy spoke for itself. Watching me out on the field during practice was one thing, but if this session went well, this weekend, I'd step out onto the field for the first time in almost a year. After months of PT and strength training, all my doctors had signed off, and I just needed Chase's approval before I could rejoin the team.

The last nine months had been both the best and worst of my life. Despite playing admirably, the Hawks lost the championship to the New York Rebels, my former team. The loss stung, but it also fueled us. The entire team worked hard during spring training and was ready to start the season. Me? I was even more determined to be there to help the Hawks take home the trophy.

This time last year, that would have been the end for me. Baseball had been my entire world, the one stable thing I'd built my life around. But now, despite my career being at a standstill, I wouldn't change a single thing, not when Brianna was there with me every step of the way. After everything went down with her ex-husband, I'd asked her to move in with me. She immediately said yes, and we got to work transforming my home into one suited for both of us. The place looked completely different now, with homey touches, pieces of Brianna everywhere. We'd even turned one of the guest rooms into a library for all her books, and most nights when I trained late, I'd find her in there, curled up in an armchair with her e-reader clutched against her chest.

Even if I never walked back out onto that field, I'd be good. Our lives would be filled with more happiness than I ever dreamed about, but I wasn't ready to let go of my dream just yet. If I could play, I wanted to. As much as I loved being with Brianna, I missed being a true part of my team. Even though I trained with them and attended almost every game, it wasn't the same as being out on the field. I missed the rush, the adrenaline, that moment of perfect harmony when we all came together to make a play.

I wanted that. Craved that. And while most guys my

age might head happily into retirement, it wasn't the right move for me. Not yet, at least. I had one more championship left in me.

Now, hopefully, my body would cooperate.

Chase sighed, running his hand through his hair. "Looks pretty good to me. Can't play the whole time, but you can get out there for a few innings as long as you promise not to push it too hard."

I smirked at him. "That shouldn't be a problem."

Chase rolled his eyes. "You forget I've been with you since the beginning, Ramos. I've seen how hard you've worked to get back into the game." He clapped his hand on my shoulder. "I'm signing off on you."

"Really?"

"Yeah," Chase said as he gathered his stuff. "Your knee looks good. No twinges, no pain. Seems like you're good to go."

"That means he can play?" Brianna asked, clasping my hand a little tighter.

"Yeah," Chase said. "He's ready. But don't let him skip out on his exercises, Bri. Make sure he sticks with it, especially after a long game."

She nodded. "Of course."

I rolled my eyes. "Don't let the doe eyes fool you, man. This one is worse than you. She had me running drills at five in the morning last week." My eyes widened. "The sun wasn't even up yet."

"Knew I liked her for you." Chase patted my shoulder as he headed toward the office, leaving us alone in the training room. Brianna rummaged through her bag, pulling out her car keys. Before she walked toward the door, I reached out and took her hand, pulling her to stand between my thighs. She ducked her chin, trying to avoid my eyes, but I refused to let her. "What's on your mind, angel?"

She smiled at me. "That I'm so proud of you, my love."

Her eyes glistened, and while I was sure that was true, something else lurked in the corners of her gaze. I brushed my thumb over her cheek. "And?"

Brianna sighed, running her fingers along the bridge of her nose. "Okay, I might be a little nervous about you playing again. Last year, when you got hurt..." Brianna trailed off, and I knew exactly what she was picturing. She sucked in a slow breath before reluctantly meeting my eyes. "I'm worried about you."

"I'm nervous too, Bri." I pulled her into my chest and kissed the top of her head. "But we can't let fear hold us back, right?"

With a snort, she rolled her eyes, all too familiar with our mantra. After everything that had worked against us in the past, we'd agreed early in our relationship to be open about our fears and concerns. Some days, it was easier than others, but we learned to lean on each other during stressful times. Brianna helped me through my recovery, keeping track of my exercises and pushing me to keep going when I wanted to give up. She also loved to reward any progress with sexual favors, which helped with my motivation.

As for me, I'd been by Brianna's side during the aftermath of her ex's confrontation. While Brianna had decided against pressing charges, wanting to move on with her life, she did take out a restraining order against him. Todd couldn't come within a hundred yards of her, which seemed to work, because we hadn't heard from the asshole since. Good thing too. I was still dying to get my hands on him after everything he'd done to Brianna.

Her family was another story. Some days, she struggled

with keeping up her boundaries with her mother. While her brother, Jason, and his family were frequent guests in the Hawks' outfield, Brianna had kept her distance from everyone else. They met up every few months, but their relationship wasn't what it used to be.

It helped that our friends had taken the place of her family, providing us with unwavering support and love. Even though I was still on the reserve list, we had dinner every week with the team and often celebrated with them after big wins.

As Brianna studied my expression, she eventually nodded. "Can't let it hold us back." She reached out, playing with my baseball hat. It felt good to be in the Hawks' colors again, to feel like more than a benchwarmer. The only thing better was having Brianna by my side every step of the way. "I love you, Damien."

"Love you more, angel." I leaned back and searched her expression. "What do you think about flying out with the team next week? Check out Vegas with me?"

She smirked at me. "I'm sure I could be convinced."

"And while we're there..." I toyed with the hem of her sweater, "maybe we could stop by one of those little chapels."

Brianna pushed back, searching my expression. "Did you just ask me to marry you?"

I smiled back at her. "I know you said you'd never want a big wedding again, but think about it. All our friends will already be there, and we can keep it small, just like you wanted."

"You're serious?"

"Of course, I'm serious," I chuckled, pulling her closer to me. "I love you, Brianna, and I'm more than happy to have you in any capacity. But can't lie, angel—I'd really like you to be my wife. To see my ring on your finger." Reaching out, I kissed her forehead. "Just think about it, okay?"

She shook her head, and my stomach sank—but then she smacked me on the arm. "There's nothing to think about. I'd marry you anywhere, Damien Ramos."

"Really?"

Brianna shook her head. "Always swore I'd never get married again, but being with you is the best thing that ever happened to me. So, yes. I'll marry you, Damien. In Vegas, back home, wherever you like." She pursed her lips. "You don't want to have a big, traditional wedding?"

"No," I chuckled. "I don't care about the details, I just want you there. Well, you and Mari and the rest of my family. But as long as the people we love show up, everything else is just extra."

"Then Vegas it is." Brianna leaned in, kissing me softly. "But first, you've got to get out on that field and win this series."

I pressed her closer to me then kissed her deeply. She let out a content whimper as my lips claimed hers. Disbelief filled me; how did I get lucky enough to have Brianna in my arms? There were so many moments of doubt, so many times when we almost fell apart before we even began, but I'd go through it all again—the fear, the pain, the uncertainty—if it meant ending up here, with this woman.

As we broke apart, Brianna held out her hand. "So, Mr. Ramos, you ready to do this with me?"

I shook my head as I climbed off the table. "Thought you'd never ask."

ACKNOWLEDGMENTS

One of my favorite parts of writing any book is this moment. The time I take at the end to think about all the people who helped me get to this place. I am beyond BLESSED to have so many amazing people in my corner, and could not do this without every single one of you.

My family—you are my rock, the sole reason I am able to put these ideas down on paper. I am incredibly lucky to have such a great support system in my corner, and I am thankful for you guys every single day.

My friends—the ones who are spicy readers, and the ones who stare at me in horror when I describe my latest five star read, thank you for always having my back. For understanding when I have to push plans for deadlines, and letting me daydream about fictional characters with you.

Maeghen—I don't have words for how much your support means to me. Not only are you the BEST hype person on the planet, you've helped me stay organized, support my crazy ideas, and help push me to become a better writer. I am incredibly grateful for you!!!

Brittany—(AKA my lifesaver) For so long, I put off

hiring a PA because I didn't know if it would be the right thing for me. But you have made my life so much better! You anticipate my needs, support my readers, and just make it so much easier to focus on my writing. I appreciate you so, so much!

To Alexa at Fiction Fix—thank you for being my editing fairy godmother over the past two years. I couldn't do any of this without you! You're so talented and always take the best care of my books.

Lemmy & the Luna crew, and Ellie at LoveNotesPR— Thank you guys for handling my ARCs and making sure they get into the right readers' hands. You guys take so much off of my plate, and let me focus on writing. It means more to me than I can ever put into words

To my amazing beta readers--Meghan, Cas, Nikki, Katie, and Brandi, you guys are the very best! Thank you so much for taking time out of your busy lives to read through the early and unedited versions of my books. I love reading your reactions and watching as you experience this story for the first time. I am so lucky to have you guys on my team.

And last—to my readers. Whether you've been with me since the beginning, or if you are just finding my books now, thank you. Thank you for investing your time in reading this story, and I hope you enjoyed it.

Love you all!

ALSO BY KC BROOKS

SAINT STEPHEN'S LAKE SERIES:

(Un)Expected

A Dislike to Lovers, Small Town Romance

(Cole & Alex's Story)

(Un)Planned

A Grumpy x Sunshine, Workplace Romance

(Calla & Theo's Story)

(Un)Spoken

A Brother's Best Friend, Single Parent Romance

(Adam & Victoria's Story)

(Un)Rivaled

A Second Chance, Accidental Marriage Romance

(Devyn & Gray's Story)

ERIE CITY HAWKS SERIES:

Single Glance

A Single Dad, Baseball Romance

(Cam and Hadley's Story)

Double Down

A Friends with Benefits, Baseball Romance

(Brianna and Damien's Story)

Triple Threat

A Secret Baby, Baseball Romance

Coming Spring 2026

ABOUT THE AUTHOR

K.C. Brooks is an avid romance reader who has always dreamed about turning her ideas into a book of her own. She lives for sunny days, iced cold coffees, and stories that make your heart ache for more. When not living in the fantasy worlds of her books, she resides in upstate New York with her husband, two children, and her golden doodle.